Acclaim from readers

"Combines Sci-fi, mystery, and suspense with numerous lessons about life that makes this book a must read."
Sandra Broudeur Brooklyn, CT

"Grabbed me from the first page."
Don Zileger Santa Fe, NM

"Nik Colyer weaved a story that captured my interest to the point where I couldn't stop reading."
Cheri DeBevois Klamath, CA

"Riveting. . .I loved the way the story continued to shift between the man and woman."
Kathy Crossman Biose, ID

"The charactors were so real and the desert seemed so alive."
Tom Lanning Phoenix, AZ

"I kept trying to do something else last weekend, but I couldn't put the book down. Read it straight through."
Francine Morgan Reno, NV

"What an adventure. Left me wanting more."
Sara Hentzel Boulder, CO

"Excellent tale! What a surprise at the end."
Richard Lancing Austin, TX

"A wild read with marvelously unpredictable twists and turns along the way."
Melissa Marosy, Woodland, CA

Maranther's Deception

Nik C. Colyer

Singing Reed Press

Book design by Tilly Sinclair   Cover design by Zoe Alowan

First Singing Reed Press trade paperback edition: March 2005
Singing Reed Press trade paperback ISBN: 0-9708163-4-0

Publisher's Cataloging-in-Publication Data
(Prepared by The Donohue Group, Inc.)
Colyer, Nik C., 1948-
    Maranther's Deception/Nik C. Colyer. 1st ed.

    p. ; cm.
    ISBN 0-9708163-4-0

1. Desert Servival--Fiction. 2.Women shamans--Fiction.
3. Sonoran Desert--Fiction I. Title.
PS3553.04784 M37 2005
    813/.6   2004106518
Singing Reed Press

Thanks to my editor, Bobbie Christmas.

Printed on 100% post-consumer, chlorine free paper
in the United States of America
10 9 8 7 6 5 4 3 2 1

for
Arthur Newfli

Author's Note

The following novel came to me one winter night during the pre-dawn hours as a single wild dream. The dream lasted only a moment, but it gave me the seeds of this story. I thought it appropriate that I share with you, my reader the note I scribbled as I sat on the edge of my bed in the dark. Be warned, as usual with my writing, *Maranther's Deception* takes a left turn in the first pages and leaves the dream, never to return.

Traveling in Mexico with a Mayan woman, we come across an ancient abandoned native village with great stone masonry. We stop to explore the ruins, go into the first building and it becomes a maze of rooms.

We can't find our way out. The further along we go the more the rooms begin to fill with furniture and household items. It looks like someone lives here after all. After too much effort, sure each door will lead to the outside, we find our way to an alley but are forced to go through yet another door. I turn as my friend steps through the door and disappears. I realize too late that some force was trying to separate us all along. I run through the same door and out into the open only to face a huge bull. It chases me away from the village and over a steep embankment where I hit my head and pass out.

Later, a carload of natives finds me and takes me to a local doctor who tells me about a local medicine woman's mischief.

Hope you enjoy the story.
Nik

Maranther's Deception

One

Stranded

I awake with a start. My sleepy gaze drifts from the unfurled sun visor to a sand-packed windshield, and I'm reluctant to roll my head to the right. I must be in a nightmare. This can't be my wife asleep next to me.

Leigha is stretched out on the fully reclined seat. Her head rests against the door, just below the sand-packed passenger window. I gaze at her chiseled face. I drink in her masses of salt-and-pepper curls, tangled and twisted from a night of sleep.

I look past her at the dark window, then swing my stiff neck around to scan the other windows. My new Volvo is completely buried in Sonora desert sand.

I lean forward and pull myself up to peer out a thin slit of light high on the windshield. Through my crack of a view, I see a brilliant new day.

Trying not to awaken Leigha, I pull my basketball-player legs past the steering wheel and climb into the backseat. When I roll down the left rear window, sand pours on the seat with a rattlesnake hiss, then to the floor. Leigha stirs, but doesn't wake. I sit in silence until she settles, then I put on my leather hat, climb through the window, and scramble up a slippery trough of crystalline grains. It's here, on a bright desert morning, where I'm forced to confront the reality of our predicament.

Last night, the wind howled, sand blew across the windshield, and my wife came unglued, showing me just how afraid she was of the desert.

"You worked every angle to get me out in your damn desert, didn't you?" she said, while the car was buffeted by the storm. "You just had to get me out here."

"We're okay, Leigha," I'd said. "We'll get help when the winds stop blowing."

"Why'd I listen to you?" She covered her tear-stained face with both hands.

I put a hand on her shoulder. "Because you wanted me to go to the theater with you. If I recall, the trade-off was a whole season of thespian hell, for two weeks out here."

"It isn't worth dying for."

"Leigha, we're not going to die. We're just stuck in the sand. We'll get out in the morning."

"If we get out of this alive, I want to go home. I'm not staying out here another day."

"What about yesterday, when we saw the flowers?"

"What about it?" she asked. "We're going to die."

My wife was facing the old ghost she'd lived with for

thirty-six years; since she was nine.

"Honey, I've already gone to three plays. If you want me to go to the final ten of this season, you have five more days to be out here. Otherwise, I'm going back to watching basketball."

There was a long silence before she said, "If we get out of this mess, I'll finish the five days in this hellhole, but we're going back across the border. I hate Mexico."

"That's fair."

"We're going to find a decent hotel, Martin Vandorfor. No mice, and no bugs."

"Something like that first place in Albuquerque?"

She dropped her hands, and her face relaxed a little. "Yes, like Albuquerque. In this last week, that was the only place that was decent."

A sudden gust of wind buffeted the car, and Leigha tensed again. "I can't stand this," she screamed. "Get me out of here." She reached for the door handle.

I yelled, "Don't open that door."

"I've got to get out of here, Martin."

"The jumping cholla cactus is in the wind. The little tuffs will stick to your skin, then break off when you try to remove them. They itch like crazy."

Her hand dropped from the door handle. "Oh great, another desert thing to be afraid of."

I sighed. "Tomorrow, when the wind dies, everything will be better, and you'll feel different, I promise."

She scrunched up her face. "I won't feel any different. I hate this desert. Take me back to Phoenix."

"But Honey, going to movies and sitting next to a pool isn't exactly being in the desert."

"It's as close as I want to get."
"Out here is where you're going to face your demon."
"I don't want to face any demons right now. Just get us out of here alive and back to civilization."
She reclined the seat, reached up, and turned off the overhead light. In the dark she said, "Just get us out of here."

Two

Oceans of Sand

That was last night. Today it's calm and sunny. I'm standing on a trough of sand, in a wide valley between two mountainous dunes, next to a mound that was once my new Volvo. When I reach the top of the slippery hill, drifts of bleached sand force me to shade my eyes. Rocky crags loom over both sides of the twenty-mile-long bowl-shaped valley. Because of last night's storm, any evidence of humanity no longer exists.

I pull out my cellular phone, but Mexico is no place to try to get a signal.

With the desert sun blinding me, I'm forced to climb into my car. When I slide in through the back window, Leigha awakes.

"Where are we?" She rubs her eyes.

I lower myself to the front seat. "We're in the desert, and it's beautiful outside." I emphasize beautiful.

Yesterday, we drove down the hill on a deserted gravel road. The walk out will not be the vacation hike in the desert wilderness I'd planned for Leigha.

"The car is buried," she says.

"Yes, I know."

"We're stranded in the middle of nowhere."

"Just temporarily." My voice comes out a little too confident. "We have plenty of food and water, and I know where we are. I've hiked this part of the desert many times. I know it like the back of my hand."

True, I had hiked this area before, but the part not so truthful is that without the road to guide me, I have no idea which canyon we came down. I hope once we hike out of the valley, I'll find the road again.

Leigha's next words tell me another gale brews. The second tempest will be much bigger then the one we survived. It will be a storm with sharper barbs than the jumping cholla cactus.

Her voice rises a half octave. A rose color flushes her cheeks. "You bring us into this godforsaken country, then get us stuck in the sand?"

In her eyes, I read childhood traumas. I don't want her to face those old demons this way.

"Leigha, I'm not lost. We'll easily hike out of here and call a tow truck. In a couple of days we can be on the road again."

"A couple of days? A couple of days! Martin, what do you think I am? You get us stranded in the desert, and now we have to hike a couple of days to get out of your mess."

It takes many hours to wade through the quagmire

of her fears. When we finally climb out of our despair and scramble through the back window into fresh air, we're met with a warm afternoon and a brilliant blue sky.

Having purged herself of fear and resentment, Leigha looks at the drifts of white sand with guarded interest. She asks the first non-blaming question all day. "What should we do now?"

"We can't get across the dunes by dark," I say, "and it isn't good to be caught in the wind. Let's pitch a tent here and see what the night brings. If the winds kick up, we'll sleep in the car."

To my delight, the night is calm, and I show Leigha the wonder of desert stars. By the way she ooh's and aah's, it may be her first experience. Her amazement makes all the whines and moans of the prior week, all the screams and yells of the day, worthwhile. After hours of pointing at constellations and watching shooting stars, we climb into our tent and make love. The night ends with us asleep, wrapped in one another's arms.

The blazing morning sun forces me up and out of the tent. I look at my digital watch and read 7:35, March 12, 2014.

As usual, Leigha has been out of bed for hours. I smell bacon and stumble over to our little one-burner camp stove atop a cleared area on the Volvo roof. The blowing sand stripped every trace of paint.

"You'd better eat hardy," she grumbles. "We have a long walk ahead of us." She piles the bacon onto a piece of paper towel and drops a bowl of slimy eggs into the pan. She glares. "You just better get us out of this, or I'll, I'll never. . ."

Not really interested in what she'll do, I don't pursue the subject.

While waiting for her to cook breakfast, I retrieve one of Leigha's overnight cases from the car, drag the tent and our two day packs out by dismantling the backseat, then jam the suitcase into the open window. It'll block the sand from filling the car in our absence. We'll only be gone a few days, but the sand could create a disaster.

At half-past nine, before we start across the dunes, I assemble my fishing pole, tie a pair of red boxer shorts to the tip, then lash the pole to the antenna.

Leigha gives me a curious glare.

I shrug. "Who knows, another sandstorm might bury the car completely. I plan to find it when we return."

When I finish, she puts her straw hat on and looks south. "Okay, Martin, which way?"

The dirt road that crossed the old lake bed was arrow straight. I sight the position of the car and get an idea of the direction we might have come from. I've got three ravines to choose from, but with my bad luck, I'll guess the wrong one. If I ever find the correct canyon, we'll pick up remnants of the old road and find our way, but I'm frightened that we'll run out of water first. I don't say anything to Leigha.

When we take our first steps onto the miserably loose sand, I realize crossing the dunes will not be easy. After thirty steps, my calves ache. A hundred feet to the top of the first dune is an impossible journey in itself.

After an hour of climbing the hot dunes, I'm exhausted. At the top of an especially high mound, I look back in shock when I spot the top of the car. We've gone barely a mile, with at least four to go. I'm not sure we'll make it at all, much less by night, but I say nothing.

Leigha trudges ahead as I numbly follow, climbing one twenty-foot-high dune and sliding down its backside. At the top of each third mound, we lie exhausted, gasping for breath. Each rest period, the heat increases.

By two o'clock, I look ahead. We've crossed less than half the distance to solid ground. My bad leg is bothering me, and I can't go another step.

Leigha collapses onto the burning sand. "Let's take a break." She pulls out a tin of sardines, and we ravage the slippery little fish.

The hot sand refuses to allow us to stay seated for too long, so soon we're forced to be on our way.

By late afternoon, Leigha steps onto the first solid object, a large flat rock.

"We made it!" She stumbles across fifteen more feet of sand and stands atop a second boulder. She crosses ten remaining slippery yards to firm earth.

I'm close behind. It feels good to step on solid ground.

Leigha says, "God, my calves are numb. I never want to look at sand like this again."

We stagger behind a round rock the size of a house and sit in the afternoon shade. She removes her boots, massages her calves, then lays back.

We finish half of the first canteen, and I look for the second.

"Oh my god," she says. "I left it on the front seat."

"You what?"

"You were in such a rush, I forgot it. What's the big deal? We'll be out of here in no time."

I haven't told her how long it'll take to get back to Whiley's campground. One canteen isn't going to do it.

I look across the dunes, and our double footpath cuts across the otherwise unspoiled sand. My gaze follows our tracks to the only discolored object in the white brilliance. I spot my red shorts atop the fishing pole, and I know I can't cross the sand again.

Determined to find my car next time, I place three boulders in a straight line to point directly at the car. Once finished, I lie close to Leigha.

"Martin! Wake up, Martin. We slept too long."

I open my eyes and see blackness. When my vision clears, Leigha's silhouette is outlined by a billion stars.

"Oh my god, what time is it?" I press the night button and look at my watch, which reads 8:30 March 14, 2014. "Wow, we really went out. It might be easier to set the tent up out on the sand."

"I told you," she says. "I don't want anything to do with sand ever again."

"We didn't bring pads, and the sand will cushion us."

She's quiet for ten seconds, then her voice comes out of the darkness. "Okay, whatever. Get the thing set up."

I don't have the heart to tell her this won't be our last night in the desert. I'm worried about water. We used a lot crossing the dunes, and we still have thirty miles to walk back up the canyon, if I can find the way. I don't want to traipse around looking for the road, and without enough water, we don't have any time to spare.

I erect the tent, and with grumbling from Leigha, we climb in without dinner. Once we are settled, she asks in a child-like voice, "Are we going to make it, Martin?"

In a muffled tone, I say, "I think so," then feign sleep to avoid any further questions I can't answer.

The rising sun blazes into my eyes through the open flap of the tent. For the third time in my adult life, I'm up before eight. One thing is consistent; Leigha is already busy. I poke my head out of the tent at her disgruntled face. She's trying to brush her hair.

"How are we doing this morning?" I ask.

"I hate this place. Get me out of here."

"As soon as we get the car out, I'll take you home."

"You're still going to the theater."

"Sure, I'll go." I'll agree to anything at this moment.

She pulls the brush through another tangle of hair. "Will we reach the campground today?" Hope is in her voice.

I don't want to make things worse in an already rotten situation, so I don't answer.

"Well?"

"Well, what?"

"Can we get there today?"

I take a deep breath and look at her. "We have a long way to walk, especially since it's uphill."

"What do you mean? We drove down the road in a few hours. Surely we'll be able to walk to the campground by nightfall."

"Maybe by tomorrow night."

"Tomorrow night? Do you expect me to stay out here in your crappy desert for two more days?"

"I don't expect you to do anything. Unless someone drives down here, which is highly unlikely, we'll need two nights to get back."

"But. . . I can't stay out here."

I want to save her. I want to magically get a helicopter out here and carry us back to Whiley's. Short of finding a stray phone signal, there's nothing I can do. I try a call, but get only a vague hiss. To save the battery, I turn the phone off. Maybe I'll get a signal when we get higher up the canyon.

After eating a dry granola breakfast, we heft the packs to our shoulders, step off the sand, and begin a slow trek up the valley.

I secretly pray we'll find the road.

Within a mile, I'm relieved to see signs of a road, but it doesn't look the same. Unlike the graded washboard we drove along two days before, the trail is little better than a rutted wagon path.

The trail worries me, but the terrain looks familiar. I decide to follow my instincts and continue up the hill.

After midday, a breeze kicks up, and late afternoon, exhausted from the long climb, I yell over the building wind, "Let's get the tent set up before the chollas fly."

She points to the base of an outcropping. "Let's build it under those rocks, out of the wind."

Wow, she's getting a feel for being out in the wild.

We make camp on the leeward side of the rocks. The tent's up, and Leigha is inside before I shout over a gust of wind, "Be back soon."

We've walked less than ten miles, so I don't expect to see Whiley's Campground, but for an unknown reason, I want to look. No, more than want, I must look. I feel obsessed.

I scale the round boulders and pull myself over the first ledge, only to see taller boulders. I have a good view of the valley we came from, but not of our destination. Disappointed, I turn back toward the tent, but something draws my attention.

Three small adobe structures are tucked under a tall rock ledge. Although badly weathered, they stubbornly stand in the strong wind on a wide flat boulder. From the condition of the buildings, I'm sure no one has lived in them for decades.

I climb onto the rock as the wind turns to a gale, then battle my way ten yards to the first building. The rotted door shifts in the howling bluster. I feel the first cholla prick my bare neck. As I pass through the open door, I have to duck low to clear the twisted mesquite support. The building is tight enough to keep us protected. The sod roof, though not at all waterproof, is hard-packed and keeps the wind out.

I remain bent to keep my head from hitting the three-inch roof-supports. The single room measures ten feet square. Under the sand and rubble, the dirt is compacted, and the visible parts of the floor are polished from use. A small adobe hearth sits in one corner. To my delight, someone left a stack of weatherworn branches next to it. This last find, in an environment where real firewood is unheard of, looks too good to be true. I nudge the pieces of wood with my shoe, then peer up the chimney.

With the excitement of my find, I sprint to the ledge, climb down, and find Leigha huddled in the tent.

"Where have you been?" she shouts over the wind.

"I found a place that's safe."

Leigha looks at me with a familiar sneer. "Don't goof with me."

"I'm serious. I found an old building that will protect us from the wind better than this tent. It has a fireplace and wood. Let's get out of here."

"How far do we have to go in the wind to see your building?"

"On top of those rocks." I point at the boulders.

True to form, Leigha refuses to break camp until she personally inspects the new location. Ten minutes later, we hastily disassemble the red tent. With our two packs hoisted onto shoulders, we climb the rocks and scurry across the open face of the flat boulder. The wind pushes us forward.

Once inside the building, I lower my backpack into a corner, dig drifted sand away from the door, and fight it closed. A weathered branch pivots at the center of the door, stretching across and locking it to the jamb. I scoop rubble from the corners of the building and make a pile at the bottom of the door to seal the gap at the floor. Once the door seals, the room settles.

I dig inside my side pouch and retrieve one of my trusty flint and steel kits to start a fire. Why I brought two is beyond me, but I did. When a small flame bounces merrily, I add a handful of sticks. Soon, the little blaze warms the hearth. The wind whistles outside, but our tiny room feels cozy.

Oceans of sand

We spend a half hour carefully picking tufts of cholla cactus from our hair and clothes, then plucking at one another with tweezers to work out the visible spines.

Too exhausted to attempt cooking, we eat jerky and smashed bread for dinner.

"We're not going to sleep on the dirt, are we?" Leigha asks. "There are bugs."

"We'll set up the tent."

Once assembled, the top pole of the tent touches the ceiling. Strange to see an eight-foot round tent inside a ten-foot square room. If the fire wasn't contained in the little hearth in the corner, the tent wouldn't fit. We settle into our sleeping bags as the last of the fire sputters. In the light of the remaining flickers, the room assumes an eerie quality. Something isn't right, but I pass it off to mental exhaustion. Before falling asleep, I habitually peek at my watch: 9:15, March 15. I almost miss looking at the date and release the light button before realizing the year is wrong. I push the tiny button again: March 15, 1974. Nineteen seventy-four? The old Seiko has been reliable, but I've had it for fifteen years, and maybe it's time for a new watch. I settle in next to Leigha for a well-deserved night's sleep.

Three

Missing

The morning is as windy and chilly as last night. Our pile of wood dwindling, I put on my rain coat in hopes that the cholla cactus spines aren't able to penetrate the waterproof fabric.

When I search the other buildings, they all appear in better condition. Yesterday, only ours had passed as an enclosed shelter. The others were simply walls of crumbled adobe disintegrated from the weather; three sets of walls, each in its own stage of decomposition.

As I race between buildings to find scraps of wood I notice two with rotted, but serviceable roofs and count three more half-decomposed foundations, some with adjoining walls. Last night, three existed, but today six structures form a single line to the far end of the almost level boulder.

Blowing sand can make it hard to see. I must have missed the other adobe buildings, but it's odd; I've always had good night vision. I pass off the thought and search for a stick here, a scrap there, working my way back to our cozy bungalow.

I open the door, bend low, and pull it closed behind me. When I turn and look through the tent door, Leigha sits bolt upright in her sleeping bag. Her face is bone white.

I drop the arm load of wood and kneel. "Leigha, are you okay?" When she doesn't answer, I strip out of my rain suit, throw it in the corner of the room, try for a fast brush of cactus spines off my face and hair, and climb inside the tent. "Leigha, what's wrong?"

Her colorless lips move as she tries to respond, but no sound emerges. Her terrified look runs gooseflesh up my back. I take her in my arms, and she melts into a trembling mass.

A minute later, a scratchy murmur emerges from her lips. Her first sound is unintelligible, but eventually she forms the single word, "Ghost."

I hold her away from me and look into her face. "What does that mean?"

"I. . . I s-s-saw a ghost."

I've never seen anyone suffering from shock, but Leigha definitely suffers from a form of it. I follow ingrained instructions from long before, snuggle her into the sleeping bag, and pull it over her for warmth. I get the canteen, quickly strip, and climb in next to her.

When I wet my T-shirt and blot her face, she relaxes, closes her eyes, and goes into a deep sleep.

Do you let shock victims sleep or not? Why don't I know? I should. I was a Boy Scout. Hell, I passed as an

Eagle Scout and later did a tour overseas in the Army. Me, the guy who usually has all the answers, and I don't know.

She isn't physically hurt, and she's breathing. When her color returns, I decide to let her sleep.

After a while, I get out of my bag and quietly gather the discarded wood. As I turn toward the adobe fireplace, I freeze. Blood drains from my face.

When I left to gather wood, we had one small stick. Now, a stack of freshly chopped, coffee-colored limbs sits on the original bleached sprig. Sharp edges of my measly wood scraps cut into my arm until I'm forced to put them next to the mysterious dark branches.

A stone carving the size of a silver dollar sits atop the pile. I pick it up and study a wide-hipped, ample-breasted woman. A new leather thong threads through the eyelet at the top of the woman's head. The jade green stone feels smooth and soft to the touch: soapstone, I believe.

I build a small fire and add three sticks to the blaze while studying the pendant. Where did it come from? How did it get here? Who in the world would know of this place, except Leigha and me? Who would brave the wind to deliver such an odd gift? While I finger the silky amulet, I realize there won't be any answers for the moment. Maybe Leigha saw what happened. Her one word keeps returning. I'll wait for her to awake.

As the fire dances merrily, the wind outside howls harder than ever before. I get back in bed to wait out the storm. Wishing I had a book to read, I glance at my watch: 7:47, March 16, 1944.

My watch is going screwy. I tap the face repeatedly, trying unsuccessfully to get the correct year.

Fire warms the building, but the extra stack of wood worries me. The little amulet is an anomaly, but I decide to deal with it later. I cuddle up next to Leigha, then fall asleep.

When I awake, I stoke the fire. While it sparks up, I wonder again how Leigha's fright connects to the pile of fresh wood and the one word she spoke."

With nothing else to do, I study our predicament, the blessing of finding the adobe buildings, how much walking we've done, and how much we must still do. I contemplate my buried car and what it will look like once we get it out. I think about our lack of water in our barren environment. I consider many things before I hear my wife stir. Once she's awake, I ask, "What about the ghost thing?"

Her pallor returns. "I thought I'd dreamt it." There's a long pause before she continues with a quavery voice. "An old woman walked through the door with an armful of wood. She didn't open the door, but simply walked right through."

"Someone left wood stacked next to the fireplace." I hold up the pendant. "I assume that same person left this."

Leigha looks at it, then slips the pendant in her top shirt pocket.

"Hey, that's not yours."

"What?"

"The pendant I handed you."

"What pendant?"

Missing

"The one in your pocket."

"Of course, silly. I've had this pendant for years."

"I've never seen it before I picked it up by the fire."

"Are you kidding me? My lucky pendant has been with me for as long as I recall. Last year, we had to take it in and have a new leather strap made, don't you remember?"

"We did nothing of the sort. I've never seen it."

"I can't believe you don't remember."

After an awkward silence, she breaks the tension by changing the subject. "The old Indian woman walked through the tent and my sleeping bag like I didn't exist. I could see into her like a jellyfish, like in all the ghost movies we ever saw. I felt something when she walked back through the tent to go out the door. I don't know how to describe it, like a shiver of coldness. Only her friendly attitude kept me from running out into the wind."

I need time to digest the meaning. I need to distract myself from the insane evidence that some kind of spirit visited Leigha. I don't believe in spirits or ghosts, but the pile of dark wood and the pendant mean something. Someone has been here bearing gifts. My mind searches for another explanation. While I battled my way through the wind, Leigha could have gone out and returned in time to pull such a prank, but I know her. A joke would be the last thing Leigha is capable of. I can't remember one time when Leigha ever thought of spoofing me, much less doing it on such a grand scale. Even if she wanted to, there would be no way to find fresh-cut wood, and what about her claim that the pendant was hers all along?

21

When I run out of logical answers, I'm left with confusion and more than a little fear. When I get scared, I eat to calm myself. With something in my stomach, I'll think better. I root into the backpack for food.

"We have to get out of here!" Leigha says in a distant voice, while she fingers the stone amulet. "We have to leave. Something is happening; I don't know what, but it's bad."

"I wish we could leave," I say. "The wind is stronger than the other night at the car. I battled to get to the next building. If we try to go anywhere, we'll be asking for real trouble. When the winds blow, the desert is no place to be."

She snaps, a flash of anger in her eyes. "Look here, you son of a bitch, you got us here; you better get us out!"

Her glare, her needle-sharp tongue, her insistence for me to do something, is the last straw. "There's nothing I can do right now," I scream. "If you want to go out and walk in that wind, be my guest, but I'm not interested in getting lost and dying on the open desert."

"Something is going to happen if we stay." She pulls the pendant out and fondles it nervously. "I feel it in my bones. We must find a way out of here, and we have to do it now."

I open the last protein bar. "There's nothing to do until the wind dies."

Leigha eats each morsel I hand-feed her, but her eyes stay wide, her face filled with a shadow of fear.

Missing

Martin has no idea what kind of danger lurks in this old building. We need to get out of here, and we need to do it now. I step out into the wind and quickly realize we'll be forced to wait out the storm. I'm faced with one undeniable fact. We're stuck in this nightmare, at least until morning, and I'm certain some kind of disaster will happen.

The first afternoon out of Phoenix, I could smell the vaguely familiar, disquieting odors of the desert. The scents brought up old memories. As Martin drove south, I kept my window up and my attention on my computer. I wanted nothing to do with his ugly barren world. We made a deal, though, and Martin attended the first three plays, so it was my turn.

Martin was such a jerk. He kept distracting me from my computer, to see the so-called sights. I wanted nothing to do with the desert, but like a man, he had to push.

Luckily we stayed the first night in a campground, because I wouldn't have stood for setting up a tent out in the open with bugs and rodents crawling about. I also wanted one last shower before we traipsed off into his cactus-filled hole in the earth for a week. How I would endure a whole week without a shower, I didn't know; neither did I think it would be worth it, but I was committed.

Most of the first night in the tent, I dreamed of vague desert experiences I couldn't remember once awake.

The next morning, determined to make the best of my situation, I tried to act friendly. We were going to be together in this desolate country for some time. Being on good terms with my gangly, "I've-got-to-be-out-in-the-desert" husband was important, but I secretly counted the hours until we would return to civilization. The deal forced me to take part in whatever kind of "fun" Martin had in mind.

Along the gravel road, the desert looked barren and hostile. The first time Martin coaxed me out of the car, I found myself more than a little nervous. Old memories continued to crop up, though I couldn't grasp their significance. Once I saw the variety of plant life, far beyond what I could've imagined, I realized it wasn't a wasteland after all, at least not this part of the desert. By midday, I got so engrossed in the landscape, I nearly forgot my fears. Every plant in the desert was in full bloom.

At dusk the wind kicked up, and he assured me it would settle once night came. I wasn't happy when he parked in the middle of a dune-filled valley, but I got out my computer and worked until I fell asleep.

Sometime during the night, he started the car, jammed the shift lever a number of times, and gunned the engine until I couldn't stand it any longer. I thanked the gods when he gave up and turned the engine off.

The next thing I remember, Martin slid through the back window dragging a load of sand in with him.

We were buried in the desert. I was reminded of a long-ago experience. The memory came to me in a single flash, but just as quickly, it disappeared.

Missing

After hours of arguing, Martin and I emerged from the car onto the drifted mounds of sand. What could be worse than being trapped in a dark car, hopelessly stuck many miles from the nearest civilized outpost? I want to define my word "civilized," because the outpost called Whiley's has little to do with civilization. It does have a phone, though, and we need to call a tow truck.

Once I accepted that we would have to walk out, I tried to make the best of a bad situation. Fear nipped at me, but I kept reassuring myself of my maturity. Childhood fears had no place in the current situation. If we were going to emerge in one piece, my apprehensions would have to be set aside. Once we were stuck inside that crummy little building, terror jumped to the forefront. When I witnessed the faint apparition of an old woman, the experience threw fuel onto an already overheated imagination. "Martin, we have to get out of here, right now!" I told him. "Something's going to happen."

Martin and I huddled inside our zipped tent for the rest of the day and through the night. The next morning, once I put my amulet around my neck, the full impact of what happened hit me. Even then, it took a long time for understanding to sink in. I wish I had my computer to calm my nerves.

Leigha and I spend the day huddled in the stout little building. I don't know about her, but I'm thankful for its protection. The winds kick up another notch by noon. The howl sounds louder and more violent than I've ever experienced. By mid-afternoon, after staring at the door for hours, the only interesting thing in the room, I realize it's changed since last night. I remember weather cracks between the roughly hewn boards, but now the afternoon daylight barely peeks through. There was a large gap between the door and floor. I'd covered it with sand. The gap is gone and the door fits tight. Small dabs of pitch fill in the few minor separations. I get up to take a close look at the workmanship. The jamb and twisted branch beam frame over the door is carefully shaved so the door has a tight seal.

After the short interlude with the door, nothing else keeps my interest, and the day drags on. Late in the afternoon, having taken an uneasy nap, I glance at my watch yet another time and read 5:58, March 16, 1933. The time and day of the month look accurate, but the year! My watch is winding backward at an incredible rate. Without drawing Leigha's attention, I tap on the plastic face of the watch again. I'm reluctant to mention the problem to her. She has enough on her mind.

With nothing else to do, Leigha and I doze as the day turns into night and darkness adds a spooky quality to the hurricane-force winds. When I awake later, the fire is reduced to embers. I toss the last of the gift pieces of wood into the hearth and scramble into the sleeping bag. I hope for a warmer day when the sun rises. I snuggle in and close all the remaining openings in the sleeping bag, then watch in curious horror as the same old woman Leigha described passes through the closed door. She's dressed in layers of thick cloth, carrying another stack of wood.

Leigha sleeps, and I'm not about to wake her. The translucent grandmother walks right through the tent, as if it isn't here. A cold shiver runs through my body as she steps through me to the hearth. Without a sound, she drops the arm load of logs. When the sticks hit the floor, they make no noise. She turns and retraces her steps. She passes Leigha and leans over to finger the little stone pendant. When she reaches the door, she turns and looks at me with a gentle gaze. Her mouth forms words, but I hear nothing. Her entire withered face smiles as she turns and passes back through the locked door. I get up and inspect the new wood, handling each stick as if it will disappear.

Thoughts of what I've just seen run laps in my head until I'm finally able to fall into a slumber. With Leigha cuddled at my side, I sleep through the remainder of the night.

The next morning, before I'm fully awake, the wind is quiet. I open my eyes and try to focus on the fingers of daylight piercing the few holes along the ceiling. The brightness of a sunny day filters into the room. I reach over to wake Leigha. True to form, she's already out of bed. She's probably been up for hours, sitting on the rocks to watch the start of a new day. I hear restrained bumps and periodic steps in the gravel outside the door.

The inside walls of our little building, unlike the day before, look smooth and polished. Earlier, patches of adobe had decomposed enough to allow the stacked flat rock under-base to show. Now, every wall looks fresh and carefully finished. I sit up, look about, and see the smooth dirt floor, hard packed and recently swept.

Did our ghost friend come in during the night and repair the building? It's the only explanation. Although the roof held well in the wind, last night it had been in dire need of repair. Today it's sealed. The building is in complete repair. There can be only one other explanation. I must be dreaming.

I pinch myself and feel the sting.

I get out of my sleeping bag, dress, walk to the door, and rotate the crossbar. When I bend and step through the small opening, I smell something cooking.

"Leigha, did you see what happened. . ." My forward movement stops. My heart flutters. My mouth drops open. I feel faint. It takes concentration to maintain an upright position. Three steps back, I put my hand out behind me to steady myself on the building.

I expect Leigha to be preparing our breakfast, but my mind is forced to leap into the abyss of a darker possibility.

The old woman, the apparition who brought us wood, bends over an open pit fire turning a crooked wooden spit, and roasts what looks like a skinned rabbit. I stand motionless, while she turns the makeshift crank. Slowly, as if in a dream, she rotates her head and looks in my direction. She smiles a toothless grin.

"Waa. . . wha. . . what are you doing here?"

Her smile widens, and she speaks to me in a language much like the Mayan Indians of southern Mexico. With a crooked forefinger, she points at the roasting rabbit, then motions me to come to the fire.

In shock, I stumble over and sit on my haunches. "Where is Leigha?"

The old woman answers in her exotic dialect.

I try to think of a way to sign the question to her, but give up.

She reaches over with a gnarled hand and peels a long piece of flesh from the roasted rabbit. I'm mesmerized by her piercing eyes, which sparkle as she hands me the strip of meat.

"Thank you," I say absently.

The rabbit tastes delicious. In three careful, hot bites, I finish the strip. She hands me another, then another. We sit in silence on the edge of the boulder sharing the meal, until the carcass is stripped clean. When finished, she throws the bones over the ledge.

I grab a twig and draw a stick figure in the sand of a human wearing a dress. I look out to the horizon, then behind me at the six intact buildings. I shrug my shoulders. "Where is Leigha?"

I get a distinct feeling she knows what I want. She takes my stick and makes a detailed sketch of a male figure with hands cupped under its head in a sleeping position. She points at the sketch in the sand, then at me. Is she suggesting I go take a nap? It doesn't make sense. I sit stupefied. A nap is the last thing on my mind. Automatically, I look at my watch and read: 11:23, March 17, 1901.

"What is the date?" I ask.

She shrugs, looks up, and scratches at the sketch. I ignore her suggestion, then stand to look for Leigha. Not sure what else to do, I bow to the old woman, turn and step away to search the six buildings.

A small hand-hewn table stands in the far corner of the structure that houses our tent. It's a piece of furniture I've not seen before. The second adobe, in disrepair, but still functional, has a straw sleeping pad in the far right corner. A small shelf protrudes from the wall in the opposite corner. Odd artifacts sit carefully positioned atop it; teeth, a large claw, a white necklace of bone.

I inspect the remaining four buildings, each in worse condition, but I find Leigha nowhere. Considering her childhood trauma in the desert, I'm certain she hasn't wandered far.

For the next twenty minutes, I look atop and under each ledge, scour the surrounding rocks, and scan the desert below. As minutes tick by, I get more frantic, finally resorting to a yell, "LEE-AAA!" No response. I race to the north side of the settlement, search, and yell again. I direct my last try westward, where I stretch out the scream long and loud, knowing in the silence of the desert, my voice will carry for miles. I'm afraid she has fallen and lies hurt in the rocks. I'm on and under every boulder in the large outcrop surrounding the adobes. I yell Leigha's name for what seems like an hour, before I go to the old woman. She still sits quietly in front of the dwindling fire. I squat on my haunches and look at her suspiciously. "You know where she is, don't you?"

She looks long into my eyes. With a stern grimace, she turns and points at the sleeping man drawn in the sand. She jabs her index finger toward the sketch, then slowly repositions her hand, pointing at my chest.

"A nap?" I ask.

Out of sheer frustration, though I awoke less than an hour ago, I follow her instruction and go into the building. To my amazement, I fall asleep.

My dreams are odd and disjointed. Moments before I awake, I float up from my sleeping position, slip through the closed door, and see the old woman who still sits in front of the open pit fire, cooking another small creature. She turns toward me with foot-long blazing fingers of fire spewing from each of her eyes. The flames are as real as the campfire she cooks over.

Without moving her lips, she speaks in a commanding, God-like voice. "I am the sorcerer Maranther. You and your woman have been separated for now. She is safe and well cared for. Do not waste your energy trying to find her. I have isolated you to test your willingness to delve into your past. When you have both proved yourselves, the two of you will reunite. I will come to you in dreams as your work progresses."

"My work progresses?" I yell. "My work progresses? I'm not a damned high-school student. I want my wife returned, and I want her right now, or I'll. . ." I realize there's nothing I can do. I'm out in the middle of the desert, and the woman has stolen my wife. In a rage, I reach across the smoldering ashes to grab the ancient woman, but her image fades, then disappears.

I awake on my side in the sleeping bag. I'm facing away from Leigha, with the debilitating certainty that I'm trapped in the mad woman's puzzle.

With my eyes still closed, I reach to Leigha. Maybe I had some kind of horrible nightmare. I want to believe my wife is still lying beside me. All I have to do is reach

out and touch her. I long to breathe a sigh of relief, hold
her tight, break camp, and get the hell out of here.

I touch cold, open space. I turn and look into a rip
in my reality. Not only is she gone, her side of the tent
is empty. Her sleeping bag, that silly little air pillow
she thought was so necessary, her clothes, even her
backpack are all missing. I smell a faint scent of her, but
have no other proof she was ever here. I've failed her.
I've abandoned her in the one place where she needs
support. Guilt weighs on me, as I imagine her alone out
there. Her childhood drama is playing itself out again,
except now I'm responsible.

I should get up and look for her, but she is in the
clutches of that spirit. I must concentrate my thoughts
and consider all possibilities. I have to come up with a
plan, but I already suspect that the only way out of this
mess is to go through whatever the ghost woman has in
mind.

Anger surges deep in my guts. Without thinking about
what I'm doing, I leap to my feet and run outside to grab
the old woman. I want to shake my wife's whereabouts
out of her. I don't care how old she looks. I stand in the
exact spot where she sat, but she's gone. The cook fire
has vanished. The place where the flame danced looks as
though it has not seen a blaze in years.

On the ledge of the gigantic stone slab, I look out
toward the desert. In sheer frustration, I violently kick
the pile of old ashes until there are none left to kick.
Tears roll down my cheeks. I fall to my knees, surprising
myself with a long, deep howl. I'm a wounded animal.
My grief rises out of my guts and rolls out onto the silent

desert. It takes a long time for my body to expel enough guilt and grief for me to get up and think about what to do next. When I'm able to stop moaning, I stand and search the expansive valley to the west with the certainty that the old hag has taken Leigha.

Four

Lost in the Past

Half-awake, I reach over for my husband and open my eyes into ink darkness. "Martin, where are you?" but I get no answer. I don't understand. Where is he?

"Martin?"

The winds have stopped. In the prevailing silence, I hear no noise in or outside this cruddy little building, no crunching of gravel underfoot or swish of clothing. The moment I fully comprehend that Martin might not be close, my mind snaps fully awake. I hate the dark and, more so, silence.

Terror creeps up my spine.

He went out to pee. Probably standing on the edge of the boulder, sending a stream forty feet to the desert floor. I strain to hear any sound to support my theory, but I hear nothing.

As the seconds tick by, my throat constricts. My heart

35

races. My eyes strain to see if he's tricking me. I wouldn't put it past him. This one would be right up his alley.

I feel for his empty sleeping bag and my heart stops. My breath catches. There is no sleeping bag, only cold, hard-packed dirt.

In a stern voice, I say, "Martin Vandorfor, if you're in here, you had better say something right now. This is no time to fool around."

The amulet is around my neck, and I feel comfort from stroking its smooth surface.

I'm enraged, but I'll be relieved when he answers.

"Martin." I hear my voice crack.

He doesn't answer.

I raise my voice so he'll hear from outside. "Mar-tin."

In the distance, a single coyote howls.

Maybe he went for a walk, but a guy who normally can't wake before noon, has gone for a walk in the desert, in the middle of the night? I don't think so.

Something terrible has happened. His disappearance is the first indication.

Abandonment floods me. Tears roll down my face. "Martin," I cry. "Where are you? Martin, don't leave me here."

I wallow in emotion for a long time. When I finally come out of my feeling of abandonment, I need to be able to see. I want to feel the comfort of being in a lit room, even in this crummy little building. I crawl on my hands and knees out of my warm sleeping bag into the chilly silence. I feel around for my pack, which leans against the wall. When I find it, I also feel for Martin's pack, but touch nothing. As I search the side pockets for my flashlight, my fear amps up another notch.

The whole scene is out of control. If Martin is playing a trick, he's dead meat.

This is Martin's last joke and the end of his life as a trickster. When I locate the flashlight and find him in the corner with his shit-eating grin, I'm going to lay into him in ways he never thought possible.

My search for a light is frustrating, as I recklessly rip open every zipper and pull out the contents of each pocket; brush, lip balm, note pad, pen, tissue, but I can't find the light. I yank everything out of every side pocket, finger through them, then go into the main pouches. In the far corner of the bottom pouch, my hands wrap around the familiar cylinder. I heft it and push the button.

"You son of a bitch," I say. 'You're going to wish you were dead if you're in here." As the light comes on, I already intuitively know Martin isn't inside the building. I know he isn't playing a trick, though I'll be relieved if he is. The beam comes on, and for a second, I hesitate to flash it around the empty room. If he's playing a trick, he'd have revealed himself by now. Still on my knees, I spin around. When my light stops moving, my breath catches. My heart stops beating as I blink from the brightness of the light.

The ghost woman sits on an ancient chair, leaning her right arm on a small table across from the hearth. My beam stops directly in her face. Too shocked to move, I can't believe what I'm seeing.

Before I feel myself go faint, my last thought confirms my nightmare. I want to wake up and get out of here.

Blackness surrounds me. I'm in a dream. I feel the old woman's presence in the darkness. I want to scream and run, but know it's futile. I'm in a desert, and there is no place to run.

A deep-throated, but gentle voice speaks into the dark. "I am the sorceress Maranther."

The calmness in the statement makes me feel safe.

"I've come to help you remember."

"Help me remember what?"

I'm enveloped with relief. I feel so safe, I almost don't ask the crucial question. "Where is Martin?"

"Your man performs a task for me. He will return."

The gentleness in her voice reminds me of my long-dead mother.

"When will he return?"

"Whenever he finishes."

"Okay," I say. "We'll see him when he gets back. For now, what do you want of me?"

"Fear will be with you when you awake," she says. "Go toward your fear to find what drives your emotion."

In a normal situation a statement of that sort would leave me wondering what she meant, but I instantly understand. My childhood desert experience incites my fear. This dread has been in the driver's seat for a long time, too long. I have an immediate grasp of the source, a working understanding. I know what actions I'll need, but it won't be easy. "Is that all you ask of me?"

Her voice comes out of the darkness. "It will be enough for now, to remember."

She's gone, and I see only the blackness of the room.

I stand a long time, gazing over the open desert and lament my situation, before I go back into the adobe. I wonder where Leigha is. When I turn to face the building, I meet the gaze of fifteen brown-skinned people, their faces serene. I feel no judgment from them, as I would have judged, had I witnessed a crazy person yowling at the desert like a coyote. They are part of the nightmare connected with the old woman.

My anger flares again. "What are you looking at?" I kick scattered ashes in their direction. They all stand motionless as I try to destroy the pit. In the process, I accidentally kick one of the larger stones. I scream in agony, hop around with my injured foot in the air. I feel like a cartoon. Forced to sit, I rub my toe and go into another round of open sobs.

When a gentle hand rests on my shoulder, I look up with tear-filled eyes. A weathered old man looks at me with concern. Quiet and reassuring, he speaks a short sentence, but I can't understand the dialect. I fall into more wailing. His hand stays on my shoulder until I've cried myself out. He walks in front of me and squats to face me. When he speaks again, though I understand nothing of what he says, I feel his compassion, which gives me solace.

"Thank you," I say, between sniffles.

We stand, and the fully grown man is only five feet

tall. I look at the others, then understand why the door frames on the adobes are so small.

Completely overwhelmed by my situation, I plod to my bungalow and fall onto my sleeping bag. In five minutes a shadow spreads across my door. A young girl with a bowl and tortillas kneels tentatively, sets the bowl in front of me, then scurries out. I use a tortilla to absently scoop the black beans from the bowl into my mouth. By the time I finish the second bite, I'm hungry, ravenous. Only ten minutes before, I shared a rabbit with the old woman, but my watch reads five hours have passed. What happened to the missing time?

I don't know where to begin to solve the old woman's puzzle. I can't even remember her name. I lie on my back and look at the twigs that hang from the sod ceiling. So much in my own world, I'm oblivious to any activity outside. Later, the old man steps into the building and sits. At first he studies the tent structure. When he rests his gaze on me, he says something in his language.

"I don't understand." I sit up and try again in the few words of Spanish I know.

He looks over at me with a blank face and obvious incomprehension, then pulls a twig from the raw adobe wall. He draws a sleeping stick figure into the hard-packed floor, roughly the same sketch the old woman drew earlier. Although, I don't need any more bad news for the day, I'm sure it's what he wants to tell me. I nod and dutifully lie on my sleeping bag. With the agility of a cat, he stands, turns, and leaves the room. The withered guy must be eighty, but his feline movements amaze me.

I've slept twice today and a third time might be a problem, but the moment I close my eyes, I fall into a dream. The old man steps through the doorway. He sits in front of the opening as he did before. "We must talk now."

I hear his words, but like the conversation with the old woman, I don't see his lips move.

"How can we talk to one another in my dreams, yet not when I'm awake? How do you come to my dream and—"

He holds up his hand. "I will answer your questions, Kicking Ashes, but not all at once.

"We talk because in the dream world, our language is of the spirit." While he speaks, his hands cut the air in rhythmic signing movements. His gesture and style of speech make me feel like I'm watching an old spaghetti western. "We talk without spoken language," he says.

"Kicking Ashes?" I ask. "What does it mean?"

"In our village, names come from the first experience after birth. Your birth happened in our small village today. When you appeared, you kicked ashes.

"I am Running Feathers, the medicine man of this village." His arm makes a sweep and rests on his chest.

"Where did you come from?"

"Your question would be better answered by asking where did you come from. We have been in this village for three generations since the white eye banished us from our homeland. It was you who suddenly appeared kicking the pit. We are accustomed to appearances. During our stay here, we've had more than our share. Many summers ago, my grandfather learned about a powerful brujo who lives close by." He points south. "The sorcerer gets pleasure by creating chaos in our little village. In my time as medicine keeper, I've learned that he steals energy from his victims' weakness. To us, you appear, stay a day or two, then just as magically disappear for years, only to surface again. You are the latest of many under his spell."

"You refer to him as masculine, but I met an old woman."

He grimaces and makes another small hand gesture. "Man, woman, young, old, fat, thin, it does not matter. He is always the same magician that causes trouble, the sorcerer Maranther."

"Maranther is her name. You say she. . . well. . . he, takes power from our weakness. What kind of weakness?"

"We do not know the answer to your question. All the victims we have known have succumbed, withered, then died."

"Died?" I blanch. "Do you mean they couldn't figure out the puzzle, and they died?"

The old man gives a single, solemn nod. "Death is the eventual outcome, but it takes time."

After a moment to digest his confirmation, I say, "My wife and I came here together to get out of a windstorm. Last night, Maranther separated us. That's why I kicked the ashes."

"Air is an element Maranther has under control. He stirred the wind to force you into his trap."

"Maranther says Leigha is well cared for. Do you know if I can trust that sorcerer's word?"

"Trust nothing. If your woman exists on the other side, her energy is also draining, but it will take two or three moons. For now you have nothing to fear. She will not be harmed."

"What do you mean when you say many have come from other time periods?"

"When do you come from?"

"When," I ask, "like what date?"

"Yes, what date?"

"2014."

He gives me a wry smile. "Ah, yes, Maranther reaches far into the future. We live in our own time, but the whites give our year of the flowers the number 1886."

I look at my watch and the year stops me. "Oh my God! The watch is right. The date is correct."

"What is this on your arm? I have not seen such a thing."

I lift my wrist.

"Oh, yes, the timepiece you whites find so necessary. I have never seen one lashed to the arm, though, and never the flashing symbols. I would like to take a closer look when out of our dream world."

"How did I get to 1886?"

He shrugs. "The brujo is a powerful sorcerer. He has skills no man imagines."

"How do I get back to my time?"

The old man looks beyond me. "My dream ability wanes. I must go now, but I will return when I have regained strength."

"When will that be?"

He stands and turns to leave the room. His image

fades as he stops at the doorway. The blue sky shows through him. He turns, puts three gnarled fingers up and says, "Three suns. While I am gone, think about your weakness."

I awake, feeling like I've been out for ten minutes. I'm surprised to find myself in a cold, pitch-black room. I look at my watch: 5:22, March 18, 1886.

The next three days, I enjoy the hospitality of my guardians. They feed me and bring wood as I lie in a catatonic state of confusion. When I get too bored, I wander out into the desert. Without them, I'd starve. I've dropped deep into self-evaluation, searching for a weakness allowing Maranther to hold me.

Although everyone in the tribe takes good care of me, they keep their distance. Running Feathers is the only one who communicates. In the regular, non-dreaming world, the language barrier is painful. By the end of the second day, I feel lonely.

On the morning of the third day, he comes to me again in my dreams. I've missed talking to anyone.

"Why are your people afraid of me?"

"What has happened to you has happened here many times. Many travelers have appeared in our village. My people do not understand where you come from. They see you all as spirits. You come out of the future, and either you will return soon, or die trying. Either way, you come to us as a spirit.

"They are frightened by your red sleeping hut the most. We have never seen such a thing or such a color on anything except the cactus flower in spring. I admit, to have so much color in one place causes concern. To have you emerge from it is unsettling."

"It's a tent. In my world anyone can buy anything like this for a small amount of money."

"I do not understand words 'buy' or 'money.'"

"In the modern world we trade money for what we need."

"Oh yes, trading. I understand."

"I've thought carefully about my flaws, and I have too many to single one out."

"This is not an easy thing," he says. "Maranther wants your life force, and you will find him devious. One thing we have witnessed through many seasons, our brujo has strength, but he cannot maintain his energy. When he takes time to rebuild, you will snap back to your world for a short period."

"How?"

"I have never been to the other side of time, so I do not know how. The others who came before you tell me when one snaps back, the world is as it was."

"Does it mean I'll be with Leigha?"

He shrugs. "I do not know these things."

"Since I'm stuck here, I'd like to learn your language. When we're not dreaming, will you help me understand the names of things around us?"

Running Feathers smiles. "You are the first white who wants to learn our language."

I have too little time before the old man runs out of energy. I need answers before he disappears.

"I don't understand. What do I do when I discover my weakness? Maranther never explained."

"I do not know, but I do know Maranther will return

soon. When he does, prepare your questions carefully. He is compelled to tell you the truth, but remember, this sorcerer is a coyote. He has learned to wrap the truth in confusion."

He pauses and looks at me with searing black eyes. "My strength slips. I must go to the waking world, but I will return." He rises and floats out the door.

When I awake, I lie on my back thinking of my weakness. I have many flaws I've never faced, and I have no idea where to begin, or which ones are important. Also, what am I supposed to do, once I remember?

I spend the rest of the day on my bed pondering my dilemma. Before dark, I slip into sleep. The moment I doze off, the old woman appears at the opening of my tent.

She sits cross-legged like an eastern yogi. "Ah yes, you have been thinking." Like Running Feathers, her lips don't move when she talks.

Her form has shifted. I can't put my finger on it, but she has changed. I'm distracted by the subtle variation in her physical looks and at first, find it hard to articulate my questions.

I ask, "What do I do with my weakness when I find it?"

"Yes, it is a good question," she says. "Not one of my other students has asked so early in training."

"Training?"

"I search for students to learn my knowledge. Some students grasp what I teach, while others wither. You show promise. I am happy to have you to work with. My last student took a moon before she even asked your question. When she did, it was too late. She didn't have enough strength left to use the answer."

"So what is the answer?" I ask directly.

"There is a saying among my people. 'Weakness is strength, without knowledge.' A good proverb, don't you think?"

"Answer my question first before we go any further. What do I do with my weakness when I find it?"

"Not what you do, but how you do it that is important. The how lies in your ability to concentrate and focus your mind on your one task. Not many have accomplished your assignment, but your ability to ask the question so soon gives me hope. Do people from your time think faster? Your woman has also asked the same question."

"Leigha," I say. "You've spoken to Leigha? Is she all right?"

"She is being well taken care of, as I promised."

"When will I be able to see her?"

"When you have the answers, she will return."

Maranther has diverted my question. "What do I do with my weakness when I find it? I want to know the answer."

The old woman fades, and I reach out with a fierce gaze to hold her. Her eyes flash and bore into mine. I feel the top of my head open. An enraged, God-like voice booms in my head. "Never put your measly intent on me, you little worm. I am Maranther."

The pressure increases. I'm weak in my knees. My stomach cramps. I feel like vomiting. "The answer," I demand weakly. "What's the answer?" It's the last of my strength.

She screeches like a hawk. Pressure increases in my skull. I'm about to lose my mental grip. The last thing I see is a huge eagle standing over me. It takes a fierce strike toward my right eye. Its razor-sharp beak opens. Before it touches me, I let go and float into an abyss.

When I awake, the blackness of night integrates with the void of where I've been. I look at my watch and read: 4:13, March 23. I've been out for two days. I release the night light button before I realize the date. When I push the button again, I read: 2014.

I shift to find my flashlight and feel Leigha's warm body lying next to me. I reach out and touch her. Tears flow.

"Leigha, Leigha," I sob, while I shake her, but she will not awaken. I jostle her roughly, then remember she always sleeps like the dead. Any attempt to wake her in the middle of the night is futile.

I cuddle and enjoy the comfort of her warm body next to mine. Before I fall asleep, I vow first thing tomorrow to get the two of us out of this damn desert.

The late morning sun blasts through a hole in the roof. In the corner of the building where the adobe hearth was, a boulder the size of a small car rests. It apparently fell from the cliff above, crushing one corner of the building. I reach out for Leigha, but she's gone. I bolt out of bed and into the chilly morning air, then run outside. The adobes, which stood in such good repair when I last saw them, have crumbled into nothingness. Lines of rocks show where buildings had been long ago. I look at my watch in shock: 2048.

"Lee-aaa," I call, already knowing Maranther has

separated us again. A dark depression grips my throat, while I fight back my tears.

Hours later, I drag myself out of self-pity, refocus, and look around. The rock crushed the building, but on closer inspection, it happened years ago. My intelligence grasps what's going on, but the rest of me reels from the shift.

Although my tent sits in direct line of the falling rock, it is unharmed, but precariously perched atop the pile of rubble. I pull the tent and my sleeping bag to a safe flat spot.

After reorganizing the tent, I walk to the northern corner of the boulder and look toward the old gravel road Leigha and I had driven a few days before. A band of asphalt covers the spot where we pitched the tent. I descend to the center of the road and stare at the ribbon of flat blackness. Apparently it is no longer a new road, though the broken white line is reasonably fresh.

A low-pitched sound rumbles from higher up the road. I turn as a large beat-up truck barrels around the bend. Its engine thumps from decompression as it careens downhill. Dumbfounded, I forget to step out of the road until the truck is upon me. The driver blows his horn, and I quickly step aside. I look into the cab and catch a flash of a burly arm with the middle finger extended.

"Asshole," the deep voice yells as the truck thunders past. Some things are universal throughout time.

My eyes follow the brake lights until they disappear around the turn. The thump of the engine fills the air long after the truck has gone out of sight. A moment later, a low, sleek car zips by and follows the truck down the hill. I take three steps back onto the shoulder as a motorcycle zings past.

I consider catching a ride from a passing car to get help, but I wouldn't know what to say.

"Can you help? I'm here from thirty years ago and my wife is caught in the 1800s." They'd lock me in the loony bin for sure. It's inviting to stay in the year 2048. If Leigha was with me, I'd seriously consider it. Thirst finally drives me to step closer to the middle of the road and flag the next vehicle.

Within thirty minutes, three cars pass me. As each approaches, it speeds up, ready to run me down if I don't move. The fourth, a dented yellow van, blond surfer at the wheel, pulls to the side of the road. I run to his open window.

"Where you going, buddy?"

"Thanks for stopping. I'm not going anywhere; I'm thirsty. Do you have any water?" I point behind me. "I'm camped over the hill and ran out of drinking water."

He reaches over the seat into an ice chest and hands me a quart sport bottle of chilled spring water. "You need a ride or som'thin'?"

"I'll need a ride later." I crack the seal on the plastic bottle and take a long gulp. "I have things to take care of. Can you spare something to eat? I'm starved."

He hesitates, then pulls out a sandwich. "Hey, man, you sure you're going to be all right? The desert's no place to go without food or water. It'll swallow you and spit your bones out. I could get you over the border into Yuma in an hour."

I reach into my pocket and separate a ten-dollar bill from my cash. "Is Whiley's campground up the hill?"

"Yeah, sure, 'bout fifteen miles."

I hand the bill through the window. "Let me pay you for the water and sandwich. Can I buy a second jug?"

He looks at my money, then at me. "What's wrong with you, man? What the hell am I going to do with old money? Besides, I've got only one jug left, and I'm gunna need it for my trip. If you don't need a ride, I'll be takin' off."

From his blanched expression it's apparent that I've shaken him. Nervously, he pulls his shift lever down into drive.

"Too much to do right now, but thanks." I step back as the van pulls onto the road and disappears downhill. I study the money. "Looks okay to me," I say aloud, then put it in my pocket. I take another long drink and open the sandwich. The smell of tuna bursts from within the wrapper. My taste buds go nuts. I wolf it down.

An hour passes, another dozen cars, but none stop. With great reluctance, I climb the rock ledge and return to the crumbled adobes.

The bottle of water is gone by the time I get to my tent. If I'm going to survive out here, and I won't leave without Leigha, I'm going to have to find a source of water and food. The way time jumps, I'm not sure where I'll wake next.

I remember fuzzy phrases about conserving energy and water. They come to the surface, as I try to think of what to do next. The memory is hazy, but I draw from those wilderness classes at Boy Scout camp as a kid. I sit in front of the decomposed adobes on the ledge of the huge boulder and try to reach into those playful, rambunctious days of my youth.

I remember going to camp and survival classes, but little else comes forward. If I'm going to survive out here, I'll have to resurrect my early training. After an hour of concentrated effort, a clear memory of the snaring class comes to me. I jump up, go into the tent, and retrieve a roll of fishing line I'd seen in an earlier search. I'm forced to braid the light line to make it strong enough for my needs.

I climb off the rock, walk three hundred yards out into the desert, still in sight of the adobes, and find an area that might do well. A twenty-foot-long V-shaped run is needed, so I stack thorny bushes along the two sides. When the loop of the snare is positioned around the only opening at the point of the trap, I hide it carefully. As an anchor, the other end of the line goes around the base of a cactus, then to a thick branch pulled tight to create tension.

With time on my hands, I take a walk around the wide part of the V and attempt to drive any potential wildlife into the trap. Having failed a number of times to herd anything other than a lizard into my trap, I go to the shade of the boulders.

Water may be my more critical issue.

The natives who had taken care of me had plenty of water, but I didn't have the foresight to find out where it came from. My mistake may cost me as the days heat up. Sitting still in the shade is my only alternative. I stretch out under the cool boulder and doze.

I awake in the dark. Only starlight helps me find my sleeping bag. I climb into the bag and feel my thirst and pangs of hunger. I glance at my watch: March 24, 2016.

The next day, though it's not as hot as the previous one, I set a new snare, then stay under the boulders in the shade to conserve body moisture. If I get through the next few days, I hope to travel to Running Feathers' time and learn of his source of water.

In late afternoon, I climb off the boulder and walk out onto the desert to find a rabbit hanging from the woven fish line. I'm hungry enough to bite into it, fur and all. On the way back to the adobes, I use my pocketknife to puncture a hole under its ribs. The knife pulls down, and the creature's organs spill out onto the ground. I remove the skin and fur, a difficult task, but eventually I drop the remains on the gravel and finish my walk to the settlement. When a blaze dances in the same pit where the old woman sat, I make a beginner's attempt to build a spit and roast the meat. Long after dark, I take my first tentative bite of the tough flesh. In my extreme state of hunger, old shoe leather would taste good. The rabbit is delicious. I reduce the carcass to bones in a ravenous frenzy. Satisfied, I roll onto my sleeping bag under a black sky. Moments before I fall asleep, thoughts of water, or better yet, cold bottles of beer, swim around in my head.

The old woman soon appears. "I am Maranther," she booms. Has she returned to finish me off? I attempt to back up, but find myself pinned into a sitting position. Fear squeezes all of the air out of me. I'm expecting her to shift into a ghoulish troll or a grizzly bear, then attack, this time to end my life, but the transformation isn't life threatening at all. Instead, she shifts from the withered, fossilized old hag to a woman in her early fifties. She acts jovial. With a smile, she says, "You have passed the first test."

"Which test?"

"The one of survival. Some could not make it even this far." She reverently places a hand on her chest. "My heart sings to know you are still with us."

A serious look crosses her ever-changing face. She frowns and speaks in a low voice. "The second chore will be upon you soon, Little Worm. Be careful and move with much caution."

I prepare to ask my one question, the one that got me in so much trouble last time, but her playful, intimate nickname for me throws me off. Finally, I open my mouth. "What do I do with my weakness?" The woman fades, then disappears altogether.

In the pre-dawn blackness, I ponder the dream and wonder what the old woman means by "move with much caution." Unconsciously, I look at my watch: 2:14, March 25, 1956.

I'm slipping back in time, just not fast enough.

What was Maranther's real first test? It couldn't have been simple survival. Anyone can survive in the desert in early spring. There must be more. Is the next duty to find water? If I'm truly going to survive, I'll need to accomplish this task soon. Where is Running Feathers? Where are his people when I need them? They know where to find water.

Will I be able to get to Running Feather's time? Will it

be a few more jumps, like last time, or will I leap past his time? What do the skips in time mean? How does time change? All morning, thoughts run through my brain.

Of course, I can't believe I didn't see it before. The jumps in time directly connect to sleep. This must be the second task. The old woman said to move with caution. She must have meant figure out how time works and move with it.

I spend many hours in careful thought about her warning. Do I have more to be cautious about? Was her warning a clue, or could she be leading me on to waste my time? I know I'm close to the answer, but I'm not yet sure what it is.

In a flash of inspiration, I suddenly understand the sleep-time connection. The more I sleep, the more months and years slip by. To get to Running Feathers, I will need to sleep either more time or more often. As a first experiment in my new understanding, I set my watch alarm to 3:45, a little more than an hour. It takes a while, but I finally fall asleep. When the watch beeps, I look at my wrist and read: 1949. The concept is right. I'm on the right track, I just have to fine-tune it.

I ponder Maranther's warning while resetting my watch.

The next time I wake, I look out at a brilliant mauve and scarlet dawn. My watch reads: 1933.

I notice, no, more like feel someone watching. I look along the line of adobes and see no one. I search the desert floor. I glance behind me and see nothing. A wall of boulders, but still I sense a presence. Accidentally, I look toward the cliff. A huge, tan-colored cougar sits high in the shadows. Its color matches the stone. Only dilated yellow eyes stand out. Its ears flatten. A pink tongue protrudes from a half-open mouth. But its eyes. Its eyes freeze me with fear. I'm unable to move. Any second it will leap off the ledge. I sit motionless. The muscles of the cougar's front legs ripple. My mind races. Adrenaline pumps. I'm ready to bolt, but I'm glued to my spot. My hand rests on the ground. I feel for something loose. My fist finds three small stones. I pull them into my grip. It isn't much. I'll have one chance. I'll have to land my rocks hard, right on its nose. I'm not sure I can move at all.

The cougar's legs bunch. Time slows. The big cat is airborne. It snarls.

Of all things to think about at the end of my life, I hardly expect my mind to spring back and relive the shadowy vagueness of that damn summer camp so many years ago. Vividly, I remember getting off of the bus, excited about a week with kids my own age.

The cougar flies through the air.

I remember a feeling of freedom. I relive meeting my three roommates: Johnny Fulbright, Frank Gunter, and I can't remember the name of the last boy, but I do remember his demeanor, his angelic looks. He had the cherub face of the Greek god of love, Cupid. His pudgy little cheeks were soft and slightly flushed, as if someone had pinched them. I remember the contrasting sullen stare, but I cannot remember his name.

Bullet-like, the cat pierces the calm air. Its trajectory is like an arrow. My throwing arm freezes as my mind continues exploring a distant past.

I see the first tentative nods from the other boys in my cabin as we stand with our packs and suitcases. We stare at one another. I must have been eight. It was the first time I'd been away from home. I was finally away from my over protective mother, who hadn't wanted me to go. Fortunately, dad supported me.

"If the boy wants to go to camp, he should go," my father insisted in one of the only times he took my side in a dispute.

The cougar is in the air, super slowed in time. It's twenty feet from my face. I'm nineteen feet from death. It's eighteen feet from tearing me to shreds. The cat is so close, I see saliva drip from its mouth. Another roar rolls past me. Without any purposeful thought, because I'm thinking more about my weak-spined father at the time, my right arm gathers strength and springs into action. The already-too-large head of the cougar gets larger. My arm swings hard.

My mind refuses to concentrate on the immediacy of the moment. My thoughts continue a journey through memory lane, a past I haven't thought of for years.

The other two boys are not important as I concentrate on the cupid-like boy. I strain to remember his name. Who was he? What happened to him, and why does it stick in my craw? I'm angry and sad at the same time.

My arm swings hard. I feel the weight of the stones. They leave my fingers at breakneck speed.

I try to remember the next sequence beyond the opening of the cabin door at Camp Rolunda. Rotilla? A smile crosses my face. We called it Camp Rotunda, because of the overweight kids and counselors. Neither of those names is quite right, though, but close. Why we gave it the nickname opens another flood of memory.

This is a hell of a time to think of such unimportant reminiscences. I'm ten feet from being mauled, and all I can think of is summer camp forty years ago?

My blood pumps. The mountain lion's outstretched paw touches the ground two yards in front of me.

I've never had much of an aim, consequently was always picked last for baseball. The stones head directly for the cat's nose. My old baseball buddies would be proud. My eyes strain to see what will happen. The feline is so close that I smell the wild odor of its breath. I want to close my eyes. I want to give myself over to fate, but I'm forced to watch. The largest of the rocks hits directly on the soft skin of its snout. I wait for the lion to flinch, but it doesn't. It's all over. There will be little left of me for Leigha, if she ever comes to find me. Some bones maybe, if they're not dragged off.

I'm cougar breakfast. I can't comprehend the next thing that happens. I imagine the razor sharp gouge of its claws, the weight of its body slamming against mine, a merciful bite in my neck to end my life quickly. My own blood spills out onto the stone slab. My life drifts away. I'm prepared for my own demise, but nothing happens. Have I already disconnected from my body and don't feel the attack? Am I numb to life? Am I dead?

I blink to clear my vision, but the illusion persists.

The first stone, which struck dead center on the nose of the cat and should have made it flinch, if only slightly, vanishes, swallowed up as if it never existed. The second smacks one ear, and the third flies directly into the cat's gaping mouth. The cat does not care. It keeps coming, inches from my face. I've given over to death with morbid fascination, until I hear the first of my rocks ricochet off the overhanging cliff. Did I miss? When the stones bounce a second time, the cougar simply disappears.

I'm shaken to my core. My stomach wretches. My mind races for explanation, until I hear Maranther's deep voice echo off the walls, "Beware!"

My body goes into convulsive shivers. I'm unable to move or control my trembling.

After an hour, I'm calm enough to disassemble the tent and reassemble it inside the adobe. I don't care if a rock might fall on me. I close the door and drop the latch for protection. I sit motionless until dark, grasping for something solid.

I repeatedly return to Camp Rotunda and the moment our counselor opened the door, a critical moment, but I can't remember past that scene.

Long after dark, before dozing off, in a quick flash, I remember the name of the little cupid boy: Jake Snyder.

He'd been the one I'd mistakenly chosen as a pal, but I can't remember why. I fall asleep thinking of Jake and wondering why his memory leaves a nervous knot in my stomach.

When I awaken, I quickly look at my watch: 1903. My thirst has doubled. I close my eyes again, frantic to get to the 1800s. Although I float, teased with the promise of sleep, I don't quite get there.

An hour later, I climb from my bag and go out to a turbulent sky with thick storm clouds in the distant west. Thirst has driven me to imagine the smell of moisture. I try not to think about thirst. Instead, I occupy myself by braiding another three strands of fish line. To take care of my less immediate need, I return to the chaparral to set another snare. I'm stuck in 1903 for the rest of the day, or until I get tired again. If I'm forced to go without water, I may as well try to get something to eat.

Dark billowy clouds are upon me. A few fat drops of water splat on the gravel. I lift my face to the sky, open my mouth, and lap a drop or two, an unsuccessful enterprise at best. When I get back to the adobes, the sky opens and dumps torrential amounts of water. I swallow whatever rolls off the rocky cliffs in chocolate rivulets. After drinking my fill, I gather the plastic bottles and canteen, fill them with murky liquid, then scramble for anything that will hold water; a frying pan, two aluminum cups, a cook pot. Once all containers are filled, I strip my clothes and stand, arms spread, under the warm cloudburst. I haven't taken a shower since Leigha and I left the campground eleven days ago. Typical for a desert storm, the rain stops as abruptly as it started. The clouds roll away toward the east and the sun bursts through, baking any trace of moisture off the surface of the earth in minutes.

My thirst satiated, I lie naked on the boulder to dry off. I think of Running Feathers and his people. They disappeared between the years 1886 and 1887. I wonder if something catastrophic happened to the community. The modern world could have overtaken them. They may have been forced to move to a city or a reservation. I make a mental note to ask him the next time I see him, but realize he wouldn't know. They haven't reached 1887 yet. When they do, there will be no one left to tell me.

The day drags on with a heavy molasses slowness. As darkness fills the sky and a sliver of the waxing moon shines on the western horizon, I finally feel tired again.

In the early morning, much before dawn, Running Feathers comes to me in my dream. "How are you, Kicking Ashes?" he asks, without moving his lips. "We have waited for your return."

"You're a sight for sore eyes, Running Feathers. You won't believe where I've been." I give a short rendition of what happened during my absence. His eyes widen when I get to the part about the cougar.

When I finish, he says, "Tell me more."

Once I tell the details, he says, "Maranther has taken a liking to you. The cat's appearance is an omen. Pay close attention."

"What does it mean?"

"I do not know, but I will consider the events. We will talk later about your sign. For now, beware, not of Maranther, but of other dangers."

His next words rush out in a blur. "To draw your woman's attention, build a shrine for her in the adobe. It must have many objects she will recognize."

He fades as I yell, "Where do I get water?"

"A half-day's walk toward. . . the. . . set. . . ng sun." His sentence breaks like a distant radio transmission. "Stay overn. . . ght and return . . . morning."

"How do you get enough water to live?" I ask, but his faded image disappears.

I awake parched, late in the morning. My mouth feels like coarse sandpaper. I look at my watch: March

27, 1827. I take a tentative glance out of the tent and feel faint. I see only the huge, flat boulder; the endless sky; and the cliffs above; no buildings, no settlement, no cook pits or sign that Running Feather's people ever existed. Until this moment, things, though bizarre, had a logical sequence. I've traveled back and forth in time twice, but the random leap past Running Feather's time implies that I may never see any specific date again. I hope the randomness isn't at the whim of that sorcerer Maranther. I've jumped one hundred years into the past. It frightens me to think my time leaps might expand. When the loop reverses, I may go ahead as far. Maybe I'll get to the year 3000. The possibilities numb my mind.

If I have to do this kind of traveling, I should be in a city to see the technology. Instead, I sit in this damn unchangeable desert. I'm not even sure if my watch shows the right date. I wish Leigha were here.

I'm alone and might continue to be alone for years. I might be destined to jump back and forth in time, with Running Feathers and that damn Maranther as my only companions. After a long while, bored with self-pity, as a last ditch attempt to bring myself out of despair, I ramble into my past for happier memories.

Leigha and I had been together for three delightful years before we found ourselves blessed with Tommy, a handful from the moment he came out of the womb. Sidney came to us two years later. Unlike her older brother, she was a quiet, introspective child from the first time she could see the world around her. Once we became parents, our attention went from each other to our two wonderful kids.

For the first time in hours, I smile with the thought of the kids and our home, but soon a fret of apprehension reappears. Am I ever going to watch them grow up?

In my entire life, I have never felt as lonely as I feel. With little else to do, I wait for the sun to set and think back to the lost days of summer camp. As hard as I try, I cannot put together more than scattered pieces of memory. Vague feelings of loneliness and unease radiate around the edges of that week.

I attempt to get past the counselor entering the cabin, but try as I might, there is no getting past the moment.

I fall asleep in a futile attempt to remember more.

In the morning, I look at my watch: March 28, 1842. I'm elated to be moving forward in time again.

I lie in my bag until the day warms, constructing a plan to fulfill Running Feather's suggestion. Soon I'll build a shrine for Leigha. When the sun peeks over the boulders, I'm forced to get up and glance out of my tent. No buildings, but signs of the little band of people lie about on the big boulder. Three makeshift lean-pole structures sit in the far corner of the huge rock. Pottery and drying racks stand near the edge, overlooking the southwestern part of the desert. Strips of half-dried jerky and several skins hang from the racks. Clothing sits on the rocks, drying in the sun.

Everything is here, except the people. I wait around for an hour, but no one shows. Eager to get on with my plan, I leave the contents of my pack behind a hidden rock shelf and strap the empty pack on my back. I grab the full canteen, walk to the drying racks, carefully pull off two of the long strips of dried meat, and stuff them into my pack. I step to the north end of the rock and look to where the paved highway, years in the distant future, will be, a road where Leigha and I will drive along, then two nights later pitch a hasty tent to get out of the wind. God, time travel is not for the weak hearted.

After I climb off the rock, I carefully orient myself to follow the cut of the land in my return journey.

During my descent down a long, winding wash, I leave myself a trail by stacking boulders, three high, in obvious places every few hundred yards. Who knows what year I might return to, but the rocks give me a sense of security, however false, in an ever-changing situation.

Over the years, I've hiked hundreds of miles through the desert. As silent as the desert floor is, I've always been reminded of my closeness to civilization by the sound of air traffic. Too few moments existed when the drone of an airplane engine didn't interrupt the silence of the endless sky. How many days in this ancient desert has it taken for me to realize those background noises are missing? I hear the crunch of the gravel under my every step, the never-ending lonesome caw of a pair of ravens who follow me, and the ceaseless breeze.

I'd always wished for true silence during my earlier vacation treks. I wanted a silence without airplanes or distant rumbles, expressions of men and their machines. Now, I'm left with the sound of the truly silent desert, a hundred years before technology, and I long for sound, something more than the lonely caw of the two ravens overhead.

I round each turn, continue to stack rocks, trying to

recognize rock formations and outcroppings. I'm not sure I'm following the same ravine, because I didn't watch when we hiked the hill who knows how many days ago. When I walked on the road, I didn't need to pay attention.

By late afternoon, I climb over an outcrop of boulders and to my delight, instead of the valley, it is a body of water. My water jug feels low, and there's a distinct possibility the lake won't be there after I wake in the morning. With five or six miles to go, I drain my canteen and double my pace to reach the lake before I need to sleep. Late at night, by the light of a quarter moon, I arrive at the huge body of water.

Thirst about to be quenched, I lie on my belly and put my face to the surface. I pull a long warm mouthful of the cooling liquid. The next instant, I spew the brackish murk out into the mirrored lake and try to rid myself of its metallic taste.

This water, even if I could swallow it, will make me sick. I'm forced to wait in the shade of a large boulder for the lake to disappear.

On the morning of the second day out, I look at my watch: March 30, 2014. Sixteen days after the first wind storm, and I stand on the edge of these slippery dunes once again. If I'd stayed at the adobes, I might be with Leigha right now.

I walk along the edge of the sand for a half hour before finding my piled rocks. Sighting over them and searching for the top of my Volvo, I see only that blanket of whiteness. I look over the dunes and spot a saddle shape on the far ridge, then boldly step out onto the loose sand. My car and the canteen Leigha left on the front seat must still be there somewhere.

I think of the canteen all night, dream of its contents. Too weak to make it up the canyon to the water at the adobes, I might make it to the Volvo.

The fishing pole should still be tied to the car antenna. Is the alignment of the rocks accurate? If the car is out there, I have one chance to find it. I won't be able to make the journey back uphill without water. The first step on the loose sand reminds me that this part of the hike won't be easy. By the time I'm over the first dune, I know I might not make it to the car. Luckily, the day is mild, and the sun hides behind stringy high clouds.

I walk with single-mindedness, ever watchful for the V-shaped notch in the distant mountain. A few hours pass before I become discouraged with my snail-like progress. I crawl to the top of yet another dune and see nothing but the white sand and that ever-constant notch in the distant crags.

The day moves slowly as the sun climbs high, peaks, then journeys toward the western horizon. By the end of the day, I find myself in a dehydrated nightmare. I claw up one side of a dune, check my position, then tumble down into the next trough. After each descent, I crumple into a heap, gasping for breath, then gather enough energy to scale the next wall of sand. As dusk settles on the big sky, I lie exhausted in the valley of another dune. I might not make it after all. I might die right here on the sand.

I get a sense for what Leigha went through as a little girl, lost in the desert with her friend Sara. Thirst is ever-present and I may expire from lack of moisture. If I weren't so beyond the ability to observe anything other than the next mountainous dune, the next billion grains of sand to climb, I might be concerned, but I'm unaffected. I'm no longer curious.

An hour later, I'm beyond thirst and have forgotten water is a part of my quest. I've overlooked my search for anything except the notch in the distant cliffs. The mechanical rhythm of my climb and tumble has become an ancient ritual. I'm compelled to do it, but no longer have any idea why.

Drained of energy, unable to consider even one more climb of another dune, I drop in the cool evening air and fall into a thirst-filled slumber.

Maranther comes to me in my dream. "If you lose your concentration, you will die here." A grandmotherly smile spreads across her face. I've seen this grin before, a benevolent helpfulness I don't trust. There's little else to do in this dream, though, so I listen.

"Why is it that Whites never learn the rules of the desert?"

Dry and shriveled, I feel weak as a kitten. I respond out of anger, try to lift myself and grab at her. I succeed in expending what little energy I do have and collapse on the sand.

"First, you kidnap my wife," I murmur, because it's as loud as I can speak, "then you give me an impossible assignment, and you expect me to succeed?"

"You are close to the answer, little worm, closer than any White." She smiles and hands me a skin of water. "You'll make it if you can keep your focus."

I point the skin toward my chapped and bleeding lips. I squirt the cool liquid. Water has never tasted so good, but too quickly I realize I'm not getting refreshed. It's only a dream. I throw the bladder at the old woman. "What are you doing? Why do you torment me?"

"You are close to the answer," she says, then winks out.

Instantly, I'm wide awake. Light and airy with the delight of being awake, I stand, look down, and see my heavy, worn-out body lying in a fetal position on the sand. Am I dead? Have I left my body on the desert sand forever?

These questions have little bearing on my elation, my delight to have energy and to feel free of the wasted body I left behind. I jump with exuberance and rise into the night sky. For one fleeting instant, from fifteen feet above the crest of the mound, I see the sparkling sea of dunes lighted by a quarter moon. Feather light, I touch my feet on the ground.

I jump again, this time with more effort, and find myself fifty feet above the desert. I look at the bowl-shaped mountain range, spinning as I float toward the earth. On the way down, I catch a glimpse of a smooth dark object in a sea of sand. My car is less than a hundred yards north of where my body lies. When I land, I awake inside my body. The buoyant feel of dreaming is replaced by fatigue and thirst.

The moonlight shines on the dune looming over me. My mind refocuses and I remember the dream. I recall flying into the sky and looking at the moon. I saw my car only four dunes away.

My determination returns. My will revives. I rotate onto my knees for the thousandth time and crawl the wall of sand. When I reach the top, I roll, loose-jointed, down the far side. I right myself and continue until I fall exhausted on the crest, my belly across the ridge. I'm unable to go another inch.

Cramps from lying in the awkward position force me to move. It takes a monumental effort to push forward and drop down the leeward face of the second dune. At the bottom, I dream again. When I jump high into the air, I see the top of my car only two hills away, less than a hundred feet. When I return to my body, I force my hands to pull me along on my belly up the next dune.

I don't remember scaling either of the last two peaks, but during the night, I come to consciousness and find myself lying on top of my paint-stripped Volvo.

Driven by thirst, I begin the laborious task of digging out the open back window. In my depleted condition it takes an hour to pull away enough sand from the buried suitcase and remove it from the opening.

As dawn illuminates the blackness of night, the hole that leads into the Volvo takes on a dark, menacing aspect. I slide through the window onto the sand-filled back seat and reach to the front passenger seat, feeling the cool, life-saving canteen. In semidarkness, I heft its weight and guess it to be a wondrous three-quarters full. I unscrew the cap and take a drink. Cool moisture, liquid gold, runs down my dry throat, but in the next second I spit and hack it out, in an attempt to expel the metallic rankness. The water is worse than the brackish muck of the lake.

What happened to the water?

With a canteen of undrinkable water in my hand and no energy to return, even to the edge of the dunes, I'm sure to die. I take another sip to swish in my mouth and wet my lips, but the taste is so bad, I'm forced to spew it out.

I sit for a long while in my debilitated state, until the light of day slips in. When I look around, my wonderful new Volvo has decomposed beyond recognition. The headliner hangs in shreds. The foam seat cushions push out of rotting upholstery. The steering wheel, split and cracked, shows sections of the round steel rod that runs through its core. The dash has crumbled into yellowed plastic. Still unable to piece together what's happened, I look at my watch in shock: 2067.

Crazy with the certainty that I'll die, I scramble out of the car and lie in the morning chill. The sun peeks over the mountains and casts golden rays on me. Without a clue of what to do to get myself out of this utter catastrophe, and certain I won't make it another day without water, I consider drinking the fifty-year-old liquid inside the canteen.

I'm prone on the sand next to the rust-pocked car. My mind twirls, not with possibility, but with consequence. How stupid of me to be in the desert without water!

In the turmoil of my fear and isolation, my mind goes to summer camp. Another piece of the forgotten puzzle falls into place. I remember camp survival training. I climb into the car and reach for the glove box and the emergency poncho I always kept tucked in a corner. When the door opens, a spider the size of my hand greets me. I jump back to a safe position and watch as it casually climbs onto the seat, then to the back of the car and out the window. In the glove compartment, next to tissues and a pair of gloves, I find something unexpected. I lift Leigha's rotted velvet pouch, unroll it, and her gold and topaz necklace slides out into my hand. I slip the pendant into my front pocket.

Next, I pull out her extra lipstick. The tube shows corrosion, but when I slip the cover off, the lipstick, though melted, radiates brilliant crimson in contrast to the drab rot of my car. I'm getting sidetracked.

I rummage deeper into the glove box until I find the plastic-wrapped poncho. The clear cellophane crumbles to the floor, but the plastic of the poncho still looks reasonably pliable. With care, I unfold and inspect it for possible rips.

After forty years, I'll finally use one of the survival techniques I learned at Camp Rotunda. I'm careful to fold the poncho back into its original shape and climb out into the warming air.

On the roof of the Volvo, I tear two pieces of plastic three feet square. I still need something to stretch it, but see only white sand.

Back in the car, I pull four headliner support wires, stick them in the sand three feet apart, dig a shallow bowl, and carefully place the first piece of plastic in the contour. The second piece of plastic stretches to the four corners of the wires, creating a second dish suspended a few inches above the first. I adjust it to slope toward me. I have never tried this method of water distillation, but I know, at least theoretically, it's supposed to work.

I pour the water from the canteen and fill the bottom plastic dish, then lie in the warming sun fifteen minutes before the first droplets form under the upper plastic. The evaporation method works. Within minutes, drops of water roll to the edge of the plastic and fall with delightful regularity. The water drips into my hand, and I lap it like a thirsty dog. I can't hold my hand steady.

Drips of lifesaving water fall on the sand as I slide into the hot car. After a frantic search, I shakily pull the metal ashtray from the center console and turn it over to dump the paper scraps, when I get another wonderful surprise. Leigha's wedding ring, the original wedding ring she lost so long ago, falls into my hand. We tore the house apart, looked in the garage, searched her workplace and mine. We combed the trash. We even had the car seats removed, in case it had slipped into an unseen corner. We looked for months before getting a replacement.

I slip the ring into my watch pocket, take the ashtray out into the sun, wipe it clean, and place it under my dripping evaporator. Impatiently, I watch each droplet gather in the bottom. With little else to do except wait, I remove the ring from my pocket and fit it on the first knuckle of my pinkie. The moment it's on, more recollections flood in.

I have distinct memories of going with Leigha to shop for our first wedding ring. We'd gone to every store in town. We visited art shows and talked to individual artists. Each time I thought Leigha had decided on a ring, she wanted to see another jeweler. In front of one more jewelry store, we'd begun to argue.

"I'm tired of looking at rings," I said.

"You're tired of searching for the most meaningful symbol of our marriage? Getting a ring is important to me."

"You've looked at a hundred rings."

"I'm hurt you won't go with me to pick our wedding rings."

"I've been going with you for a month. Pick a damn ring, and let's get on with life."

The argument is clearly etched in my mind, as if it happened yesterday. I had said the worst of all possible things. A fire truck blasted by, drowning out my shouts. The drunks lined along the wall, not ten feet from us, giggled and nudged one another. A pigeon flew over us and dropped its splatter on my new jacket. We looked at one another and burst into laughter.

I study the ring for the minuscule chip on the edge of the diamond. During our sixth anniversary celebration, a brick slipped from the shelf on the barbecue and hit Leigha squarely on the ring. We scrambled to remove it before it cut off circulation in her finger. She cried after the jeweler explained the damage.

The ashtray is a quarter full, maybe a single swallow. I lift it to my lips, empty the contents, and replace it.

I slide into the car and search for more of Leigha's belongings.

If anything will draw her to me, it will be this ring, but it's good to have a number of other articles to offer, too. I find her office keys, a beeper, and a pair of gloves. I put to immediate use a stale tube of lip balm that had obviously melted and congealed many times.

I carefully put the cache into her small makeup bag, then climb out of the sauna into cool, open air.

The second mouthful of water is heaven. I slosh it around before swallowing.

Within the hour, the heat has evaporated every drop. I save a swallow in my jug for the long journey home, then carefully fold the plastic poncho. Before my disaster is over, I'm sure I'll need its services again.

Leigha's things in my pack, I begin the return journey across the loose sand. With a single swallow of water for the impossible trek across the dunes then up that endless hill, I already know survival is questionable.

When I finally make it to the top of the first dune, my attention is drawn to another in a long string of amazing sights.

I am mesmerized by the mirage coming fast across the floor of the desert, a tractor trailer truck barreling south in the heat, then passing five or six hundred feet east of me. The familiar thump of its loud diesel engine reaches a crescendo, then fades, as the vision dissolves into the heat.

I smile, but not too wide. My chapped and bleeding lips can't handle much movement.

My crawl toward the road takes forever. Three more slippery dunes later, my stamina gives out. I collapse in the sand, afraid I'll expire a hundred feet from the road. It would be ironic. After nearly dying on the desert dunes with a portion of a canteen of water to save me, I can't make it a hundred yards to real safety: to automobiles and trucks, to water, maybe food and people.

With short bursts of energy and too many long rests

in the blaze of the sun, I crawl, without realizing it, out onto a long, black ribbon of hot asphalt. It stretches, arrow straight, across the valley. I take another extended rest, then creep to a signpost and pull myself up, ready to flag the next car.

I stand in the shadow of the diamond-shaped road sign, the only shade for miles. I rest my scratchy eyes from the glare. As a reward for my successful effort, I swallow the last few drops of water and look over the heat waves for the approach of a vehicle. Far to the north and south, nothing moves.

I've arrived, all right, on a completely deserted road.

When I have a moment of clarity, I can't recall seeing another car or truck pass during the entire two hours I crossed the dunes to the road.

Maybe I'm hallucinating. Maybe I'm still lying on sand and just think I'm standing here.

I stomp my feet and don't feel soft sand under me. The earth is solid, but I can't be positive.

"I think the road is solid." My dried croak scratches out the short sentence, which surprises me. I haven't spoken in a while.

I unhand the signpost, turn south, and begin a slow, purposeful, gait toward the mountains.

I've stumbled for half an hour, putting one foot in front of the other, until far off in the distance, I hear a familiar sound. A yellow automotive apparition appears miles up the road. As it comes close, I step out onto the middle of the asphalt and weakly wave my arms.

A battered Chevrolet truck pulls to a halt and three bronze-skinned people stare, slack-jawed at me while I wobble over to the open window on the driver's side. They look Mexican, so in a gravel voice, I say the only Spanish words I know, "Agua, por favor?"

They produce a full gallon jug and hand it over. I'm so shaky the driver has to open his door, get out, and help me lift the jug to my lips. The smooth liquid pours into my mouth. Some spills onto my chin. I never thought simple water could taste so good. When I pause to catch my breath, I thank him and his family one at a time. He helps me hoist the jug to my lips again, and I drink greedily until the bottle is half empty.

When I fear I might finish off the last of their water, I lower the container. He gives me a smile and waves me on.

"Do you have food?" I mime eating.

His coal black eyes glint. He smiles, turns away, and speaks in Spanish to the plump woman who sits in the middle. She reaches into a well-worn grocery bag and produces four fat tamales.

While I unwrap one and stuff it in my mouth, he motions north. With a single bite, the tamale is half finished. I shake my head and point south. He gives me a weary smile, gets in the truck, and restarts the ancient engine. After he grinds the old floor shift into first, he looks at me with a sympathetic expression and says one word, "Maranther."

The truck rattles to the pavement and rumbles away. I stand with three tamales, the remaining water, and a body full of goose bumps.

"He knows about Maranther," I say aloud as I watch the truck evaporate into the heat waves.

I devour the remaining tamales and feel satisfied for the first time in a week. Revived, I take another long drink from the jug and turn south. For good reason, I have renewed vigor in my step. I continue my journey.

Soon, a magenta, hovering creation slides in from the north. With no wheels touching ground, the machine slips past my waving arms, effortlessly tracks across the remaining miles, and disappears into the hills. Fifteen minutes later, another beat-up, rusted-out ranch truck towing an equally antiquated horse trailer lumbers along the road. I smile when I hear the engine wind down. The brakes squeal, and the old rattletrap slows to a stop.

"Where you goin'?" asks a hulk of a man wearing a sweat-stained, cowboy hat pushed back on his forehead. A stub of a half-chewed, unlit cigar protrudes from the side of his mouth.

"Just up the hill. Can you give me a lift?"

"Sure thing, buddy; jump in." He pulls a pile of boxes and papers toward him to make room.

As I climb into the trash-littered cab, he says, "Hell, man, you look like somthin' the cat drug in. What's you doin' out in the middle of the desert? Did your car break down?"

"If I told you the story, you wouldn't believe me," I murmur with what's left of my voice.

It takes three tries before my door fully closes. When he lets go of the paper, it slides against me. He tromps on the gas as the rattle-ridden truck slowly pulls away.

"Don't see people walkin' round this part of Mexico often."

"I'm on vacation." I don't feel like filling him in.

"You must be thirty miles from the nearest town."

"Yeah, I know."

"Could be dangerous out here, 'specially if it was hotter."

"Yesterday, I almost died out there." With my thumb, I gesture back west toward the valley.

"Shee-it, man; you ain't tellin' me you hiked out there in the dunes. Hell, dune sand is slipperier-n'-snot."

"It's slippery, all right."

"I don't know how you climbed even one dune, much less. . . How far out there did you go?"

"Five miles or so."

"Well, you're lucky it's not summer. The sun would cook your bones by the end of the first mile."

"Umm," I murmur.

"Where you goin'?"

"I'm not sure. Up the canyon eight or ten miles. I'll know when I see it."

"I'm goin' past Whiley's."

"I won't be going that far."

"There ain't nothin' between here and Whiley's. What you gonna do?"

"I've got a camp to get back to."

"Humph," he grunts. The robust, desert-dweller color drains from his face.

The truck leaves those dammed white dunes and starts to grind its way into the hills. He shifts into second.

To my relief, following our short exchange, he stops asking questions. After being alone in the desert for weeks, it surprises me how little I have to say.

Three miles into the hills, I ask, "What's the date?"

He looks at his thick wrist. "April second."

"The year," I ask nervously. "What's the year?"

He looks at me suspiciously. "Why do you want the year? It's been the same year for months. You haven't been out here that long, have you?"

"Three weeks."

"Then you should know the year."

"Please, just tell me the year. I need to know."

"Twenty sixty-seven, just like it's been for the last three months."

I look at my watch and confirm the date.

We ride along in silence for another five miles.

"I knew you'd wanna know the year," he finally says.

Does he know what I've been through? Does he know about Leigha?

I say nothing. The truck continues to creep up the hill. When the climb gets steep, he's forced to shift into first and poke along at a fast walk.

I think about Leigha and pray she's all right. I wonder if the original wedding ring will draw her attention.

We near a familiar bend. I carefully scan the terrain.

"I'll want to get out around the next turn."

"You're gonna get out here?"

"Around the next bend, I'm almost sure."

He turns his already blanched face to me. His good-old-boy accent disappears when he speaks, and I'm unnerved for the second time today. "There's a legend in this part of Mexico. They say an old sorcerer called Maranther haunts these canyons. He captures people and catapults them through time. My friends claim to have met some of these people, but I never believed it."

"She's a woman," I say.

"Huh?"

"Maranther is an old woman."

"Hell, man, you ain't jokin', are you?"

"Maranther's got my wife."

"Your wife? What's she doing with your wife?"

My voice breaks. "I don't know. I haven't seen Leigha in three weeks. I've got to find her."

"Is she in a different time?"

"I don't know. One thing's for sure, though."

"What's that?"

"I'm definitely in a different time."

The truck rounds the next bend, and I recognize the rock wall. "Drop me here."

The driver slows the truck, pulls onto the shoulder, and stops. With the engine idling, his face still pale, he asks, "What time do you come from?"

He holds the wave of paper back as I get out of the truck. I slam the door and lean on the open window. "I live in Northern California in the year 2014. I was on vacation with my wife when Maranther abducted her. The old witch sent me on a two-hundred-year wild goose chase to find Leigha. I've been out in the desert for. . ." I look at my watch, "eighteen days, and I don't know how to get my wife back." I pause to catch an emotional upheaval from spilling all over him. "Thanks for the ride." I heft the jug. "Could I ask for some water?"

"Sure, pal. I can't wait till I tell my buddies. They ain't going to believe that I actually met one of you."

He reaches behind the seat, pulls a half-gallon jug into sight, and hands it over.

"Thanks," I say and take the bottle. "Thanks for the ride, too. I don't think I could've made it without you."

"What's your name? I want to tell 'em your name."

"Martin Vandorfor."

"You got somethin' to prove you're from the past?"

"What for?"

"I want to show it to my buddies. They're not gonna believe me, if I don't have something to show 'em."

I reach in my pocket, pull out a small wad of folded money, and hand him a five.

"Will this do?"

"No kiddin'! This is collector's stuff."

"Thanks for the ride."

I turn toward the rock wall, ready to face the desert and Maranther. I'm halfway up the wall before the truck roars to life. I look in time to see the old horse trailer swing around the bend, then I climb the ledge as the already distant sound of the truck fades. I'm left with the silence of the desert again. I'm alone.

The six adobes are less than foundations, little more than squarish mounds of dirt and rock piled helter-skelter. My red tent, which continues to travel with me through time, glares a contrasting bright red. It sits next to the circle of rocks, once the fire pit. In a crevice on the cliff sits the canteen. It also seems not to have aged a single week. I slosh the water. After a small sip, I squat and survey the familiar surroundings.

Although the saguaro cacti that dot the terrain have doubled in size and the adobes are little more than forgotten rubble, not much else is different. The rocks are the same. The sand has not changed. I stare at the brilliant and cloudless turquoise sky.

I sit in quiet contemplation until nightfall. I need a plan. I'll wander aimlessly without one, but first, I need to sleep.

The sun peeks over the cliffs behind me. I look out on another clear, warming day, then climb out of the bag and glance at my watch: April 3, 2032.

The adobes, though still in ruin, are more clearly defined. Three walls stand in defiance of the weather. A sun-bleached door frame hangs askew. I step over the crumbling wall and inside the first adobe, our adobe, where Leigha and I slept together a lifetime ago. With a small stick, I begin the laborious process of clearing out a corner of the building.

In a half hour, I find a flat rock and place it in the cleared corner. I set Leigha's retrieved make-up goodies carefully on the rock and arrange them in a loving way, using her ring as a centerpiece.

Outside, I climb down and set a new snare. An hour later, I find a small ground squirrel on the fish line. I eat a rodent lunch and take sips of water from the remains of the half-gallon jug.

In the morning, I'll have to hike in the direction of the water hole, but thankfully, I'm the proud owner of two plastic jug containers, a canteen, and a sport bottle to fill and bring back.

During the night, Running Feathers comes to me. "You must spend much time praying for her return," he says. "When you get close to her time, talk to her as though she sits in front of you. This will bring the two of you together. The closer you get to the date you parted, the more she will be able to see your shrine."

"I've learned my lesson about water," I tell him. "I won't be caught without it again."

"It is an important lesson out here." The old man smiles. "There are many lessons in the desert."

"How do you get your water from so far away?"

"We have a closer source, but I don't have time to explain. For now, you will have to go to the oasis, a day's walk from here." He points toward the south. "Watch for the sawtooth peak on the horizon. The oasis will show itself long before you reach the ridge, but it will give you a point to walk toward."

"Give me a general direction of your closer source. I'm sure I'll find it."

"You might look for years and be within a shout of it, but never discover the location. It is difficult to see."

"Can't I try?"

"Do not waste your precious time. You have much better things to do before your woman returns. If you have not reunited with your woman when we next meet, then I will take you to our secret water."

His image fades, and I awake before dawn. Out of habit, I look at my watch: April 4, 2016. Later, when dawn breaks, I turn toward the west and spot the distant ragged peak.

Since I'll be back by nightfall, I empty my pack of everything except empty bottles and begin my walk.

The terrain rises and falls imperceptibly, allowing me to keep the mountaintop in sight. Two or three miles into my trek, I find signs of an ancient trail. It must be more than fifty years after the settlement was abandoned, yet the path still exists. The desert is slow to change.

I walk with the sound of crunching gravel under my feet. If I'd been on a pleasure hike, it would be a jaunt through a beautiful, untouched desert scene. Instead, I trudge across dangerous ground, full of pitfalls, not the least of which is my dwindling water supply.

I'm supposed to find a water hole toward the sawtooth peak, but the vagueness of the direction concerns me.

More than once, the trail disappears. I'm left to look at the distant peak, my only guide. It won't take more than a single step in the wrong direction to miss the oasis altogether. I can easily walk right by it. Hundreds of possible scenarios would leave me stranded out in the middle of the desert again. I shuffle along, and I think about most of them. A number of times, when I get seriously worried about having taken a wrong turn, the trail reappears, and I'm back on track.

Although Running Feathers said the peak lies many miles beyond the oasis, all day my hike keeps directing me toward a formation of rounded boulders. The land becomes more rugged the closer I get to the formation. I scramble across ravines and climb in and out of deep gullies.

The day proves hotter than the previous one, which leaves my water jug dangerously low.

I count thirteen canyon washes before the ground levels out. The last two miles are a smooth sloping hill to the top of an arroyo. Once on the arroyo, I look in the distance and see in a small gully the first inkling of greenery. The heat creates many mirages, but the closer I walk, the more sure I am that a long string of palm trees dot the otherwise treeless environment.

After an exhausting three hour hike from the adobes, I hear the distant rustle of the palm fronds in a slight breeze.

I look into a deep depression, almost a small canyon. At the bottom, no larger than one of the adobes, lies an ancient pond. The palms circle the water hole so thick, I have a hard time squeezing between them to get to the water. Under the protection of the dense palm grove, the air feels cool and soft. The breeze manages to slip between the trees, but only enough to circulate air across the still pond. It feels deliciously cool as I lie on my belly and drink deeply from three inches of water.

After I've filled my bottles and drunk my fill, I lean against a tree trunk and let my thoughts drift.

My feet ache from the hot desert tramp, so I take my boots off and soak my toes in the cool, damp sand.

I lie back and listen to a cacophony of song birds that live in the palms. The calming effect of the breeze and cool shade lulls me into a deep slumber.

When I awake, the day has wasted away. The sun has dropped low, not yet set, but definitely not enough of the day left for me to make the return journey to the adobes.

With all the water I want, in an otherwise bone-dry desert, the safest place for me is next to the oasis.

I climb out beyond the rim of the water hole and gather scraps of wood for the night's fire.

At the far side of the oasis, I set yet another snare and hang my otherwise useless car keys on the trip line to jingle when the trap springs. Within an hour I have myself a small dinner. Although it is definitely not a rat, it must be a desert rodent of some kind. Not as tasty as the squirrel I'd eaten the night before, it still satisfies. I'm not full, but at least not hungry. Greens would be nice. Before I fall asleep, my thoughts rest on a big Caesar salad.

An ever-growing moon illuminates the landscape. I find myself wiggling into the gravel to find a more comfortable position. Halfway through the long night, I awake chilled. With the fire dead and nothing for cover, I scoop out a deep pocket in the coarse sand and lay palm fronds on top of me. Not a wool blanket, but I am insulated from the chilly early morning hours. Those extra few degrees of warmth allow me to find a fitful, broken slumber.

Out of the depth of the darkest hour, I'm startled awake with the roar of a large cat. Seconds later, a horrible life-and-death battle takes place not many yards from where I'm lying. When the struggle ends, the cat roars again, then drags its prey across the marl, up the incline, in my direction.

I know it's too close when I smell the salty odor of fresh blood. When the animal stops pulling its prey, it gives one final, long roar. I lie silent under the fronds. Time moves slowly, as the feline tears apart and eats its kill.

The cougar, and from the sound it's at least the size of a mountain lion, chomps and grinds the flesh with copious growls and whines. The animal is so close, I hear it swallow. Because the cat hasn't detected me, the breeze must be wafting my scent away from it. As long as

I lie unmoving a few feet from the carnage, I may be able to get through the incident without becoming dessert.

When first under the fronds, I'd felt warmer and cozier in my little nest. With the cougar nearly on top of me, I'm claustrophobic. To alleviate the fear, which could build into panic, I force my thoughts elsewhere.

I wonder how I'm able to draw so many disasters to me in so short a time. My mind drifts from one problem to another, always returning to my one gigantic issue: how to find my wife and get the hell out of here. With the one situation solved, all else should fall by the wayside.

Having no real answers, I soon think about the kids. Will they be okay while their mom and dad traipse around the desert in search of one another?

A trapped feeling, which has nothing to do with my current predicament, reminds me of being cornered another time in my life. I'm off again, into thoughts of my ruined car, the mortgage, my family, anything but the hidden terror of that summer camp so long ago.

Before dawn breaks, my thoughts again light upon my trapped feeling. I've touched it so many times in the last few hours, I decide to stay with it. I snap back to Camp Rotunda and the little boy, Jake Snyder, and settle on the memory of Jake, his blond hair and slight build, his tendency to whimper whenever things didn't go just right. Despite his shortcomings, I liked him.

Camp Rotunda was far from the city. I was away from my parents. The woods fit both Jake's and my personalities. We hiked the hills and swam in the lazy creek meandering through the valley. A frown crosses my face when I remember I didn't like Jake any longer.

I didn't want to see him or say a single word to him. I remember the disappointment, but for the life of me, I can't remember why. Although I approach it from every angle, the abrupt end of Jake Snyder and little Marty Vandorfor's friendship remains a mystery.

I assume the feline will go to its lair or hunt for something else when finished, anything except lie close to its catch and doze. I want to wriggle a stabbing rock to a more comfortable position, but I don't dare budge, for fear of alerting the carnivore.

After dawn, I allow myself a slow, quiet turn of my head. I look through the fronds and see the cougar asleep next to the bloody pile of meat. The cat looks much bigger than I imagined. It lies in a quiet sleeping position, a friendly come-here-kitty-kitty look on its face. It is a healthy animal. The one exception to its perfection is a deeply split ear, an old wound that healed so long ago it looks like he has three ears. A soft snoring comes from the feline, but every five minutes, it slips from sleep, opens one eye, and has a look around.

I'm stuck under the stiff fronds, lying atop a bed of gravel for another hour before I realize the cat might sleep next to its kill until nighttime. The urgency of the matter doesn't show itself until the sun rises and warms my makeshift cocoon.

I have a moment of hope when the cat stands and yawns, but my optimism is dashed when it shifts position and saunters to the shade of a palm a miniscule ten feet farther away and curls into a fetal position.

I seriously explore two possible approaches, though neither will work: I'll wait for the cat to snore again and try to slip away, not exactly a probability, even if I'm quiet. In this gravel, quiet is highly unlikely.

The second consideration is to startle the 150-pound beast into running away by going on the offensive.

Sweat rolls down my forehead and drips into my eyes. My vertebrae are crunched. I can't feel my butt. It's gone completely numb.

Out of desperation, I spring out of my pit and scream, flinging fronds in the direction of the cat. Its eyes flash open. I reach a full standing position. It leaps two feet off the ground. I flail two fronds and rattle them in its face. I run at the startled creature. When it lands, I'm less than five feet away.

It snarls and bares sharp fangs. Its eyes flash huge. I continue to yell and wave fronds, but my advance slows. Any closer and I'll touch its nose.

To my relief, the cat jumps away, toward the palms. Its retreat spurs my advance. I chase it into the thick trees. Sure it will soon realize I'm vulnerable to its claws and teeth, I stop my advance. I turn and dash back over the mound. I snatch my pack, three water bottles and the canteen, then sprint away, glancing over my shoulder.

In my retreat, I search for a weapon. I need to keep the cougar at bay if it decides to attack. I pick a large rock, but a hundred yards along the trail, I find the perfect tool and grab a three-foot segment from a rotted saguaro trunk. I scrape sharp spines from one end and run. I glance back, sure the cougar will fly at me.

I make amazing time on the trail. When I get within sight of the adobes, still taking furtive glances behind me, I look at my watch: 1:16 April 5, 1933.

I throw the saguaro club aside and climb onto the boulder. Although I missed Leigha this time around, I'm relieved to see the string of adobes in better condition. Soon, Running Feathers and his people will appear.

I go into the little adobe and study the shrine with the ring as its centerpiece. I stare at the altar for a long time before I see something different, but I can't pinpoint it until the ring catches my eye.

"The ring!" I shout. Tears spring to my eyes when I see it isn't Leigha's old ring after all.

"This is her replacement ring," I say aloud and break into a wide grin. "She switched them!"

I grab the ring and look carefully, then slip it into my pocket.

After she lost the original ring, we tried to have the same design recreated. The artist had moved to Vermont and left no forwarding address. All we had to work from was a single photo, and not even a close-up. I had not taken the picture of the ring, but of Leigha holding her friend's baby. By accident, the ring peeked out from under the blanket.

We took the photo to another jeweler, and he created a model in wax. Consistent with the first ring-buying experience, Leigha drove the poor jeweler and me crazy with changes. She shifted the design so many times, he eventually, though politely, returned the wax model.

When she realized he wouldn't finish the ring, she had him cast the design in gold and set another diamond. Once the ring was complete, though the likeness came close, it became painfully obvious it would never be the same. Leigha had sighed and accepted the new ring.

Leigha's been here, and for now that's enough. The next morning, even with the sun breaking over the rocks, the same cloudless blue sky, the same too-quick-to-warm desert under my feet, life looks much better. My watch reads: April 6, 1874. The time thing does indeed speed up. I add more years to each of my jumps.

Once I step out of the little building, it's obvious what part of the nineteenth century I'm in. The finished adobes have snug doors, and a small curl of smoke rises from each building.

I'm very hungry, but reluctant to interrupt anyone. A young boy watches me from across the boulder. I'll wait until everyone awakes before I beg for food. I step inside to build my own fire. The boy stands at my door. I kneel, turn to face him, and strike my bar of steel across the flint rod. The brilliant flash of a blue-orange spark leaps out a foot from my hands. The light momentarily fills the dim hut. I look his way with a grin and expect him to be mesmerized. He's gone. On the third strike, the mat of fluff sputters to life. I fan the flame, add a few sticks, then rise to close the door.

The boy steps into the doorway pulling his reluctant father. He lets go of the man's hand and motions at me with bright eyes. He wants me to make the flash again.

"Come in," I say with a hand gesture.

They shyly stand at the door.

When I flash it again, they both disappear. I wonder what kind of tale will be told of my magic.

Once the fire flares and the room warms, a knock comes at the door. I pull it open and Running Feathers steps in. He says something in his language and points at my pocket. I pull out the flint and hand it to him.

"The news of the fire magic has gotten to you quickly," I say.

He motions me to demonstrate.

I pull twigs and straw from my starter pile and stack them on the floor. He looks on curiously as I point the flint at the pile and strike it four times. When the twigs blaze, he grins and looks carefully at the flint.

I hand it to him, but he's reluctant to touch it.

When I reach out and grab his hand, then lay the tool in his outstretched palm, a worried look crosses his face. He speaks in his slow dialect. It sounds beautiful, but completely beyond my ability to comprehend.

I motion for him to try, but he hands it back. I grab the steel and strike it across the flint, then hand it to him again. He looks suspicious, but cautiously pulls the two bars together. The first flash lights his face. He laughs nervously. Three more strikes, and he returns it.

I hold my hands in a gesture of refusal and hope he'll get the message. "A gift," I say.

Once he understands my intent, he beams.

He pantomimes the sleep gesture, and I realize that we'll talk then.

"I need to eat first," I say, while I rub my belly and motion food going into my mouth. In childlike delight, he sparks the flint again, pulls a leather pouch from his waist, and reverently places the tools inside.

After he leaves, I turn to the blaze and warm my hands at the hearth. Minutes later, he returns with a basket and pulls out the leg of a large bird. Turkey, or maybe eagle; something big.

I bite into the meat, and it tastes metallic, or sharp, like Limburger cheese. It definitely isn't turkey, or at least not any turkey I've ever eaten.

I swallow the first bite and smile. "This is good."

He pulls out half a cooked squash and hands it to me. I haven't seen a vegetable for weeks. I set the leg aside to devour the yellow meaty substance inside the hard skin. On the first bite, my mind leaps to summer camp so many years before. Since my week at Rotunda, I've never liked squash, but even cold, this one has a wonderful nutty flavor. The memory takes me to the first camp dinner, which, now that I remember, consisted of the vegetable. Every meal at camp had squash. The smell has a double edge to it. One side reminds me of how happy I was to be away from my mother and on my own. I had already met Jake. How excited I had been to have a friend so quickly. The other side of the smell brings a vague heaviness.

I haven't eaten squash since, though I can't understand why. It tastes delicious. I devour my food and wash it down with fresh water.

Running Feathers piles a small group of twigs and takes out his new striker. He sits back in delight when it smolders after two tries.

I gnaw on the last of the bird leg.

"Do you have more food?" I make a lame attempt at pointing to the basket, then at my mouth.

While he's gone, I wonder about summer camp and its connection with squash. Why did I have an aversion to that particular vegetable, when it tastes so good? Why, after liking Jake so much, did I not ever see him again? Why have I blocked him out of my memory? Explanations are dormant in the recesses of my brain, but until now, my life has been too busy to consider the questions.

I step outside into the crisp morning air, and every little sound the tribe makes is audible in the silence. A baby fusses in the third structure. I hear murmurs from the end bungalow, a man's deep voice and the higher pitch of a woman, probably his wife, in the middle of a discussion. I want people around. I love being near people. Although I can't communicate, I'm still delighted being with them. After my loneliness, the rich sounds and odors of this little village leave me fulfilled.

Running Feathers returns with more of the metallic meat, and I eat until I'm stuffed.

Once the relentless sun warms things up, I sit outside my hut for an hour to just watch the people. Running Feathers steps over and sits like an eastern yogi across from me.

"Show me your water source?" I pantomime drinking from a cup.

He looks at my awkward motions and corrects my signing.

I try again, this time I'm sure I have the movement. My hand moves across my face and points toward my mouth with four fingers, their sign for water.

He stands and walks away. I wonder where he's gone, but a moment later, he returns with a skin of water.

"Where is your water?" I point at the boulders above us.

It takes a while to communicate using my poor excuse

for sign language, well, more like charades, but when I get my message across, he leaps to his feet, gathers armfuls of empty skins, hands half to me, then leads the way up a path through and over the boulders above the settlement.

I ask him how water can be on the top of a cliff, but he doesn't understand my question.

With so many twists and turns, I'd surely get lost on my own. We walk and climb without communication. We stop once for a short rest during the half-hour trek. Three times I'm sure we are able to go no higher. We're at the top of the world, and three times we come upon another, taller group of boulders.

I pull myself over what must be the steepest ledge. Running Feathers turns me around to see a panoramic view of the desert north of us. The valley is a lake again. The distant mountains beyond the water are tinged in mauves and lavender. They might be a hundred miles away, but in the vagueness of the desert, they could be three hundred. There's no way to tell.

Running Feathers turns me south, and I face not the top of the world, as I had guessed from the arduous climb, not a peak that overlooks a three-hundred-sixty-degree view of the desert far below, but simply more desert. Behind us the land is as flat as a valley, as open and seemingly lifeless as only desert can be.

We step toward the east, off the highest ledge, and walk on a flat, gravel surface that stretches out for ten miles. The hike continues along the edge of the cliffs, then abruptly drops down another vague path among the boulders. Running Feathers leads me between two huge rocks into an area the size of a basketball gym. It's easy to see why he had to show me. Even with a map, I'd have never found his little hidden bonanza.

We walk a few yards, winding between boulders, as the dry, scruffy life of the desert shifts to luscious green tufts of grass and reed. He leads me to the far side until I feel slushiness under my feet. Another ten steps in the slurpy mud, and we come to a pond the size of a city bus. Hot and thirsty, I want to jump in the pool to cool off. I begin to strip my clothes, but Running Feathers frowns and shakes his head. Reverently, he kneels and carefully drinks directly from the pond. With a narrow path through the thick reeds, I have to wait my turn. When finished, he stands and allows me to drink my fill. The water tastes sweet and fresh.

Our side of the tiny pond is shallow, so one at a time, Running Feathers hands me the water skins, twenty-two in all. I carefully fill them and hand them back.

We stay at the pond for an hour until he stands and loads skins on my shoulders. He seems in a big hurry after being quiet for so long. Once he hefts the remaining skins on himself, we backtrack along the path, then down through the maze of boulders. I watch for landmarks to retrace my steps later. Walking with heavy skins is cumbersome. I'm glad we're headed downhill.

By the time we arrive at the settlement, the sun has warmed the day. A passel of children greets us, taking the water bags.

When we've unloaded, I wander through the camp, watch women cook over open pits. Children play at their feet. I see no men around and make a mental note to ask Running Feathers. I like being in this community. I want to put off sleep for fear of making another leap into loneliness. I drink in their humanity.

I miss Leigha and worry about her, but the quiet, quaint settlement is enough for now. I won't be able to rescue her until I solve Maranther's puzzle; neither will I return to civilization until Leigha and I go together. How long the unraveling will take, I don't know, but it looks like a long stay. For now, with my water jugs full and my belly satisfied, I'm happy to sit in the sun with my back against the adobe and soak in the warmth.

I watch my neighbor as she roasts a rabbit. The young woman rotates the carcass on its wooden spit. With each revolution, the flesh turns darker. My mind wanders as I observe. I think of our barbecue at home, how, just for fun, we'd cook slowly over mesquite charcoal. We'd use an electric spit and turn a piece of meat bought from the supermarket. The contrast of these two worlds boggles my mind. I recall the sweet smell of fresh-cut grass in the yard on a summer day.

In this little settlement, the food being cooked has been caught for sustenance. The villagers go about their daily life. They talk to one another and smile a lot. They deal with their children with stress-free faces. From my seated position in the warm sun, they look much happier than people in modern society. My mind drifts as I doze on the edge of sleep. The calmness of the day lulls me.

With a sudden shift, the afternoon takes on another mood, an added energy. The warm tranquility ends, as if a thunder cloud has gathered. A gusty breeze blows from the west as Running Feathers approaches. "Kicking

Ashes, I have waited all day for you to doze. You fight sleep like a small child."

The lull of the village stirs to an atmosphere charged with anticipation. When I jump to another time, the weather is always different.

"I didn't want to leave your village," I say.

"You cannot stop the passage of the present time by staying awake. It will drive you crazy, and you will do unexpected things."

"I only stayed awake for a while. I'm lonely."

"I do not envy you. It must be difficult to awaken in distant years."

I shrug, accept the inevitable and point toward the door of the adobe. "I left the shrine for Leigha as you suggested, and she took the ring. What should I do next?"

He raises his eyebrows. "I do not know what follows, but she took the offering. This has never happened before. It is a good sign. You have done better than the others."

"You mean to tell me others caught in Maranther's maze were also couples?"

He nods. "Many, but there is one who is still with us."

"Why would Maranther choose couples?"

"I do not know."

Still baffled, knowing my time is short, I move on.

"Who is the other traveler?"

"He comes to us every five or six years and claims to have been trapped by Maranther many years ago. His name is Nathaniel. He originates from a time before our settlement."

Lost in the past

I'm intrigued with the possibilities of talking to someone who's been trapped and survived Maranther's damnable time loop, but I have a few more questions before Running Feathers leaves my dream. I ask, "Why are your people afraid of me?"

"You and all the others are like ghosts to us. At times you are in solid flesh, then at other times, you appear vague, like a spirit. As fast as you appear, you disappear. You come to us one day, then not again for years, but you never age and we never know when you will arrive. We built a sixth adobe away from us, so you and others like you can come and go in peace. Maranther has condemned you to his world, but we are simple people. We do not understand magical things."

"But why afraid, especially the children?"

"Men of magic usually are feared and respected. Men of magic can do wonderful things to help, or, as in your case, disrupt lives. My people have also heard of your magic fire stick. Anyone who has one must be a powerful sorcerer."

"I gave the flint and steel to you. Haven't you told them?"

"Yes, I have, but they think you must be even more powerful to give such a thing away." He grins. "My standing in my tribe has risen because of your gift."

"You said others came before me. How many?"

"We have been the victims of Maranther's mischief for the sixty-two winters we have lived on this rock and we count fifteen spirits who have come and gone."

"Fifteen people have been forced to go through the same insane ordeal?"

Running Feathers nods. "Most have perished."

"Is there nothing you can do to stop her?"

"Her? To us, Maranther appears as a man."

"Your man comes to me as an old woman."

"I now know our sorcerer can shift into four human and two animal shapes."

"Maranther has pulled this kind of crap for years, and no one knows how to stop her?"

"What is crap?"

"Mischief."

"Yes, no one knows how to stop him."

I change the subject. "Why did we leave the pond so quickly this morning?"

"A presence stalked us. We have had trouble with a mountain lion lately. Around water, the predatory animals like to hunt. Lions are strong medicine in our village and we do not like to disturb them."

"I ran into a cougar at the oasis." I tell him a short version of the story.

"It might have been Maranther," he says. "A lion is one of his animal shapes."

"But my lion had a split ear, maybe from a fight. The Maranther cougar was perfect in every way."

"Hmm," he murmurs. "A real lion gives you a sign to pay attention. I have never heard of a mountain lion lying next to a human. They sense humans. No one ever sees them. I will have to think about your event."

Too many things to contemplate, but I'll have plenty of time to think after I awake. For now, I need questions answered. I know Running Feathers and his people will be gone when I wake up.

Lost in the past

"Where have the men in your village gone?"

"Elk hunting." His face drops into a sad stare. "I'm sorry, Kicking Ashes, but I do not have enough energy to stay with you. Keep your woman in your thoughts, and she will feel you. You've made the mistake of letting your energy run out of your soul while you search for the answer. You must stay here and build your strength. You will need it."

His image fades, and I awake refreshed and cheerful. I look at my watch: April 8, 1799. I've been asleep for two days and jumped further back in time than ever. I wonder if my next series of jumps into the future will be as far.

Within the next five boring days, I jump from 1799 to 1979. My decision is to stay close to Leigha's shrine. On the evening of 1979, certain I'll leap right through the time I might meet her, I keep my thoughts focused on her and the years we've been together.

I remember the weekend we went off by ourselves to San Francisco and roamed the city. The morning of the first day, we walked out of the hotel into the skyscraper canyons. The fog came in so thick we could see only the base of each building. Well bundled, we walked from Market Street up the hill to the traffic-filled streets of Chinatown. People smiled and greeted us in passing. Leigha commented on the friendliness of the city. After a while, it became comical the way people looked at us. We'd been obliged to say good morning or nod to each person. The city was alive that day.

We've gone back many times since and we were never able to recreate the feel of that special occasion. On a foggy day in our past, San Francisco welcomed us with open arms.

Next, I remember our first camping trip with the kids. I'd talked myself blue trying to convince Leigha that camping would be good for everyone. We left Friday afternoon. The whining from the kids had stopped only after we arrived at the mountain lake. Once we ate, Leigha relaxed and enjoyed herself. She was afraid of the canoe, so we spent the next morning coaxing her into it. When we floated quietly out on the smooth lake, it took the rest of the day to get her out of the sleek little boat.

I used the camping experience as a reminder, when I talked her into our desert trip. After months, she finally relented and agreed to our ill-fated adventure.

In an attempt to keep myself occupied while I think about her, I bring up hundreds of Leigha memories.

In the pre-dawn hours after the sixth excruciatingly boring day, I awake and find myself lying next to her. Thinking it an illusion or dream, I lie in a half-dozing slumber waiting for her to vanish. When I realize it is her in the flesh, I bask in the feel of her warm body next to me. I listen to her soft breath and pull in close. Tears roll down my cheeks. Ten minutes later, she stirs to find a better position.

"Leigha. . ." I shake her gently. "Wake up, Leigha."

"Mmm. . . wa. . . what? It's still dark, Martin; let me sleep." She rolls over and tucks her sleeping bag around her shoulders.

"Leigha, we have to go." I'm gentle, but I won't let her fall asleep and possibly lose her again.

She mumbles and groans. "Why so early?"

"It's dangerous for us to stay. We have to get out of here before dawn, before the sun rises. Something tells me Maranther is not paying attention. Before she wakes, I want to be far away and out of her influence."

"Who is Maranther?"

"I'll tell you later. We have to get out of here, now."

"Okay, okay, I'll get up."

Slowly, she wiggles out of the sleeping bag into the chilly morning air. I hurry her into her clothes and help get her pack loaded. Each time I look at her, tears well up, poised to flow again.

Darkness surrounds us. With flashlights in hand, we hoist our backpacks and walk to the edge of the boulder. I look at the dusty old road, and I'm relieved to see it in the same condition as when we drove down in the Volvo. With a flash of my light, I get one final look at the decrepit adobe structures, then say a silent good-bye and good riddance to my home for the past three weeks. I'll miss Running Feathers and his people, but I won't miss anything else.

We climb down the rocks to the road and begin a forced march up the hill. When dawn breaks, we're far away from the adobes, miles up the winding road. We don't stop, or even slow, but I admire the beauty of the early morning desert, the vivid colors of dawn, which continue to spread across a partly cloudy morning.

"Martin, please don't walk so fast, I can't keep up with you."

I'm ten paces ahead and speak without breaking my stride. "If we're going to get free of Maranther, we'll have to cover twenty miles to Whiley's by nightfall."

"Who is Maranther?"

"Answers to your questions must wait. I can't talk and hike at the same time. I don't have the extra breath."

"Why do we have to go to the campground now?" she asks. "What's the hurry?"

"We have to get out of this mess."

"What mess?"

"I can't explain right now. It'll take too long."

"I wish you would tell me what's going on."

By mid-morning, Leigha stops and puts both hands on her hips. "Look here buddy; we gotta get something straight. I'm not some cow for you to herd along. I need to stop and rest. You go on if you want, but I'm finished for now."

I stop and turn. "It's critical we get to civilization before either of us falls asleep."

"Who is Maranther, and what's sleep got to do with anything? We haven't seen anyone since you got stuck in the sand the other day."

Where has she been the last three weeks?

I drop my pack in the sand and face her. It's as good a time as any to tell her, I think. She'll figure it out on her own, sooner or later, but exactly how do I approach the subject? My cheeks flush. "We got stuck in the storm last month, Leigha, and you know Maranther."

Defiance sets hard in her face. Her voice cracks. "I don't think so. I haven't met anyone in this damn desert since we got here. Who is he, and why do we have to get away from him?" She refuses to respond to the "last month" part of my statement.

"We met one person, Leigha."

"Who? I don't remem. . ." She blanches. "You mean the old woman is Maranther?"

I nod.

"It was a dream, and it happened yesterday morning, not three weeks ago."

I look at my watch, then read the date aloud, "It's April fourteenth. We've been in this desert a month to the day."

She steps over and looks sideways at my wrist. "Your watch is wrong. We went to sleep last night, and you rudely awoke me this morning with a wild tale about getting away from Maranther. I went along with your little scheme, because I thought all along something bad was going to happen, but so far, it hasn't."

I look at her dumbfounded. My thoughts race as I try to catch up with the change of events. Is she right? Have I traipsed around the desert in a dream? Has my exhausting month been a horrendous nightmare after all? I sit on a flat boulder beside the road. My muddled mind goes from one event to another during my ordeal. I distinctly remember almost dying in the desert, nearly being eaten by the cougar. It's so real, so solid in my memory, it's impossible to consider it didn't happen. Everything comes clear when I remember the ring.

I point at her hand. "I found your wedding ring."

She looks at her hand and blanches. "Where did it come from?" For a moment, she smiles as she studies the details of the original ring.

"When I went to the car, I found it in the ashtray."

Her face comes alive. "The ashtray, of course. I took it off when I went to the gym. I remember now. It was loose, and I lost it while swimming the day before. Luckily, it was easy to see at the bottom of the pool. I put it in the ashtray for safe keeping until I got it home."

She's happier than I've seen her since we started this damnable trip. The ring proves that the month has not been a dream. It affirms that my experience is real. The question is, how did Leigha lose a month? How did she sleep thirty days? Rather than call it to her attention, I decide to let her bask in the wonder of having her ring. It's important to get her on the road before she asks more questions. The inquest will come soon enough. For now, she's happy.

"Let's get going. We have many miles to cover."

Without a word, she shoulders her back pack and we continue.

Leigha glows with vitality. There is a bounce in her step and a joyfulness in her stride.

I, on the other hand, feel drained and washed out. My lips are somewhat healed from the chapping I suffered in the valley, but the rest of me feels wasted. I've pulled my belt tighter two notches during the month of hell, and I'm ready to pull in a third notch. Not that I mind a tighter belt. My normal 190 pounds had been going to seed the last few years. The month of a forced diet has thinned me to my old fighting weight.

I follow in an exhausted stumble, as Leigha takes light quick steps along the gravel road. The sun warms, and beads of sweat pop on my forehead. A weary tiredness overtakes me, but I'm determined not to stop again. If I do, I fear sleep will have its way. During the nightmare march up the road, I wonder just how far Maranther's influence extends. I hope Whiley's is far enough away. Maybe Maranther won't be able to follow us once we're around people of our time.

By late afternoon, exhausted beyond any ability to think clearly, I call a halt, and we step under a saguaro.

We sit in the shade. Leigha looks at the ring for the hundredth time. "Come on Martin, tell me the truth, when did you find the ring?"

"I found it a week ago," I say without thinking about where our conversation might lead.

"You mean you found it when we stayed in Phoenix, and you didn't give it to me?"

I don't have enough nerve to give her an answer, especially an honest answer. I fear what the truth might do to her.

"I'm not blind, you know. You've dropped a lot of weight and worse yet, you look drawn and haggard. This kind of exhaustion can't possibly have happened overnight."

"I don't know what happened," I say, then let the rest of my explanation die. I don't have the energy to try to convince her of the impossibility of the events.

Her voice softens. "Tell me what you do know."

I say nothing and stare at the desert, wishing we were on the pleasure hike I had planned. I've lost my awe for silent and stark beauty. Since survival became an issue, I now long for my barbecue with its aromatic smoke rolling across a fresh-cut lawn. I crave the chaotic screams of my kids. I want normalcy, yet even if we're able to get clear of Maranther's influence, my memory of the past month will leave nothing normal.

"I. . . well. . ." I stammer, not knowing where to begin or how much she already suspects. Can she take all the news in stride and adjust to the missing month? Will she emotionally implode from the strain? I don't need a collapsed woman on my hands.

"Martin, what's happened? I see you went through something. While we've walked, fragments of last night keep coming to me. My dream was so bizarre, I haven't been able to piece together even one complete scenario. I need your story to help put it in perspective." She looks at her hand. "Let's start with the ring. Where did you find it, and why did you wait until today to give it to me?"

"I didn't give it to you, Leigha. I left it last week for you on the altar in the corner of the adobe." I fish into my pocket and hand her the old one. "Running Feathers told me to leave it. He said it would draw your attention." My lower lip quivers. My eyes fill with tears. As if a dam has burst, I blurt out the entire story of her missing month. Between sobs, I recount the missing weeks, one day at a time.

She scoots over, and we hold one another while I continue to unravel the truth. After I finish, she kisses me and the old Leigha and Martin passion blossoms. She lays me on the sand and removes my dusty pants. I spring to life inside my shorts, and she gently holds me in her wonderfully familiar way. I'm too weak to help, and don't want to. I love the rare times when Leigha takes command.

She stands, slowly slides off her Levi's, then she sits on me. After a long languorous rhythm, a deep shudder rumbles through her body, and she leans forward to kiss me. Excited from her moans, I find myself trembling. I continue to thrust into her until I climax. She pulls me closer, kissing me deeply as my sex releases.

We lie on the sand, Leigha atop me, her legs splayed, her chest resting on mine, her head relaxing on my shoulder. I visualize the smoke of the barbecue and hear the kids in the back yard. I smell our fresh-cut grass. I'm home.

I awake at dusk, and she's gone again.

A chill runs through me. Why did we stop and why did we have sex? While we made love, I knew I'd fall asleep, but for some idiotic reason, I did it, anyhow. I miss her already. I miss her sleeping next to me. I miss her smell in the dry, nearly odorless air. I miss talking to her. I'm alone again.

A brilliant burgundy sky shifts into the darkness of another ink-black night. I look at my watch: April 15, 2051. If I could, I'd be kicking myself across the desert. "Damn it, damn it, damn it!"

Still exhausted, I return to sleep. Maybe Maranther will come to me. I want to vent on her. I want to grab her filthy clothes and shake her.

I wake in the morning refreshed, but not energized. I'm alone again and depression descends. Mechanically, I look at my watch: 2089. I re-pack my gear and stare at the long ribbon of blistered asphalt. A hundred steps downhill toward the adobes, I realize it might be a week or two before I'll have any opportunity to connect with

Leigha, much less get her out of this desert.

Instead of returning to the adobes and isolation, I'll continue uphill for real food, anything but jackrabbit. A cold beer wouldn't be bad. My taste buds flutter. A beer sounds good.

I stash my backpack behind a prominent saguaro, then finish the journey Leigha and I started yesterday, seventy-five years ago.

I walk less than two miles and the familiar sign, as big as the building it sits on, peeks over the rugged terrain. I want to kick myself. Two short miles might have put us out of the clutches of that sorcerer.

In ten-foot-high, faded brown block letters, the sign spells out: Whiley's Campground. When Leigha and I stayed there, what seems a lifetime ago, the camping area was small and quaint, with gravel parking pads spread out over the desert. Now the pads and roads are paved, electricity installed. The place has lost its desert charm. One thing hasn't changed, though. Even now, only a few campers are spread out on the huge lot.

I hope the little restaurant still exists. The memory of something to eat other than rabbit or rodent makes my mouth water. Maybe I can get a burger and fries. Another mile, and I come to the outer fences of what looks like a prisoner-of-war compound. The rusted chain-link fence that surrounds the parking lot has a thick strand of old razor wire curled loosely on the top. Every few hundred feet a mercury vapor light stands. The enclosure, so incongruous with the vastness of this past month in the desert, inconsistent with my memory of the campground, almost forces me into meltdown.

After hell month and the loss of Leigha again, it doesn't take much for me to cry.

In my wasted stride, I take twenty minutes to walk around the massive acreage and find the front gate. A small chain-link door stands next to the larger car entry. I pull at the rusted latch, squeak the door open, then walk across the inner driveway. The building, a huge, army surplus Quonset, sports a wood frame wall at one end. From up close, other than heavily peeled paint, it looks like any normal building with square corners, windows, and doors. What's left of the paint has curled off the wood in long green ribbons. Three steps, which lead to the front door, are desert-dried, stacked, rough-hewn timbers. One of the double screen doors hangs ajar. I pull the screen open. It moans in protest. The wood finish is cracked and sun-bleached, slightly short of the scrap pile. They've seen much use and many halfhearted repairs. The tarnished brass latch, from a period long past, sports a deep purple glass knob. I twist, and the knob squeaks. The latch gives way. As I push inward, the door scrapes across gouged linoleum.

My senses and salivary glands come alive. The smell of cooked bacon wafts out on a blast of hot air. Three slow ceiling fans spin high above my head. More than a dozen faded red Formica tables, with four matching chairs each, are evenly spaced on the concrete floor.

Three men play cards in a dark corner. I step in, turn and push the door closed behind me. Two of the card players shift in their seats and look in my direction. A middle-aged couple sits at a table in the center of the room. The pudgy faced guy stops in the middle of a bite.

His poised fork doesn't move. His mouth doesn't close. His eyes widen. He doesn't blink. The redhead who sits with him, her back to me, clanks her fork on the plate and turns, then gives me the same stupid expression. To my left, close to the front door, a grizzled old guy with an iced drink in his hand sits at the end of the long bar that stretches most of the length of the building. He hasn't turned, but stares at me through the full-length mirror.

It's been a while since I've been in any social situation, if one could call this odd assortment of humans social.

I coax my trembling legs to carry me a few more steps to the bar. The middle-aged redhead, her mouth open, follows me wide-eyed across the room. Except for my dragging feet, the room is silent. At the bar, I settle on a faded red plastic stool. A large bald man, dirty apron wrapped around his wide midsection, saunters out from the back room. His mouth also drops. He cautiously walks toward me.

"What can I do for you, buddy?"

My voice comes out in a dry, splintered croak. "Can I have some water."

Without glancing away from me, he grabs a glass from below the counter and turns a spigot. The sound of the liquid rushing into the glass makes me impatient. In an instant, I finish the glass and put it on the counter.

I attempt calmness, to hold back my anticipation. "Another, please."

I want to leap behind the counter to hold my head under the spigot. I want to drink gallons and let it splash over me.

He serves a second, then a third, and a fourth. I empty the glass as quickly as he fills it. After the fifth, I replace the glass to the counter half empty.

"Thank you," I say. "Thank you."

I reach over and grab the well-worn menu from the metal rack. The light green paper has seen many greasy fingers. It shows discoloration along the edges and small splatters of old food, but I don't care. On the second page, I find what I'm looking for. "I want a hamburger, well done, extra mayo."

"Sure, pal. Want fries, too?"

I nod.

He disappears behind the partition.

The old man who sits seven stools away sets his empty glass on the counter. With a decided slur, he says, "Where the hell you been? I mean, hey, you look like shit."

I try for a smile but don't make it. I imagine the look on everyone's face when I start my story about being bounced around through time by an old hag sorcerer. Instead I say, "I've been lost in the desert for a month."

The guy is too drunk to carry on more than a single-sentence conversation, so he responds with a muddled, "Oohhh."

I turn to the water and finish it as my hamburger sizzles on the grill behind the partition. I feel the stares of five people drill into my back, but I don't care. I'm going to eat something other than burnt rabbit.

"What's ya doin out in the desert?" the drunk asks.

Without a glance at him, only at my glass, I say, "My car got stuck in the sand, and I had to walk out."

In the bar-length mirror, I notice a tattered image

facing me. My usually well-kept hair is tangled and filthy. My face is caked with dirt, lips cracked and bleeding. An image of an old prospector or a drunk comes to mind.

The cook steps from the back. "Somethin' to drink?"

"Cold beer."

"We only got one kind."

"I'll take it."

"I'll have another," says the guy at the end of the bar.

My mouth waters as Baldy leans down and removes two bottles of frosted Coronas from under the counter. He pulls a cold glass from the same compartment and is about to pour the contents of the bottle into the glass when I shout, "No! The bottle. I want it in the bottle."

He sets the beer in front of me and slides the second one to the drunk.

"Thanks." I put the mouth of the cold bottle to my chapped lips. The first gulp leaves me amazed. I don't know why, but tears well up in my eyes. I rarely drink, but this beer symbolizes safety and my inclusion into civilization. The second swallow is as wonderful as the first. Too soon the bottle stands empty on the counter.

During my savored ecstasy, the cook returns to the grill. I smell the sizzle of a burger and hear the familiar boil of fries. Five minutes later my plate arrives. After eating lean rabbits for the past month, a greasy burger and fries looks incredible. I feel everyone watch as I crunch through the bun, lettuce, and delicious meat.

I munch loudly, with much unintelligible comment, and tears come to my eyes again. The fries taste glorious. I order another beer chaser. I'm in hamburger heaven.

The burger doesn't last as long as I want, so halfway

through eating it in big, wolfing bites, I order another.

"Doesn't look like ya got much to eat out there," the drunk quips. I'm surprised he's able to notice anything.

"Rabbits," I say between swallows. "Lots of rabbits."

He takes a swallow of his new beer. "Lucky it's not summer, you wouldn't have made it a week."

"Talbert, leave the guy alone," the cook yells from behind the partition. "Can't you see he's eating?"

I want to talk to someone, anyone, but a drunk isn't exactly my first choice.

The last of my second beer disappears, and I feel giddy. The owner might be forced to sweep me out from under the bar, if I have another.

"Can I have another water?"

He sets an ice-filled glass pitcher on the counter.

"Drink all you want."

Two more glasses are gone as I eat the second burger. "I need a room with a shower."

"Sure, pal. They're not luxury suites, but they're only eighty-five dollars."

I wipe my mouth with a paper napkin. "I don't mind. I'll pay for everything now."

"Sure, let's see." He rolls his eyes, looks at the ceiling and says in a sing-song voice. "That's seventeen-ninety-five each for the burgers and fries, six each for the beers. It comes to forty-eight and eighty-five for the room for one night. Let's see, 133 dollars and sixteen percent tax, twenty-ninety-six with a grand total of $154.16."

I try to hold my surprise. I'd expected prices to rise since 2014, but I'm not prepared. I brought 500 dollars in cash and a fan of credit cards, but at this rate the money won't last long. I pull out my wallet as the cook turns and rings each sale separately on a hand-crank cash register. Smoke and grease have stained the chrome yellow.

He looks back as I eye the ancient machine. "It's been here since the building was built back before the turn of the century."

"What's that?"

He slaps his hand on the thin slab of yellowed marble resting below the widely spaced keys. "The register, of course. It's the only object in this building that's worth anything."

I give him a wry smile and look in my wallet. Mixed with the money are myriad reminders of what I'd been doing before I got stuck in this damnable desert. I pull out two hundreds and set them on the bar.

The ancient register stops. He looks at me. "We. . . uh. . . well. . . what I mean is, your money hasn't been in circulation for fifty years."

"I've got credit cards." I flip the folds of my wallet.

He reaches up and wipes his head. "Sorry. Credit cards haven't been in use for decades. Where have you been?"

I look at him and feel crushed. "If I told you, you wouldn't believe me."

He goes pale. "Well. . . once in a long while, we get someone who comes in off the desert like, you know, torn up and looking like warmed up death." He pauses for a moment. "It's happened to me three times since I bought the place seven years ago, back in '47. We have a legend in these parts. It's a story so far-fetched, if guys like you didn't walk in here, I wouldn't believe it."

I look at my useless hundred dollar bills and choke out one word: "Maranther."

The three guys in the corner stop playing. The drunk drops his glass.

The proprietor retreats a step. "You're caught in the Maranther thing?"

I nod and stare at the bills. "Maranther has my wife. I've been in the desert for a month trying to find her."

The room is quiet. The drunk asks, "When are you from?"

He sounds much drunker than a minute ago.

"2014."

Everyone in the room gasps.

"We came by here a month ago on our way to the hot springs."

Tears roll down my cheeks. "We were on a vacation." I bawl and drop my head to the bar.

"It'll be okay, pal." The cook puts his big hand on my shoulder. A moment later, he hands me a paper towel.

"Food and room's on me. Go through that door and turn to your left." He points toward a faded blue entry at the back of the building.

He hands me a key. "Three bungalows face the desert. Take number two. Get yourself a shower, and I'll bring you shaving gear. Take a load off your feet. I guarantee that you'll feel much better in the morning."

"Thanks." I sniff and take the key. Wobbly from the beers, I walk to the rear of the building, turn left, and go through the door. The sun blasts me, and I have a hard time adjusting to its brightness.

The little cabin is as he described. It's not the Hilton,

but neat and clean. The shower feels wonderful. As I step out of the bathroom, I see scissors, shaving cream, and a razor on the counter. I carefully trim off the long stubble and shave my face smooth again. When I recline on top of the bed, I zonk out.

Five

Nathaniel

When I awake, I feel a sharp, stabbing pain at my side. It's quiet and dark, only the repetitive sound of the high-pitched hoot of a distant owl. I get up and flip the wall switch, but the light doesn't come on.

Well, I can't have everything. I feel my way to the bathroom, relieve myself, then sleepily climb back into bed. No covers are in sight, but the night is warm. I can't find my pillow in the dark, so I lie on my back and fall asleep once again.

Morning reveals a bright, sunny day. I feel rested and refreshed; my world has reconstructed. I'm back in civilization, but something is out of place. Not until a small sparrow lands on the edge of a large hole in the roof and knocks down loose dirt do I become aware of the difference. I take a quick scan of the room and see rotted furniture, a shattered wall mirror in the front corner, and a punctured TV on its side on the floor. A quick glance at my watch confirms my suspicion: 2154, a hundred forty years into my future.

I want a bacon-and-egg breakfast with all the fixings; toast and jam, but, most of all, I want black coffee.

Although my room is trashed, I hope the restaurant is still open. I hope I can trade the ring for supplies and a regular breakfast.

I walk through the open door frame, turn right and follow the glass-strewn concrete walk. My hopes droop when the faded blue door that leads into the restaurant hangs askew on one small hinge. Any wish for breakfast vanishes when I push the door aside and step into the destroyed remains of the restaurant. The only things left under the open shell of the rusted Quonset roof are two broken tables, one bar stool with a bent leg, and a litter-strewn concrete slab. Both wooden ends of the building have either rotted or been carted away. Disappointed, I find my way through the trash to the nonexistent bar. I look toward the place where I'd seen my face in the mirror. Still half asleep, I rub my eyes, then spot a low cabinet with closed doors. I'm thinking maybe canned goods and take steps toward the cabinet.

"Already looked. Ain't nothing but a big tarantula."

I leap away from the deep voice, turn and put my hands up for protection. A young man stands with long, blond hair, a matching goatee, and two even rows of white teeth. His smile is arresting.

His lips curl as he lets out a bellow of a laugh. "Sorry to scare you, but I've been waiting around for hours for you to wake up." He swaggers over, holds out his right

Nathaniel

hand, and tips his overly large cowboy hat with his left. "Nathaniel Gerald Bishop," he speaks in a thunderous voice that echoes off the tin roof.

I reach out to shake. "Martin Vandorfor."

He grabs my hand and crushes it, grinding the bones. "Well, I've been waiting a long time for you to get this far out in history." His British accent, or is it Australian, mixes well with a slow Texas drawl.

"How did you know I was coming?"

He lets my hand go, and I flex my fingers. "Running Feathers told me two weeks ago. I timed my jumps to catch up with you. I've been awake for a day and a half waiting for you to show up here. I'm going to need a little sleep, pronto."

"Why did you wait for me?"

"Together, mate, we're going to foil that Maranther. Sorry, I can't answer any more questions right now. I need to sleep, and you'll have to sleep with me."

I raise my eyebrows. "Excuse me?"

"It's not what you think. We have to sleep touching, so we can bounce through the same time zones together."

"How do you know this works?"

"Saranden and I jumped for months, before the idiot went bonkers and dove off the boulders at the adobes. Something about moving through time makes a person a bit wobbly."

"Who's Saranden?"

"My Mexican friend."

"I thought Maranther only trapped couples."

"Couples seem to get trapped in Running Feathers's village. Like me, there have been a number of single men traipsing though time, but I'm the only one who's ever landed in that old Indian's camp."

"No women?"

He yawns. "Only in couples."

"Curious."

"One of the smaller curiosities of this entire business, I can assure you."

I lean against one of the tables and cross my arms in front of me. "How long have you been in Maranther's maze?"

"Coming on five years."

"If you've been traveling through time for five years, how do you keep from going crazy?"

"Hell, I don't know, probably a solid constitution. I've gone through three companions during that time though. All fine people. I hated losing 'em, but I'm ready to get back at Maranther. He's been a pain in my ass for too long."

"How do you propose sleeping together?"

He bellows another deep roar. "Hell, no, I ain't going to sleep with you. You're too ugly. We sleep feet to feet, with one leg tied together. As long as we touch while we sleep, we jump together. Once we confront Maranther, if we're tied together, he can't separate us."

I blanch. "Confront Maranther? Why would we want to do that?"

"Do you want to get free of his meddling and get on with your life?"

The question needs no answer.

I follow Nathaniel to the cabins. We pull two filthy mattresses onto the litter-strewn floor, and he ties our ankles together with a piece of twine from his back pocket.

I'd slept soundly the previous eighteen hours, so try as I might, I'm unable to doze. As soon as Nathaniel is flat, he's out, and I'm left with the eerie experience of being pulled through his time travel. My watch shows we're sliding back through the years.

Umm, more burgers and another cold beer or two would be good, but my hopes are dashed when the walls of the cabin vanish. I marvel as the Quonset hut disassembles itself, leaving Nathaniel and me lying on the sand. For hours, time rushes by. When it stops, my watch reads: 11:14, April 17, 1912.

With Nathaniel snoring, I'm afraid if I untie myself, there might be another abrupt jump, which would leave me behind. Later in the afternoon, I finally wake him.

"How long do you want to be tied?" I ask.

In a sleepy voice, he says, "We only leap so far, then it ends. As soon as the scene around us stops changing, you can untie yourself and let me sleep." He rolls over as I disconnect myself.

After stretching, I set a snare and resign myself to rabbit once again. One thing for sure; there's an ample supply of them.

By dusk, I've snared my meal and built a fire. I take my first bite as Nathaniel stirs.

"Yumm, dinner." He steps to the pit rubbing his eyes, then pulls a chunk from the carcass, and gnaws on the tough meat. We're silent during the ten minutes it takes to devour every morsel of the stringy flesh.

"What's the plan for getting out of here?" I ask.

He throws the last of the bones aside and takes a long pull from his canteen. He replaces the cap. "Maranther isn't able to sustain our image for long. We pass through his time, but with every pass, he gets energy from us."

"You've seen Maranther as a he. She comes to me as an old woman."

"You caught that, huh? There's significance to the shift, but I haven't been able to put my finger on it. He comes to me as a middle-aged, rich landowner. Anyhow, at one time I confronted him, and the time thing went wild. Hell, I leapt so far back in time I thought I was going to see dinosaurs."

I pull at the sleeve of my shirt to show him the watch. "Last month, when this all began, I did the same thing. I kept track of the time, and it went off the scale."

He looks over. "I've seen wrist clocks before, but not like yours. Can I have a closer look?"

I unsnap the band and hand it over.

"So, you say, with your timepiece you're able to track the days as well as the years?"

"Yes, but normally when I jump, the time of day and day of the month remain consistent. Only the years jump around, but when I stood up to Maranther, everything went crazy."

He hands the watch to me. "Things take on a whole different light. It confirms suspicions that Maranther's control dissipates after a confrontation."

Nathaniel and I sit in silence staring into the blaze.

I add a piece of dried saguaro to the fire. He picks his teeth with a splinter of bone. "What I hope to do is have you confront Maranther while I sit in the shadows. As soon as you can no longer hold your own, I'll take over, then back to you, and so on. We'll be able to drain his energy and get back to your time."

"But my wife. Maranther has my wife."

"I don't think it's a problem. Before we face off with Maranther, we'll find your wife. Maybe she can help."

I think about it, then look at him, "What happens to you when we jump together?"

"I'll be stuck in your time. What date are you from?"

"2014."

"Better stuck in your time than this damn merry-go-round."

He picks up a stick and drops it in the blaze, then looks at me. "What happened to your wife, anyhow?"

It takes ten minutes to tell of Leigha's disappearance.

"That Maranther is a relentless trickster, but I think we have a real advantage, now that we know what year it is. Much easier to get to an exact date. Your clock will come in handy."

I follow his lead and separate a splinter of rabbit bone to pick my teeth. "When you jump, how do you decide when to land? I don't have any control."

"When I travel alone, my jumps are random, too, but you noticed what happened when I slept and you stayed awake?"

I smile when the plan dawns on me. "One person stays awake and watches the time, then wakes the other when we want the journey to end."

"Exactly. For years I've jumped around looking at buildings and natural changes for indications of the passage of time, but with your timepiece, the accuracy will be precise. Hell, we'll probably be able to calculate it to the day. We need to get our sleep patterns close to one another, though. Maranther is a wily coyote. He'll find a way to separate us, if we aren't vigilant. He knows what I have in mind. He's probably preparing traps for us as we speak."

I look into the flame. I think of the cougar at the oasis and wonder if it was another Maranther trap. My mind flashes to when I accidentally found the adobes in the windstorm. Had a trap been carefully laid for us then? I think further back to the day I got the car stuck in the sand. Was the windstorm the original trap? If I go further, I see consistent disasters following us across the Southwest. Did our vacation debacles lead us to this part of the desert? Does Maranther have that much range in her field of power, or is this coincidence? The thoughts give me chills.

We lash our legs together, and the two of us sleep through the night. In the morning my watch reads April 18, 1689. Nathaniel's jumps boggle my mind. Our last leap took us two hundred years in a single night.

He awakes, stretches, and puts his hat on. "We've got a long walk ahead of us. We better get goin'."

"Where we off to?"

"Back to the adobes, of course."

"Is it necessary?"

"It's one way to get to Maranther. We must be in the territory of our original entrapment. Also, how else do you expect to find your wife?"

"You got trapped on the boulder, too?"

"I camped there one day to get out of the wind. The

next morning, my horse was gone and the floor of the desert looked different. It wasn't long before the adobes appeared. I hadn't realized I was jumping until I awoke two mornings later in front of 'em."

"Why didn't you walk out and back to civilization, once your horse disappeared?"

"Let's start walking, and I'll tell you the story."

He takes me across the desert, over open country, no roads, no sign of man.

"You know where we're going?"

"I've been out in this part of the desert for five years. I can smell that boulder."

"All right, you lead, but continue your story. I'm all ears."

We crunch through the gravel, winding in and out of desert scrub and saguaro. "Sometimes my horse would wander off, but she always returned after a day or two. It was a joke she played on me when she got annoyed. I knew she'd return, so I decided to wait her out. I couldn't carry all my gear without her. When the adobes magically plunked on the boulder, I knew something was up. Not until much later, when the buildings crumbled into ruin, did I realize I was traveling through time."

I catch up with him as we turn and march down an open wash. "What happened to your horse?"

"She never came back. Maybe Maranther ate her for breakfast or somethin'."

"If Maranther draws energy from people," I say, "how have you been able to survive?"

"I don't know, but time travel doesn't bother me."

I look to my right and see an odd expression on his

face; confusion, or maybe a poker face, like he's hiding something.

The hike down is much easier then my earlier trudge up that long slope. By late the next afternoon, we stumble to Running Feathers's water hole, drink, and rest. The afternoon sun leaves long shadows while I fill my two jugs and Nathaniel's three skins. We hike among the boulders. I'm lucky Nathaniel knows his way. The trail has not been created yet, and I'm lost after the third turn.

We arrive at dusk. I set a snare as Nathaniel gathers wood for the night.

At first light, my watch reads: 1423.

When he awakes, I'm cooking another rabbit. He gets up, puts on his hat, and saunters over to the fire. The carcass hasn't begun to cook, so he warms his hands on the little blaze.

I turn the greasewood stick crank. "At the rate we've been jumping through time, we'll see dinosaurs soon."

"Yeah, Mate, I know. Maranther's been jumping me for a long time. Each loop goes further."

Three days later, we bottom out at 793, I hope A.D., and start the long uphill climb through time.

During the jumps, I long to be in the Mediterranean, or England, where I could really see changes. I want to observe buildings, to watch entire towns spring out of the forest, experience the change of political forces. I'd love to live in ancient Rome and look at the Parthenon while it is still in good condition. The desert changes so little. Except for the cactus, everything is the same.

While cooking another rabbit over the fire, I look

up. "I'm starving eating these skinny jackrabbits and no vegetables. I long for a salad or cooked broccoli."

He looks at me. "What's broccoli?"

"I can't explain, but it would taste wonderful right now. Last night I dreamed of swiss chard and brussels sprouts, two of my least favorite vegetables."

"What are those? Do they grow common in your time?"

"As common as the day is long."

"Maybe being in your time won't be so bad."

"You just wait and see."

"For now, you can get your green vegetables here." He steps to the boulder and reaches under a long crack. When he brings his hand out, he has the scrapings of a greenish mass.

"What is it?"

"Lichen. It grows under rocks and in the cracks of certain kinds of cactus."

"I can't eat lichen."

"If you want your greens, you'll eat it." He hands the mass over. I take the spoon-size glob and touch it with my tongue. It's flat and tasteless, but my body wants it. My taste buds scream for more. I drop the wad in my mouth. "Not half bad."

"Tomorrow, I'll show you a cactus you can eat."

"Your green matter will do for now," I say, "but I'll still dream of broccoli."

On the morning of the fourth day, my watch begins an upward swing. By the sixth day, we're close to 2014. In the corner of the adobe, I reset Leigha's small shrine, carefully placing each item in order of importance, the last being her replacement diamond ring. I push a stick into the ground and slide the ring onto the shaft.

Six

Leigha's Memories

I remember, Martin and I went to sleep in our tent in that crappy little adobe. On the second night, he disappeared. In the middle of that same night, when I heard some noise and peeked through the door, the old woman sat on the edge of the boulder in front of a strange fire watching it burn in a peculiar, fascinating way. I couldn't take my eyes off of it. The old woman seemed so safe and warm, I relaxed and drank the tea she offered. Her body glowed in the light of the queer flame. At first, the tongues of fire frightened me, but they became soft, yielding, and warm. Soon, I felt so comfortable, I sprawled on the earth next to the fire and its dancing flickers. The old woman hummed a sound vaguely familiar. It was a melody so gentle and hopeful, it lulled me to sleep, like the gurgle of a small brook on a quiet night.

When I awoke, I still felt her friendly warmth. With

that afterglow, I wasn't even worried when I found that Martin and all of his things were gone. Somehow this strange woman soothes my fears, and I have an odd trust that Martin is alright.

I remember the horror of my childhood. I wanted to revive my friend, but no matter how much I tried, Sara slipped away.

I feel the loneliness of that day, crying for my best friend, crying for myself and the distinct possibility that my life would end like hers. For a moment, old feelings flood in. For the first time in thirty-odd years, I feel again the guilt of not having done enough. It lasts only a moment until I step outside and the old woman appears. When she does, I'm safe. Tinges of the memories still linger, but helplessness and despair disappear. With the ancient, oddly dressed woman who doesn't look like she could care for herself, much less both of us, I have an irrational feeling of safety.

"You comfortable, Senora Leigha?"

"How do you know my name?"

She waves the question aside with one arthritic old hand. "It does not matter."

Her words calm me.

"Would you like to eat?" she asks.

I feel vast space around us, like we are in a large and empty stadium. I look to see if we are in a different place, but the familiar adobes still sit atop the giant rock, tucked under the cliff. Everything looks the same, but the vastness persists.

The old crone turns the roasting rabbit and motions me to sit across from her. She tears off a strip of meat and hands it over. I'm hungry, but don't like handling my food with my fingers.

I look up at her. "I want a plate, a fork and a knife to cut the meat. I'm not about to tear at the food with my teeth like an animal."

She smiles, reaches behind her, pulls out a wooden bowl and small stone hunting knife, then places the strip of meat in the bowl. The knife looks quaint, but I can't eat with such a rudimentary utensil. I remember the Swiss army knife in my backpack, one of those fat ones with everything, including a spoon and fork.

I set the bowl on the earth and go into the building, bending as I pass through the pint-sized doorway. The tent and all of Martin's things are gone. The only things remaining are my pack, sleeping bag, and the small air pillow to rest my head. Forgetting about the army knife, I turn toward the old woman and look through the door. "Where is my husband?"

"He will not be with us for a time," she says. "We have sent him on an errand."

I look around in hopes that he left a note. He usually writes a quick note. He's that kind of guy. He wouldn't disappear without letting me know when he'd return. I look carefully under my bag and pack. When I find no note, I walk to the door and look at the old crone. "Where did he go?"

"It does not matter." She points toward the open desert. "He's out there, and we will see him again."

"He would never leave me alone. We're on vacation, for God sakes." I feel a frantic nervousness in my voice. I try to calm myself, but it persists. "I never wanted to come to the desert. I know he would never leave without telling me."

"It's an important journey," she titters, then sweeps her hand. "He's on an errand for us. I promise he will return."

"What am I supposed to do without him?"

"Think about your friend Sara. Think about what happened during that part of your life."

"How do you know about Sara?"

"Let us say I know much about you and your man, Martin. For now, understand that the two of you are here to find your destinies."

"How do you know?"

"I know what happened in the motel when the mouse ran up your arm. I know how you got your car stuck in the sand and had to walk out. I know you sighed with relief when your parents moved away from the gossipy little town. What was the name of that town, Leigha?"

"How do you know? How do you know about Tult?"

"I have watched over you since your birth, but I've waited since long before you were born."

"But why?"

"Let us say that you asked me to look over you."

"I never said a thing to you. In fact, before last night, I never laid eyes on you."

"Remember the second play you took your husband to, 'The Taming of the Shrew?'"

"Yes, I remember, but how—?"

"During intermission an old woman came to you and asked when you planned to go to the desert. Do you remember, I gave you a flier for a play?"

"You were that woman?"

"Do you recall the seamstress in the little town of Tult? She protected you from the peering eyes of the neighborhood?"

"That was you?"

"What about the old nurse during labor with your first child? She watched over you and made sure you were well cared for."

"You, too?"

"Now, remember your dead friend Sara."

"You weren't Sara, too?"

"No, I wasn't Sara, but I did go out to the desert with you. I showed you the way to the cave and brought the search party."

"No one came with us."

"Not there in the flesh, my dear, but I guided you."

"If you guided us, then why didn't you save Sara?"

"Sara's time had come. Her entire life had been lived for that moment in the desert. Her death set the stage for your rebirth."

"What does that mean?"

"Destiny sent you to watch your friend die. You felt the wrath of the town and you've lived with the guilt of your friend's death."

"Why was I supposed to do that?"

"Those events have tempered you and made you the person you have become. Destiny prepares you for the next part of your life. Look out on the horizon, Leigha. The possibilities of what is to come will astound you. We have so much to do in the coming years."

I turn my head to look toward the break of dawn.

Maranther's Deception

Except for the one sharp peak far off in the distance, the horizon lays flat and featureless.

I turn back and say, "If the possibilities. . ."

The odd looking fire continues to burn, but without the brilliance it had a moment ago. The feeling of vastness vanishes. The rabbit still hangs limp on the wooden spit, but the old woman has disappeared. I go on a frantic search, though instinctively I know she is no longer around. The logical side of me says she is too old and decrepit to move so fast. She couldn't have climbed down the boulder while I turned my attention to the horizon, but in one second, she no longer exists.

Again, I feel abandoned. I walk to the pit and pick up the bowl. Without the proper utensils and with no one around, I grab the strip of meat with my fingers and take a bite. Although the rabbit is tough, I mechanically chew. When I finish, I pull another strip from the roasted carcass.

I eat and for some reason, I think of my childhood friend, Sara. I watched her die of thirst so many years ago. It was the year people glanced sideways at me.

The memory of their hidden whispers: "There goes Leigha. She killed Sara out in the desert."

That was the most horrible year of my life. I felt Sara's parents' anger. Her big brother taunted me whenever he got a chance. It seemed like the whole town pointed fingers at me and chanted, "There goes Leigha, the girl who killed Sara Britton."

I suffered the last year we lived in Tult, that insidious little town nestled in the badlands of southern Utah. At the end of the interminable twelve months, to my relief,

136

my father found a new job, and we moved.

Too much time has gone by since I've thought about the particulars of that old trauma. The memories flood back in torrents. From deep inside the pain of that year, I feel once again my childhood sufferings. While I mindlessly eat dried, stringy meat, I remember the seamstress from down the street. Out of a whole town of people, she understood. What was her name? She was the only one who grasped my suffering.

I sought solace with that strange woman, so different from my mother, from other mothers or from anyone in Tult.

Once the seamstress arrived, gossip about her sizzled through our town. No one went into her shop. She was an outsider. The chatter flew like the pigeons at the courthouse: "How dare that woman move into town and set up shop right across from Williams Hardware!"

"How dare a spinster outsider expect us to welcome her with open arms!"

"The gall of that woman to be in business for herself, when a woman's place is in the home."

Before the accident, we kids pulled vicious pranks on her, knowing the town approved.

I can't recall her name, but I remember how much pressure we all put on her to pack her sewing machines, pack her fancy ideas, and go back to California.

After the accident, I looked for places to hide from peering eyes and found none. I took long walks by the river, or into Salsbury Forest. Eventually, I found they too were not safe retreats. For a while, I wandered alone, until one day when I came upon Sara's big brother Billy,

Sally Farnsworth, Becky Slader, and Freddie Conche. With Billy's rage to spur them on, they chased me deep into the forest. When they caught me, they kicked me and called me names. Billy did the worst damage when he punched me in the face and left a deep cut above my right eye.

For the first time in years, I feel the faded scar hidden under my eyebrow.

After they'd finished, they laughed, and taunted me from an ever-growing distance. When I stood to return home, I was lost. I spent the rest of the day finding my way out of the forest. For two weeks, I stayed inside, nursing my bruises and dealing with the worst case of poison oak in my life.

I never took another walk in the woods or hiked by the river again. After that day, I was not interested in being outdoors, and mere thoughts of the desert made me cringe.

Martin hauled me out here after the session with our therapist, when I relived that awful time with Sara. Behind my back, the therapist and Martin talked about how to get me out here to purge the experience and learn to enjoy the desert. They made an agreement, without my knowledge, they thought. They actually went behind my back and how professional can that be coming from a highly respected therapist.

Our trip was meant to heal the deeply buried shock of Sara's death. It looks more like another trauma will be added to my old one.

Sleeping with my leg tied to Nathaniel is awkward and painful. When I want to shift, I have to wake him to synchronize our turns. Two weeks, and I've learned to lie flat on my back with my worn-out sleeping bag pulled tight. The nightly desert chill leaves me in need of another blanket.

I look toward the southeast. Early morning colors reflect through a long string of distant wispy clouds. The mountains look like small bumps on the horizon. I glance at my watch: 2015. It's one year after Leigha and I got trapped in Maranther's despicable time loop. Although I made a Herculean attempt to stay awake, when we came around to the year 2000, I fell asleep for a few minutes and slept through my time. It may take another two weeks to go around the loop again to find Leigha.

I shake Nathaniel. "We've jumped past my time."

He groans, turns his back to me, the leather thong binds, and I wince.

"Look," I say. "We've gone past 2014. I'm getting up."

He stirs and turns his head toward me as I untie the rope. I get up in a huff and slam around the boulder. I have no idea what I'm looking for, but I look just the same. I'm moving to work off frustration. When I spot Nathaniel's empty water skins and my almost empty gallon jugs, I grumble, "I'll fill the bottles."

He yawns and stretches.

I grab the containers and walk the vague trail toward the top of the cliffs. Within a half mile, I've burnt off some of my anger.

I finish the remaining water as I reach the cliff summit drenched in sweat. Some anger lingers, so I force march myself along the ridge top to the pool.

Hot and exhausted when I arrive, I want to jump into the water to cool off, but I remember Running Feathers' comment, more than a hundred years after his certain death. I've had enough bad luck. I'll not chance drawing more by riling any possible native pond spirits. Carefully, I kneel at the edge, pull reeds aside, and put my head to the water. After even one day in the skins, water tastes like wet leather. In the plastic jugs, it grows algae and tastes alkaline. Fresh, clean water directly from the pond is a delight.

Under a warm sun, I drink and rest along the reedy shore. The day is normal for April; cool in the morning, gradually warmer, then hot by noon. There's a promise of genuine desert heat as I bask in the sun, splashing my face occasionally with the water to stay cool.

I lie for an hour until I hear a crunch in the rough gravel behind me. Nathaniel steps up and tips his hat. "Since it's going to take at least ten sleep periods before we return to your time, it might be nice to get another burger."

"Good idea. I'm sick of rabbit."

"We'll regulate our jumps right into the restaurant and eat."

"The currency changed after 2014, and I only have money minted in my year. To pay for the food, our jump has to land us in the early part of the century."

"It's no problem, Mate. We simply won't go to sleep. If we start back now and walk all night, we can eat breakfast with your current money, then spend the rest of tomorrow in the motel. Life might look a whole lot better after a shower and shave. If we stay awake long enough, we could eat lunch before we sleep."

"You've thought this one out."

"Anything to keep from eating another rabbit." We both laugh.

Once we find the gravel road, without saying much, we follow it out of the canyon into the night. To keep awake, Nathaniel tells me about himself. "When I was a boy of about ten, I came to the Southwest from Australia with my parents. They followed stories about large tracts of land to be had for the taking. If you settled the land for five years, it became yours.

"My parents found a piece of land in the highlands east of the settlement called Albuquerque, but it wasn't as easy as the stories led us to believe. Turned out that we'd built a camp in the middle of Apache sacred land, and nobody told us. My dad was tough and he wouldn't be run off by any savages. The first summer we fought Indians and scraped by. We barely made it through the winter, but Dad was determined. He held the land through frozen winters, stifling summers, those damn grasshoppers, and more hornet-angry Indians than we could count."

"What happened after five years?"

"I don't know, because I left. I was tired of looking over my shoulder and scraping by. I wanted more. One thing led to another, and one winter I found myself crossing the desert to the Pacific Ocean. I spent the next year in a steady move north to the settlement of San Francisco. It was a small community of maybe two hundred people, but they were hard working and honest. I threw in with them for five years."

"Today, San Francisco has twenty million people."

"Could twenty million people fit on that peninsula?"

"Twenty million live within sight of the city."

"That's a lot of people."

"It's pretty crowded down there."

"Is that where you come from?"

"I live two hundred miles east, in the mountains."

"Oh yeah, I heard about those mountains. What were they called?"

"Sierra Nevada."

"That's them. I heard gold was found there later."

"It's how my town was created."

"How's that?"

"Three gold mines were built in Nevada City, but the mines petered out, and they're shut down now. They've become tourist museums."

"What's tourist?"

"People who travel around. Tell me about your time. I find it much more interesting."

He continues as we round a large rock outcropping. A single saguaro stands tall into the ink-black sky with billions of stars to outline its massive shape.

"San Francisco Bay was an incredible place," he says. "You could walk out your door and hunt your choice of game. A man could bring home enough food for ten families before he got out of sight of the settlement. During the autumn and spring, so many ducks and geese flew along the migration routes, for weeks on end, they blacked out the sun with their endless numbers. With a single shot from a rifle, I could usually drop three or four birds.

"Black and grizzly bear posed a problem, though. They wandered through the settlement often. We didn't know what to do with those huge carcasses once they were killed, so after a while, we stopped shooting them and simply drove 'em away."

A dry desert breeze tickles the back of my neck with an occasional coyote yelp in the distance. Other than the crunch of gravel under our feet and an occasional jet overhead, no other sounds break the silence of the night.

Nathaniel's story continues as we push our way up the road. "The San Francisco Bay supplied us with seafood. Clams and mussels filled the mud flats, with more bass and salmon than we could think of catching. There was so much food, other than our individual gardens for greens, we hardly had to do anything to get tucker."

"What's tucker?"

He laughs. "Food, Mate, just food."

"Why didn't you stay?"

"We're coming to that part of my little story. "I met an amazing woman with the reddest hair you ever saw. She and I got married during my second year there. We settled into what could've been a wonderful life."

Nathaniel's walk stiffens, then he says, "Our first baby came a year later. She and the baby died during birth."

He pauses for a long time.

"I'm sorry," I say.

"I couldn't hang around after that. Two months later, I headed south along the coast. I've heard tales that the West Coast is filled with people in your time. I'd give anything to see the cities."

"You'd be disappointed."

"What do you mean?"

"They're ugly, sprawled, litter-filled, and noisy. The water has been polluted so much no one can drink it."

"What's litter?"

"Garbage. People throw their garbage everywhere. It's not too much of a big deal when a few people live close, but when a city has ten million litterbugs, things kind of get out of hand. Air pollution is the same. Think about a million fires built within the San Francisco area."

"I see what you mean. It could be a disappointment."

We walk in contemplative silence.

We make a bend in the road, walk up a steep grade, and when the road levels out, I say, "So, go on with your story."

"When I traveled south, I didn't meet anyone until I reached a settlement south of the fifty-mile cliffs."

"Big Sur?"

"And a fitting name for such a place. The settlement sat on one of the long sandy beaches stretching for miles. The desert emptied right into the ocean."

"That would be Los Angeles. Thirty million people live there, in my time."

He stops and turns to me. "You don't say. I can't fathom so many people in one place."

"Hard to believe, but true."

He starts walking again, and I catch up.

"I stayed along those beaches for two weeks," he says, "but the wandering spirit got me again, and I continued south to the tip of the thousand-mile peninsula."

"They call that peninsula Baja," I say. "It's Mexico's land."

"In my time, it was all Mexico."

"That's right, before the U.S. stole it."

"Baja is another fitting name. That place is barren beyond belief." He pulls a small shell from his satchel and shows it to me. "Got this in Baja."

"It's a sand dollar."

"At the tip, I ran across another little settlement and stayed through the burn of the summer. There was little to tie me to the place, so I rode a barge across the bay and wandered North through the desert. As the hot time of year began, I stumbled into the canyon of the adobes. Of course, the adobes weren't there yet. During the first night, my horse took off. While I waited for her to return, I camped on the boulder. I'm still not sure Maranther didn't have something to do with my horse disappearing."

"Maranther is slippery," I say. "I wouldn't put it past her."

"One morning the six adobes appeared, and I met Running Feathers. When he explained my situation, I didn't believe him, but after the adobes crumbled into ruin and I saw my first paved highway, I was forced to reconsider.

I step to the side of the road. "I got to take a leak."

He continues while I turn my back to him and water the sand. "During the first year of time travel, I stayed pretty close to the adobes. I returned every five or six days to get more information from Running Feathers. Once I found myself hopelessly stuck in Maranther's maze, I explored further away from the area. Hell, I've been manipulated by Maranther for five years, and I'm ready to get on with my life."

We walk in silence in the semi-dark, each in our own thoughts. The quarter moon rises over the horizon, shining a vague nocturnal luminescence over the ghostly terrain.

After thirty minutes, I ask, "Do you think we have much of a chance to get out alive?"

"Maranther's influence doesn't affect me in the same way as it does everyone else. Since we've met, I notice you wasting away, another reason why a burger or two might not be a bad idea. These jackrabbits are lean. You could use a little fat."

I think about Nathaniel's observation and wonder if Leigha is going through the same slow degeneration.

We keep each other awake with stories.

After dawn, as we stumble up the never-ending road, Nathaniel says, "Why don't you take a ten-minute nap? I'll keep track and wake you before we leap too far into the future."

"Here?" I ask.

"I'll take one after you wake up, and we'll be fresh for breakfast."

"Take the watch and wake me in ten minutes."

He takes it, and I feel a tinge of unease as I doze off.

In the afternoon, I awake. Nathaniel's short length of rope hangs loosely at my ankle with a scribbled note.

Martin says we've been separated a month. From my point of view, we've been asleep, and his story is a little hard to believe, but he looks so thin and haggard. There must be some credibility to his statement. The appearance of the wedding ring supports Martin's tale.

When we make love, it's gentle and careful, unlike our usual coupling. Martin falls asleep. Lying on top of him, with my head on his chest, I'm aware of the little stone pendant in the pocket of my shirt. It's a comfort to know I have it, though I'm not sure why.

Later, stiff from lying in an awkward position, I roll off him and find a more comfortable place. I hear his familiar snore as I doze with full intent of waking him to continue the journey. It doesn't feel like much more than a flutter of my eyelids before I return to consciousness. I fall asleep with him not more than a foot away.

My eyes flash open onto a late afternoon brilliance when my hand touches empty space. I sit up and look about.

I stand and call out, scan the area, but I already know what happened. My calls get louder. I frantically search for any sign of him.

Although it appears impossible, his explanation of the lost month makes some sense, especially now. Once the revelation sinks in and my loneliness envelopes me, I break down and cry. Although Martin's a victim of the old woman, as I am, I'm still alone in this awful desert and not sure what to do. I don't even know how to get back to the adobes, much less to civilization.

As darkness settles on the desert, I weep. I witness the sun setting, the crimson clouds, reflections that turn the desert floor into a deep blush, but I'm too confused to comprehend the beauty.

Night descends as I huddle in my sleeping bag. After hours of sobbing and cussing, I manage to fall asleep.

When my eyes open again, the sun leaps over the eastern horizon. The cool air makes me scramble to find a sweater and socks. Once warm, I roll my sleeping bag and stow it in my pack.

I hoist the backpack to my shoulders and walk out to the gravel road. Even if I could find the adobes, there's little for me in that direction. I look uphill. At least at the campground I'll eat and wait for Martin in relative comfort. I'll find out the year. If Martin is right, I should also be time traveling.

I turn up the gravel drive and toward civilization, away from the ruined adobes and vague memories of the old woman's sorcery. I walk out of the valley, more thirsty and hungry by the moment. A mile or so later, I come over a small rise and find myself gazing at the campground sign.

It's a long walk to the main building. The front doors stand weathered, dry, and cracked in the desert sun.

Any semblance of paint has long ago peeled off and disintegrated. I push one of the doors inward, and it protests with long scrapes on the deeply gouged linoleum floor. The tinkle of the little bell above the door reminds me of home, but things are very different here.

I step through the door into the dark hall. The smell of burnt grease attacks me. On my right, a wasted old man at the bar slowly turns his head. His bloodshot eyes widen. His mouth drops open. His half-drunken face reveals a toothless grin.

A rotund man steps from behind the partition. He wipes his hands across a dirty apron. One hand swipes his bald head, maybe an unconscious habit of wiping hair out of his face. "Can I help you?"

I take the single step off the entrance landing onto the smooth concrete floor and walk to the bar. "Water?" I ask in a husky voice, more frog-like than I want it to sound.

He dips a glass in a hidden bucket of ice, squirts in clear liquid, and hands it to me. "You been out in the desert?"

Something happens that is out of context with being in this greasy little restaurant. I leap out of my seat and take the stance of a fighter, spilling my glass of water in the process. I feel my blood pressure rise. My eyes open big. The hair on my neck prickles.

He asked an innocent question, but I snap at him, "Why?"

I catch a glance of myself in the full-length mirror and see my frightening expression. I see a battle stance, with disheveled hair and a dirty, weathered face.

Almost under his breath, the toothless old man at the end of the counter murmurs, "Maranther."

Baldy backs against the wall.

I defend myself, against whom, I have no idea.

The fat guy and I glare at one another. Embarrassed, I bring my arms to the bar. Why have I reacted? Why does this one word send me over? Baldy nervously swipes his imaginary hair and grabs a towel to clean the mess.

I turn and ask the drunk, a little too casually, "What did you say?"

He drops his gaze to his beer. In a frightened tone, he says, "Nothin'."

"No, what did you say?" I try to sound nonthreatening and casual, although I'm not doing a very good job.

"He doesn't know what he's talking about." Baldy slides back to the bar and towels the spilled water.

"What did he say?" I turn back to the old guy, and he shrinks into his glass of beer, eyes focused on the foamy head.

"He didn't mean to say nothing, Miss. Talbert never means to say anything. He's just Talbert, and he never says much that counts."

My voice leaps an octave. I'm feeling on the verge of hysterics. "He said something, damn it, and I want to know what it was." I can't believe I'm acting so strange.

Although Baldy looks three times my size, he appears ready to bolt. He gulps once more, nervously pulls his right hand across his sweating cue ball of a head, and gets me another glass of water. "There's a legend about an old sorcerer who's lived in this area for two hundred years. He catches unsuspecting people and spins them off through time. We've gotten more than our share of time travelers, and we've learned to recognize 'em. You have that empty, confused look I've seen many times."

"What's the word? I want to know the word."

Baldy says, "Maranther."

I'm able to brace myself and not spill the second glass. My face turns hot from the dread the word invokes. I reach for the glass. I need to focus. I lift it to my lips and take a long drink.

"You hungry?" he asks.

"Yes, but my husband has the money."

"Breakfast is on me. It isn't often we get a time traveler. What do ya think, Talbert, has it been five years?"

"Yeah, at least five."

"I can't wait for things like this to happen. It's probably one of the few reasons I stick around this rat hole."

"It's not because of me, Sam?" the drunk asks.

The cook gives him a sarcastic grin, then looks back at me.

"Your husband's got the money?"

"Martin Vandorfor is my husband."

"Ten years ago a guy named Martin came in. Wonder if it was him."

"Hell, yes, it was him," the drunk croaks. "I remember clearly." The drunk becomes animated, waves his arms, a shine in his eyes. "He came in here and ate, must'a been three burgers. He went in one of the rooms, and we never seen him again."

I'm stunned. What Martin said must be true after all. I ask, "What's the date?"

Baldy turns and studies a calender partially hidden

from my view. "It's April the—."

"No, not the month. The year; what's the year?"

"Seventy-eight."

"Nineteen seventy-eight?"

"No, two thousand seventy-eight."

"Oh."

I take a moment to regain my composure. I'm more than sixty years into my future.

My stomach makes a loud gurgle.

"Hey, you want to eat?"

"Please," I say absently. "How about a burger?"

"Be right up."

He steps behind the partition.

I sip my water, wondering how Martin and I will ever reconnect and get out of Maranther's clutches.

After Baldy serves the burger, I take a bite and fall into deep reminiscence. Why am I so jumpy with the mention of that name? I can't even think the "M" word, much less voice it. What does the name have to do with me? Why am I afraid? She was gentle and considerate. She certainly helped me through a confused period after Martin disappeared, but my memory has huge blank spaces. My inability to conjure up anything but vague anxiety leaves me to question what actually took place. I still can't believe Martin's story. His thirty days feels like overnight, but something crowds my mind. With the last bite of the burger, I decide my memories are too big to fit into one night.

"When are you from?" A voice asks from off in the distance. The question brings me back. I surface and remember where I'm sitting. Am I supposed to answer?

I dip a french fry into catsup and put it in my mouth. "Twenty fourteen."

"Jesus," Baldy says. "I wasn't even born."

There's a pause, then he gets an excited expression. "The other guy came from 2014, too. He must be your husband." He shakes his head. "This is the strangest place I've ever lived."

I take another fry, then wash it down with my water.

"What's it feel like?" Baldy asks.

I look at him.

"I mean, what's it feel like to awake in a whole new world? What's it feel like to know time has changed and things aren't recognizable any more?"

"I don't know, because I've been out on the desert, and nothing changes out there except for a cactus or two. I'm still not convinced what I'm going through isn't a gigantic hoax or a bad case of the flu.

"Oh, wait; there's one change. The road changed. The road is paved. In my time, we drove our car on a gravel path."

"Mexico paved it in 2047 to be exact," he says. "I'd just bought the place. Everyone anticipated a surge of traffic directly from Yuma, but it never happened. Once in a while, a trucker comes in to eat. A stray camper drops in here and there, but the road didn't change much."

Outside the front door, a thunk of heavy boots makes me glance at the reflection in the mirror. A silhouette darkens the filthy glass door. When the doorbell jingles, Baldy looks up.

The drunk spins on his stool and says, "Tarnation."

The door closes and dims the sunlight. The stranger

shuffles across the concrete. I recognize the gait, the lameness in his right leg, which is more apparent when he's tired. He got the limp from that motorcycle accident a month after we were married.

"Martin?"

"Leigha?" he croaks.

I fly off my seat, bound across the room and knock him against a table. While we struggle to regain balance, I notice his normally thick arms have dwindled. His wide chest has shriveled. I'm in his arms, and that's all that matters. He bursts into tears in my hug. I kiss him. He's back; it's all I dare consider.

"I thought I'd lost you forever," he says. "I thought you'd gone. It's been so long."

"So long?" I say. "It was only last night. I woke this morning and you'd vanished. Where did you go?"

We hold one another close as he calms, then speaks. "I waited at the adobes two weeks, but you weren't there, so I came to Whiley's for something other than rabbit."

He falters, and I help him to the bar. He pitches my remaining half glass of water into his mouth. When Baldy refills it, Martin empties it again, and another. On his fifth, he comes up for air.

He eyes Baldy. "I'm hungry. Can you cook me another burger or two? I don't have any current money, but I have a ring." He pulls it from his pocket.

"Keep your ring," Baldy says. "It'll be a pleasure to cook you something. Hell, once every ten years I can give a guy a free burger or two. Besides, you look much worse for wear since the last time." He slips into the back room, and the sound of sizzling fills the hall.

"What happened since yesterday?" I ask.

"Nathaniel and I traveled together, and the bastard stole my old Seiko wrist watch."

"Who's Nathaniel?"

Baldy says from the backroom, "He's been our most frequent visitor. He's come through here five, maybe ten times in the all the years I've been here. From what I'm told, he showed up at least twenty times before I took the place over."

"Kinda flashy," adds the drunk. "Toothy grin and all."

"It's him, all right," grumbles Martin. "He left me in the desert yesterday, and he's got my watch."

"It was just a Seiko," I say.

"You don't understand; the watch tells me the year. Without it, I don't know how we'll return to our time. Even if we can break free of Maranther, we won't know the year."

There's that word again. That "M" word. I tighten, ready for something unexpected. To distract my terror, I ask, "What do you mean?"

"Think about it. If we go back home without knowing the date, it will cause havoc for us and everyone we come in contact with, especially if they know us.

"If we go to the house a day too soon, we could find ourselves sitting there. It's already enough to make me crazy, but think of the kids and our neighbors. If we show up a year late, they would have given us up for dead. Nobody would have the slightest idea where we were.

"The watch is our only hope," Martin says. "Without

it, we haven't a chance in hell of getting back to our own time."

I ask, "Can't we get a new watch?"

Baldy says, "Yuma, Arizona, is a few miles over the border, sixty miles north of here. You could borrow my old clunker and drive there before dark. It looks like shit, but that car has never let me down."

"We haven't got any money," Martin laments.

"I filled the tank last week," Baldy says.

I look at Baldy. "That's very kind of you."

"We have money," I say. "The ring. We'll hock the ring and get more than enough money to buy a watch."

Martin looks at Baldy. "There's one more problem. There's a big chance we might leap before we return. We may not want to, but your car will be left somewhere between here and Yuma."

"Leave it parked in a place visible along the way, or in the parking structure in Yuma. Put the keys on top of the rear tire where no one can see them. If you don't return in a day or so, I'll dry out Talbert here, and we'll retrieve the car. I need to go to Yuma for supplies, anyhow."

"Which parking structure?" Martin asks.

"There's only one. You'll see the building long before you get there."

Martin, puts out his hand to shake. "Thanks."

"Name's Sam Ross."

"Martin Vandorfor." The two men grasp hands and shake.

Martin turns to me. "This is my wife, Leigha."

Sam reaches his big hand out and gently grabs mine. "It's my pleasure," he says.

"Let me finish cooking the burgers, and after you eat, I'll take you out to the car. It's an old wreck with some peculiarities, but it runs." He's quiet for a moment, then stammers. "Can. . . I ask you a favor?"

"Sure Sam, anything you like."

"Well. . ." He gets an aw-shucks look. "So far, my friends don't believe me about time travelers. They think I'm telling stories. Can you leave me a souvenir to prove your existence?"

"No problem, Sam," Martin says, "but what would it be?"

"I don't know, something delineating the year and placing you in that year."

Martin pulls out his wallet and rifles the contents. "Here's my driver's license, but I'll need it when I get back. I've got business cards, but no printed dates. Here it is." Martin pulls out a credit card receipt from the hotel where we stayed in Albuquerque. It looks as though it's been in there for a few years, but it has a date and Martin's signature.

"That's great," Sam says. How about if I get a copy of your driver's license, too? I got a copy machine in the office."

"Yeah, sure." Martin hands him three plastic cards. "How about you take the credit cards, too. I've got these outdated ones."

He takes them and studies the top one. "We haven't used credit cards since before I was born."

I reach in my pocket. "Here's something to date us for sure." I hand him a new tube of my favorite lipstick.

He looks at me with a blank expression. "I don't

know, we still have lipstick in our time."

"I'm sure you do, but mine was manufactured in 2014, and it's fresh. Somebody might be able to forge all the papers Martin gives you, but you can't forge lipstick and have it stay fresh all these years."

"I don't get it. I can buy a tube of lipstick in Yuma."

"Sam, it's obvious you don't have a woman in your life. We're not talking about a cheap tube of lipstick here. The metal cylinder alone is dated by its shape. Lipstick manufacturers change designs like I change socks. I'll bet the design can be dated to our exact year."

"You may have a point." He holds up the lipstick. "I'll check it out in Yuma next time I'm there. For now, I'll finish your burgers and get you on the road."

"No onions or mustard," Martin yells, after Sam steps behind the partition.

"Gotcha."

In a minute, he slips two burgers in front of us and we devour them. Sam brings in another for Martin, which he savors more slowly before he orders a third.

He takes the burger with him as Sam walks us out to the car and gets us on the road. I drive, while Martin eats.

"I thought I'd never see you again," he says between bites. "I was afraid Maranther had swallowed you up."

I tense. There's the "M" word again.

We're driving into the same valley where everything began. We're going right back into the lion's den.

Seven

The Monolith

I've been to the adobes too many times, I know each turn. I say nothing to Leigha as we roll past the wall of rock I'd first climbed, so long ago. A half hour later, the old car clunks and rattles its way out onto the long dune-filled valley. We roll down the broken asphalt two-lane, then over the flatness of the old lake bed. Halfway across the valley, I shout over the noise of the car, "Pull over."

Leigha looks at me. "What?"

"Stop here."

She reluctantly slows the car, pulls to the side of the road, and leaves the engine idling.

"We need to back up," I say and lean my head out the window, looking for the road sign I used for shade. She shifts into reverse and slowly retraces a hundred yards.

When she parks, I get out. She follows me across the dunes to our rotted Volvo.

"What happened to our car?" she says fingering the

little stone medallion. "What a mess!"

I hand dig a trench to the trunk. Even with Leigha's help, it takes an hour, but finally, we're able to uncover the trunk. I dig for the keys in my pocket, wiggle the right one into the sand-riddled lock, then fight the trunk open.

I don't expect much; rotted pairs of Levis, a shirt or two, but Leigha packed things valuable to her. While she rummages through her disintegrated belongings, I sit on a dune and drift in my thoughts. Occasionally, I hear her coo, or moan, depending on what she's found. When she's finished, we have a small bag of her personal items to carry to Sam's car. I carefully repack the trunk and close the lid. We set out across the dunes, and I bid a farewell to our car, knowing it might be the last time I see it.

After a long struggle in the sand, we come over the last dune and see Sam's clunker. I point toward the car. "Who's that?"

"I don't know, Martin. We'll have to find out."

A skinny little middle-aged Mexican man wrapped in a serape and wearing a large, wide-brimmed hat, leans on the rusted front fender.

"What do you think he wants?" I whisper.

"Maybe he needs a ride."

He greets us in a language I don't understand.

"Hola," I say in a friendly gesture, using one of the few Spanish words I know. "Do you speak English?"

He shakes his head. He doesn't even try to indicate what he wants, but silently, in the manner of a gentleman, he opens the driver's door for Leigha. Once she's in, he closes it gently, then in a lightning quick movement, opens the rear door and slips into the back seat.

"Hey, what the hell? Get out of my car right now!"

"Oh, let the little guy stay," Leigha says. "It's obvious he needs a ride."

"What if he's a criminal?"

"He doesn't look dangerous to me," she says.

The little guy, as if he knows exactly what Leigha is saying, makes a short remark, which I don't understand, but his dark eyes sparkle. He gives me a toothy smile. Gold fillings and crowns pepper his grin. I recognize the smile, but I can't place him. The car chugs away, slowly gathers speed, as we cross the dry lake bed.

We roll at a reasonable clip, until we begin the climb up the canyon. It doesn't take long for the road to bleed off any momentum. Leigha is forced to shift to third, then to a long grind in second gear. When she drops into first, the old car hunkers. I fear it may not have the power to get up the hill. When we reach what we hope to be the summit, she has to limp along in first gear, but the engine chugs doggedly.

At the top of the hill, when she's able to shift into a higher gear, the old car gains a little speed. We pass a faded sign that says we've crossed into the United States of America. A second sign, in even worse condition, tells us Yuma, Arizona, is sixteen miles. Both are simple road signs. I want to ask the little Mexican what happened to the border guards and inspection stations, but after some futile attempts at communication, I know the gap between his English and my Spanish is too great.

Leigha slows, makes a left turn, and drives along a

new paved road. Since we left the campground, we have not seen another vehicle, until a sleek-bodied racing car streaks in from behind and passes us at a speed faster than I've ever seen traveled on land. Leigha and I look at one another. I look back, but the little Mexican seems unfazed. In seconds, the sleek, red car has disappeared. Minutes later a small truck flashes past; then a blue sedan. They all go at high speeds beyond my impression of what's safe, but in the desert, driving rules must be different.

In a mile, the dry desert turns into lush green pastures and farmland. A twin building looms on the horizon.

The last time I went through Yuma, miles of one and two acre homesites lined the highway. Each homestead was strewn with junk cars and skinny livestock standing on overgrazed land. As with too many small southwest towns, it looked like one large spread-out ghetto, few residents caring about the aesthetics of their property.

Beyond farmland and pastures, the only building standing is the double monolith.

"We should be getting close," I say, "but what happened to everything?"

Leigha extends her index finger at the windshield. "It looks bigger than any building I've ever seen."

I turn to the weathered little man in the back. "Yuma?" I say, in an attempt to make my sentence as simple as possible.

He cracks a gold-toothed grin and points with his crooked finger. "Yuma."

"Well, if that's Yuma, what happened to the town?"

"It's sixty years in the future, Martin. Things around

here have changed a lot in that time."

"I despise time travel," I say. "It's so confusing."

She smiles. "Yes, but it is so amazing."

I point through the cracked windshield. "Would you look at that structure? It's taller than any building I've ever seen."

"What about the design," Leigha says. "It's beautiful."

Two thick glass spires split from the main body at least a hundred stories from the ground. They separate from one another and reach for the heavens, spiraling a half turn to the highest point, maybe four hundred stories.

"Look at the six little crystal shapes at the top," Leigha says. "They must be ten stories tall."

"More like thirty."

"Yuma," says the little guy from the back seat.

Leigha looks at me. "What is such a massive building doing out here in Yuma, nowhere, Arizona?"

I wait for common signs of humanity, old dead cars, litter along the highway, billboards, but I see nothing but crops and tilled fields. The one human sign is the single monolith, which looms ever larger as we move toward it.

The farmlands turn into grassy and wooded parks as we pass under a ten-story, sculpted steel arch. Integrated into the arch are the words "Welcome to Yuma, Arizona, City of the Future."

Leigha points at the windshield. "We have a mile still to go, and it looks like the park stretches all the way to the split structure, which seems like the only building."

The road opens to a four-lane promenade, but I see

only a few people mowing lawns, digging in the gardens, and lazing on park benches.

"Everyone must live and work inside," Leigha says.

I make a quick guess. "The base of the building could easily be a mile across. How did they build such a gigantic structure out here?"

"Maybe the better question is why?"

A series of signs guide us to the entrance and down a ramp. Because Leigha is driving, I'm able to put my head out the window and look up the leading edge of the building. "It's more than two hundred stories before it begins that impossible split."

As we plunge underground, all sunlight fades, then disappears, then we wind through ten layers of a gigantic parking structure. Leigha looks for a place to park.

The little guy says something other than his one word, "Yuma," but neither of us understands his language.

Once we park, I place the keys on the rear tire, and we take a short hike to the elevator. I say to the little guy, "Your ride is over; we'll see you later." He doesn't understand, so I embarrass myself when I shoo him like a cat.

He smiles, but keeps pace five yards behind us.

On my third try, Leigha intervenes. "Give him a break, will ya? Let him go where he wants. Besides, he probably knows more about the building than we do."

The elevator opens and a group of young people pour out. They talk loud as they joke with one another. We step in. I look at the control panel. "Five hundred twenty-eight floors. The building is a mile high. I've never seen so many buttons in one elevator."

The Monolith

Our choice is easy, with the main lobby well marked. I hope the old man will push another button, but he also heads for the lobby. When the doors open, I stand like a child in a toy store.

We step into the main hall and Leigha lets out an audible sigh. "Martin, look up."

I follow her gaze to a sixty-story ceiling. The lobby, if one would call it a lobby, is a mile long and half as wide. The park-like setting sports a series of long, narrow lakes, each cascading into another. Large shade trees encircle the shores. On the lower level, shops and businesses hidden among the greenery surround the park. We've walked into the ultimate mall. Upper balconies layer atop one another practically covered with plant life. The sun streaks in through huge sheets of tinted glass as I take Leigha's hand. We stand in open-mouthed silence and look at the bustle of an entire city inside one gigantic structure. There are no cars, no horns, and no smog. People ride bicycles, walk, or stand on one of four moving sidewalks that snake through the trees and shrubs.

I say, "Let's sell the ring and get out of here."

The little Mexican guides us to a holographic map. No one seems to pay any attention to the eight-foot disc that floats knee high in the center of the hall. Three people walk unceremoniously through it like it doesn't exist. The multicolored lines of the map flash across their legs as they pass. We cautiously approach the disc, which comes alive as we walk up. The plain, mono-colored images leap into vivid lights depicting one kind of store or another.

"What do you think?" Leigha says. "The flash and

sparkle of the lights remind me of the extra bold lettering in the yellow pages."

I put my hand to my chin "I bet they paid extra for that."

She points. "This one has miniature fireworks, like a minuscule fourth of July."

"At least Madison Avenue hasn't changed."

"Oh, Martin, don't be so cynical."

The little guy grins and spreads his arms to encompass the setting. "Yuma, Arizona."

After five minutes of close examination of the colorful holograph, I take her arm. "Remember, Leigha, we're on a mission."

"You're always so pragmatic. Loosen that tight little ass of yours and have fun for once."

"Well, aren't we on a mission? Don't we have to figure things out before we get too tired and have to go to sleep? Who knows where, or when, we'll end up when we awake?"

"Okay, okay," she says. "There are six jewelry stores and two pawn shops on the ground floor."

A square foot of space opens with the mere mention of jewelry. A menu bar gives jewelry store and pawn shop options from seventeen other floors. The eight-foot hologram shifts, shows a horseshoe pattern, and indicates the seventh floor. More miniature rockets and flashing lights appear, again an indicator of the larger stores. Leigha lets loose a childlike giggle with every holographic explosion.

I've already chosen three of the six jewelry stores and two pawn shops on the first floor. The moment I've decided, five cards appear in my hand.

"Oh, my," I say.

"I got some, too," Leigha titters.

"Yuma, Arizona," the little guy says, his gold-clad smile one of delighted patience.

When I shift my attention from the map, it returns to an eerie green outline and fades. We walk around to the left and follow a paved sidewalk that passes in front of hundreds of shops. More people than I can count mill through stores and restaurants. It's the biggest shopping mall I've ever seen.

After we pass at least fifty storefronts, one of my cards beeps. I shuffle the cards, and the third flashes in bright yellow. A miniature holographic hand with long, red, sculptured nails reaches out of the card and points directly at the store. The hand moves as we get closer. It continues to point at the front doors of Yamier's Pawn Shop.

"Can you believe this?" Leigha asks.

We walk through the front door and the card turns itself off, returning to a small plastic shingle again.

A tall man dressed in a loudly striped suit steps over to us and holds out his hand. "Can I help you?" He speaks in a heavy, East-Indian accent.

I turn to Leigha, but she shrugs, so I reach into my pocket for the ring.

He grins. "Ah, first time you've been in Yuma, hey?"

I nod.

The little Mexican says, "Yuma."

The salesman holds out his hand. "Give me the card, and I return it to it's rightful place for you."

I hand it to him.

"If you don't go into a store, put the leftover cards in box at the entrance."

"I see."

"Now, I can help you?"

I pull the ring from my watch pocket and hand it over. "We would like to find our best price."

He pulls out a jeweler's loop, steps over to the counter, and studies the stone under a high-intensity light.

After a long, careful inspection, he looks up. I haven't dealt with many pawn brokers in my life, but I'm reassured to see, even in the future, they have not changed. Without comment, without a hint of expression, he looks directly at me and says, "Fifty-three thousand."

I, on the other hand, am unable to hide my surprise. My face goes from a serious negotiating expression to utter astonishment. "Fifty-three thousand?" I choke the few words with a wild-eyed smirk. I distinctly remember paying three thousand for it. Fifty-three thousand is an outrageously high price for pawn.

"Okay," I say.

The little Mexican tugs at my sleeve and shakes his head.

"Come over to my desk, Sir," the salesman says, "and we will complete our arrangement."

Our tagalong's scowl intensifies. He shakes his head.

"The little guy's got a point," Leigha says. "Let's have a look in other stores first."

"Not a bad idea," I say and hold out my hand.

The man gets a you-don't-trust-me look. Still holding the ring, he snaps, "Sixty-one, and it's my last offer."

Sixty-one thousand. A person can put a good down payment on a house with that kind of money. The price of diamonds must have gone through the ceiling.

I extend my open hand in his direction. Reluctantly, he returns the ring.

"Thank you. We may come back." I turn and walk toward the entrance.

"Sixty-nine," he shouts, "but only now, not when you return."

Ah, yes, some things never change.

After an exhausting walk along one side of the mall and then back across the other, Herold's Jewelry Mart makes the best offer, $137,000 plus an antique digital watch. He pays cash, in ten-thousand-dollar bills.

"Oh God, we're rich," Leigha says. "Now what do we do?"

"Well, for starters, let's eat. I'm starved."

"I guess the little guy has earned a meal," she says.

"I guess so."

The little Mexican grins, his gold inlays gleaming.

The hologram again helps us find a restaurant, but the bill for three burgers, fries, and condiments is more than two hundred dollars.

"We have the money and the watch we came after," Leigha says after a leisurely dinner. "Let's go."

"I can't believe what you're saying. You want to return to our cruddy little campground after being in the mall of the century? What about the clothes you wanted to buy?"

"I just want to get home. I'd love to shop here, but you already told me that everything we're not wearing gets left behind the minute we fall asleep. If I buy new clothes and we wake up tomorrow in our time, these new styles will look out of place. I just want to get out of here."

We take a long hike to our elevator. Once we're in and the door closes, the little Mexican quickly pushes a button going up.

"Hey, what are you doing?" Before I have a chance to counter his command, the elevator lurches upward.

"Oh, why not, Martin. Let's see the sunset before we return."

Wasn't it a moment ago, when she was in such an all-fired hurry to go? Women! I'll never understand.

In less than a minute, we get out on the garden roof, then look out over a flawless landscape, a spectacular sunset, and a view of the distant mountains rivaled by nothing I've ever seen. The Mexican motions us to sit on wooden deck chairs that line the wall. The backs are adjusted low with leg rests.

"Let's sit for a minute," Leigha says, "to rest our feet."

It feels good to lean my head back and rest for a moment.

I come awake with a start and look around. For a second, I don't know where I am. Maybe aboard a cruise ship out on the Caribbean, or on our second trip along the west coast of South America? Then, in one big flash of memory and inspiration, it all comes to me.

I lift myself on one elbow and cry out, "Martin!"

Silence. Has Martin disappeared and left me alone again?

"Martin!" I scream.

"What. . . what do you want?" he grumbles. To my surprise, he's still on the chair. We're attached at our ankles with a piece of twine.

I remember the little Mexican looked mischievously at me. I recall him grabbing one of each of our ankles. The second he grabbed us, everything went blank.

"We've been duped again," I say.

Martin tries to roll over, but the strap binds, and he's forced to stay in the awkward position.

I shake him. "Martin, wake up."

When he's conscious, he snaps fully awake, eyes wild like a trapped animal. He lunges to his feet, but with one foot attached to me, he stumbles, falls forward, lands on his outstretched hands, and yelps.

Martin untangles us by cutting the knot with his pocketknife. Once I'm free, I stand, stretch, then turn to face him.

In the ghostly moonlight, he looks at his watch. "Shit, the watch doesn't work. How did we fall asleep? I don't remember a thing."

I point at the string. "I remember the old man doing something with the twine, then I woke up."

He spits a single word out like venom. "Maranther."

I shiver with the mention of the name.

Martin puts both hands on his hips and glares. "That little fuck was one of Maranther's henchman. That old bitch was probably laughing the whole time."

I bend, pick up the twine, and show it to him. "If it was her, then why didn't she separate us like she's done in the past?"

He shrugs. "How am I supposed to know."

Martin paces the cement walk three times, then turns to me. "What do we do now?"

"I haven't got a clue."

He has a second look at his watch. "At least it tells the time. It's six-thirty in the morning; maybe a diner is open."

He takes the twine, jams it in his pocket, then leads me to the elevator. When it arrives and the door opens, I notice the drab, unkemptness of the compartment.

Reluctant to step in, I study the interior.

"What do you think?" Martin asks.

"I guess it's safe, but it's so old and worn out."

We step in and I settle in the corner. He pushes the ground-floor button. We shoot down, but after a long floor-passing wait, we stop on the seventy-fifth floor. When the door opens, three hulking men greet us.

"C'mon out." The biggest man speaks, in a strong New York accent. "We're not goin'a hurtcha."

Martin is a big man, but compared to these three, he looks like a pencil-necked weakling. He takes a stance to protect me.

"C'mon, man. Ya know we could come in there and take ya out, but the boss wants ya in one piece. The elevator ain't goin anywhere, so you're stuck with us. Why don't ya come along and see what he wants?" The big man smiles a crooked grin and waves his two buddies off. He steps back and says again. "C'mon, unless you give us a hard time, we ain't gunna hurtcha."

I walk out of the elevator, close to Martin and along a tattered hall toward the outside wall of glass that overlooks a panoramic view of the rising sun. The early morning colors light the hall with a golden hue. I hold Martin's hand as we cautiously cover the five or six hundred steps to the wall of glass. We walk into a plush room the size of most houses, and I gasp at its opulence.

A man with long blonde hair stands, his back to us, looking out. The structure is so clear and unencumbered by separating lines, it looks as though there is no glass at all.

I gaze past him onto the eastern landscape.

He speaks with a strong British accent. His back is still to us. "You've come a long way."

"What do you mean?" Martin asks.

I want to say something. I want to shout at him for waylaying us. I want to scream and bring the authorities, but I'm afraid this man is the authority.

He turns.

Martin growls, "You bastard. You stole my watch and left me out there to die."

His toothy grin widens. With a benevolent calm, the stranger says, "I couldn't get you here any other way. I knew there was no possibility you'd leave without your wife." He nods toward me.

"Without my wife." Martin spits the words and moves toward him. The biggest of the guards steps forward.

"I wouldn't," the guard says.

Martin stops, but continues to spew insults.

The blond man's smile holds as he waits for Martin

to finish hurling his long list of grievances.

When Martin runs out of insults, the blond man's grin slackens. "Within the walls of this building, the next phase of your task begins. Maranther tells me you're a star student."

"The next phase?" Martin's voice raises a half octave. "The next phase to what? I'm going home. I want to go back to my time, with my wife, to my normal life. I don't want to go to any next phase."

"Leave any time you want," the stranger says, "but I've watched others who came before you. I'll guarantee if you go into the desert at this time of year, you won't last more than a day or two. Look at yourself. I don't think you have much energy left, especially to deal with the harshness of late spring."

I look at Martin and say, "He's right, you know. You're wasted and exhausted. You have dark circles under your eyes."

The toothy guy turns to me. "We haven't been formally introduced. My name is Nathaniel Gerald Bishop."

"Leigha Vandorfor," I respond with a cautious smile.

I turn and see Martin grimace.

"Your husband and I spent time in the desert." The man waves his guards away, and they step into the next room. "We parted under sudden and clumsy circumstances." He focuses on Martin. "Sorry for that, Mate."

Martin leans an elbow on the wet bar. "I don't think you're sorry for anything."

Nathaniel raises his voice, "Sid."

The biggest of the men enters the room.

"Sid will show you to your room. Order breakfast. We

have pretty good food here. You'll feel better once you've eaten."

"Are we your prisoners?" Martin asks.

"We'll talk after you've been fed. I have exciting people for you to meet. We have much to discuss."

"I want out of here," Martin bellows.

"Go right ahead." Nathaniel points toward the desert. "Leave whenever you want, but I warn you, the trip will be much more difficult than you think."

I touch Martin's shoulder. "Why don't we take him up on his offer? Let's see what he has in mind after we eat. For now, I could use a little breakfast."

He turns to me. "Don't trust this guy."

"Come on, Martin, I'm hungry. Let's eat."

Resolve flushes Martin's face. "For the moment, we'll have breakfast, but I want my watch."

"When you come back, Mate."

The big guy leads us out of the room onto the balcony. The walkway overlooks the massive inner environment of the main hall. I glance over the edge and see it isn't as clean and tidy as when we'd come in with the little Mexican. The building looks much older. The trees are fully grown.

We're led down a long balcony. On the opposing wall, a quarter mile away, hundreds of people walk similar halls above and below us. A beehive quality exists inside the building. It brims with activity, but something isn't right. For all practical purposes, everything should be utopian perfect. It's what humans have been striving toward, a central living space with unlimited land to support its inhabitants; but something is amiss.

The guy leads us to a small apartment on the north side of the building, instructs us in the use of the control panel, then leaves. I'm sure I'll hear the door latch behind him, but no bolt snaps or key turns. Curious, I walk to the door and open it. To my surprise, no guard stands outside the room. I poke my head out to see the large man lumbering toward the office.

"I don't trust him," Martin says.

"Me either, but for now let's eat. After we're finished, we'll figure out what to do."

"I'm sure he has a devious surprise for us, and I don't think it'll be so easy to get away from here."

"All I know is we need to eat. Will you make a choice so we can order breakfast?"

Martin walks to the control panel and jabs his finger into a green button. A series of holograms project onto the counter. The illusion is so real, I almost smell the three strips of bacon on the plate. A series of eight possible breakfast projections flicker, one at a time, onto the counter. We each choose one. A hologram of juices and coffees demands another choice, then the projection disappears.

"What do we do now?" I ask.

"After we eat, let's get the hell out of here and go back to Whiley's campground. This place gives me the creeps, especially since Nathaniel seems to be running the show."

I unbutton my blouse. "I'll feel better once I take a long shower."

Martin strips his clothes. "Yeah, I guess you're right."

Ten minutes later, after the first shower in who knows

how long, we return to the kitchen in robes. Our meal is on the counter, and our clothes are clean and folded. A thin man in a waiter uniform stands next to the food. Martin digs into his pocket and pulls out a five.

The man holds out his hands, palm facing us. "I can't accept a tip." He speaks in a snooty British tone. "Even as measly as the one you offer. The meal comes to you compliments of Maranther." He tosses his head, turns, and pushes the cart out the door.

"Maranther?" Martin slowly lifts the stainless steel cover over our food and inhales. "Will we ever get clear of that meddling sorcerer?"

We eat in silence. Like he's starving, Martin gulps his food. I try to enjoy mine, but also find myself shoveling it in like I haven't eaten in days.

With a full stomach, I step to the large couch facing the expanse of glass. I sit and look out at untouched open desert, then feel the comfortable warmth of the day. Despite our tenuous circumstance, a sense of security envelopes me. Martin sits beside me, and I snuggle close. The next thing I know, he moves, and I'm startled out of a deep sleep in late afternoon.

I awake with a start and look out through the wall of glass. The sun has long since found its way behind us, leaving the shadow of the building stretched out for miles on the flat, uneventful landscape. A hundred miles to the east stands a saw-toothed formation of mountains, but from this distance it looks like a line of small bumps.

I move to get up.

Leigha leaps off the couch, searches the room with a wild, fearful look. "Martin?"

"I'm right here."

She turns toward me, reaches for the little amulet, then relaxes. "I thought you left."

"It's okay, I'm here."

She settles next to me as I look at my wrist. "The new watch doesn't tell how many years we've jumped. No wonder Nathaniel took my old one.

She gets up and walks into the kitchen. "I'm hungry. Let's order more food."

"What's for dinner?"

She lifts her hands to cover her mouth. "Oh, Martin."

"What?"

"The order panel looks old and filthy. The whole room is decayed."

I leap to my feet and spin around the sofa, then notice its raggedness. Paint shavings from the walls cluster on the floor. The once-plush lavender carpet allows the bare concrete floor to show through.

"We've jumped time again," I say. "From the looks of things, definitely into the future."

The printing next to the meal photos is unreadable. Leigha pushes a button. I hope for the same holographic projections, but the way things are going, I don't expect much. Nothing happens.

I take Leigha's hand, and we walk out of the decrepit apartment onto the concrete balcony.

She glances over the rail. "What's happened to all the people?"

The building, which teemed with life, has fallen silent, though faint individual noises echo up from the lobby.

"I don't know." I gaze over the edge onto the tops of an immense, ancient forest. The foliage hides the entire ground floor. "I'd guess Maranther has something to do with this."

I look across the wide expanse to see thick cords of vines, with vegetation covering the opposite balconies. The massive yellow-tinged windows cast a sickly ochre light on the greenery.

"It's so old," she says in whispered reverence, toying with the thong from her pocket. "It looks so, so used up. How many years did we move forward?"

"It must have been a lot. The building has been in disrepair a long time."

"Wait," she says. "Isn't that a baby fussing? Listen, it's the sound of children playing."

Silently we walk to Nathaniel's office, but I already know we'll find no one. We open the door and step in a room layered thick with cobwebs. No one has been in the suite for decades.

"There's nothing here," she says.

We make an about face and walk to the elevator.

Leigha pushes the first floor button, but we hear no electrical sounds. I say, "I don't expect the elevators will work."

"Worth a try," she says. After a minute of waiting, we push through the stairwell door. Echoes click from tentative steps as we move down the steel stairs. We would not be able to see, but for some long-dead engineer with the foresight to design small windows every fifteen feet. The bronze color of afternoon filters through the dingy glass.

We descend for thirty minutes until we find our way to the ground floor. I open a squeaky steel door, and we step into an overgrown courtyard.

Leigha looks above her head. "The light through the trees barely filters to the ground."

"Yeah, and it's much cooler under here."

She points across the court. "Look, there through the brush. It must be the people we heard from above."

Nine adults sit on one of many steel benches scattered across the courtyard. They give us curious looks.

"They already know we're here," she says. "We may as well introduce ourselves."

I turn to her. "The stamp of Maranther is all over this place. I cast my vote to get the hell out of here this very second."

She nods toward the people. "Too late. Let's at least say hello. It's the right thing to do."

"I don't trust anything around here."

She grabs my hand and tugs me across a hundred yards of tangled forest to the far side of the courtyard.

"What happened?" Leigha asks, when we get within yards of the small group. "Where did all the people go?"

Six ancient women and three old men stare. They're cleaning bean pods into a large wooden bowl on a metal table. They look at one another. The largest of the men, as though he talks for the group, says, "The rest of our family works outside. They should be back soon."

The Monolith

Leigha says. "I mean what happened to the thousands of people who used to live in this building?"

Everyone looks to the far end of the table where the oldest man sits. They look expectant, like he knows the answer. The children who had scampered about come closer and settle next to the adults. I get the distinct feeling they're preparing for a story.

"Come sit and relax," he says.

People on both sides of the table scrunch to make room for us to sit closest to him. I feel awkward without introductions, but one of the old women silently motions us over.

The old man says. "When I was a boy, a great number of people lived here." He pauses, fingers the black beans from a dried pod into the half-full bowl. "More years then I remember have gone by since a thriving city stood here. They called it Yuma, Arizona.

"One could hardly get from place to place for the mass of humanity. Fertile fields stretched for miles around. 'The Spires,' they called this building."

A dark-haired youth asks, "Why was it called 'The Spires,' Grandpa?"

"How about the stores?" another asks. "Tell us about the stores and what was in them."

The old man smiles, picks up another bean pod, and peels it open. "Because it was the tallest building in the country."

"What about the stores?"

"All of the glass-walled living cubicles that surround our inner forest here were once filled with small stores and restaurants. They sold the harvested food grown in the fields and wondrous things imported from far-off lands. Many years ago—"

"How many years ago, Grandpa?" a boy of five cries out.

"Well, Antone, I was about your age."

The boy beams, then climbs upon the old man's lap. The man continues stripping the bean pod, then picks another. "I was about your age when all the shops were open and busy. They gave off the most delicious smells of exotic cheeses and fresh-baked breads. Some shops sold new clothes, while others, paper goods. Many sold jewelry or household items.

"What about the toy stores, Grandpa?" a blonde boy across from me asks. "Tell us about the toy stores."

The old man weaves a tale of toys and games. He describes, in detail, many playthings I'd bought for my own kids. When he moves the story away from toys, I witness a definite shift in the attention of the children. Before long, they slip from laps and return to romping under the trees. The old man continues in a more serious tone. "People worked much harder than we do today. They labored so much, they hardly had the opportunity to enjoy their lives." The old man stops for a moment, shifts his weight on the bench, then pulls another bean pod. "There was so much abundance inside this building, but even so, many people lived poor."

"I still don't understand the word 'poor,' Grandfather," says a milk-skinned girl who stands close. She's the only youngster interested in the adult part of the story.

"These days no one lives poor, Sara, so I see how hard it is to understand what it means. When our building was full of people, a system called money existed. I still don't understand it too well, because I was a boy at the time. My guardians told me about it long after. Some people didn't have much of the money and so could not trade for the things they needed. Other people had most of the wealth and hoarded it, for what reasons I still haven't been able to figure out."

"What kind of things, Grandfather?"

He smiles, as if he knew the question was coming. "Money didn't have much value to me when I was a child, so I don't remember much. I do recollect a bright red fire truck that I wanted my mother to trade her money for."

A young woman with a round face positions roughly fashioned pottery cups on the table and pours a thin, reddish liquid.

The old man stretches his arms up and twists his body slightly as if to present the courtyard. "Our towers became known, and other structures sprang up around the country. People liked being clustered in one large building with open country around them."

For fifteen minutes, mesmerizing everyone, he tells stories of a past that fascinates me. Because he's a masterful storyteller, I want him to go on forever.

"In my youth," he says, "something happened, but it took many years before I realized what took place.

"Because we lived on one of the upper floors, I used to go to the roof to play with my friends. One day, my playmates didn't show up. I asked why and my mother said everyone was very sick.

"Not long after, she caught an illness that left her weak. For many days she hacked and coughed. With no one to attend to her, I, a lad of five, waited on her while she got worse. When she died, I didn't understand. I thought she was sleeping."

He shifts his body, puts a hand under his chin, rests it on the table, and continues. "Very quickly, few people were healthy enough to leave. Soon, almost every person had died. I was on my own in the empty building. Once the dust had settled, nineteen other people and I remained unaffected by the sickness. They tried to remove the dead, but too many had perished. The survivors concentrated on the first three floors. Eventually, they closed the doors of the rooms on the upper levels. No one has ever gone back upstairs."

When he finishes, as if someone directed the small group, everyone clasps their hands to their open mouths, makes muffled screams, and moves in a rocking motion. Leigha and I look at one another. I shrug. Everyone has closed eyes. After a minute of muffled screaming, they stop.

As if nothing out of the ordinary has happened, the old guy continues. "Since those dark times so many years ago, we've had few visitors." He pauses to take a drink of the cherry liquid. When he continues, a smile rises in his withered, old face. There's a gleam in his eye. "I count eighty summers before my failing memory lapses, but we have been lucky, and our family has grown. Last year our numbers peaked at more than a hundred. Lucy here, Martha, who works out in the fields, and Sara are pregnant, which makes three more.

"After those first hard years, my life has been blessed with this group of people I call my family."

He continues, but I find myself so intrigued by the screams-into-the-hands thing, I hardly hear another word.

When he comes to the finish, everyone looks delighted. A woman brings out another load of bean pods, and we all strip seeds into a large stainless bowl. I sidle up to the grandfather. "Why did you all scream?"

He pulls thoughtfully on his white beard. "Something I learned from my guardians after the great sickness. They had been working with a small group of people who believed every person's emotions, like anger, sadness, or frustration, needed to be routinely expelled to maintain good health.

"Their philosophy asserted that energy won't stay buried for long. One way or the other, it must be released. The question is whether it comes out in a constructive or destructive manner. You may unconsciously provoke a fight with your mate or your neighbor to release the energy, but to hold it is harmful to the harmony of both body and community.

"Before the great sickness, most people held in their emotional energy. Take what happened here, for example; the telling of the old story. A tale about everyone dying is sad and frightening, but it happened so long ago, the immediacy of the shock is small. The old culture listened to a story like this and buried it here." He rubs his belly. "It's a miniscule story, an insignificant little twitch in our body; hardly enough to be noticed. During a single day, though, we sustain many of these little twitches. A person loses energy when he goes through emotional suffering, even as small as a twitch. We don't detect such a small amount of energy, but we lose it, just the same."

His steel-blue eyes sparkle. "Think of an emotional wound you've experienced. When you think about the event, it consumes your energy."

"What do you mean?"

"You know, for example a big one like a loved one dying, or a separation, maybe a friendship gone bad. At the end of the day, with these thoughts to consume your mind, don't you feel exhausted? Remember awaking the next morning so worried that the night's sleep wasn't enough to rebuild your strength? If things persist, you'll probably get ill. At the least, holding the energy numbs us to the joy in our life."

"You have a point."

"Good example of what happens, especially when we deal with people who want something from us."

"So what's it have to do with screaming into your hands?"

"You've jumped ahead of me, son. Give an old man a chance to tell his story." He puts his hand to his mouth and makes a momentary scream.

"Sorry," I say.

"People who used to live in our city didn't understand the concept and they ran around exhausting themselves. People who lived here worked eight hours and more a day in jobs they didn't like, often with people they didn't want to be with.

"My guardians and a small circle of their close friends were experimenting with the energy-building technique when the sickness struck. There wasn't time to run from the building, because one day everyone raced about, and the next, everyone lay in bed. Those able to leave scattered the virus. We've had so few visitors since then, I assume other cities got wiped out, too." He lifts his hand to his face. I expect a muffled scream. Instead, he breaks into a sob and tears roll down his cheeks. I am amazed to see, for the first time in years, a man openly crying in front of me. No one at the table appears concerned. I feel uncomfortable and turn away to watch the children play tag.

When he calms, he picks up a cloth napkin from the table, wipes his eyes, and blows his nose.

"To openly grieve is also one of our practices."

"What do you mean?"

"It always grieves me to remember how many people died. They depleted their energies so much the sickness destroyed them. The only people who didn't get sick and die were the thirteen souls who practiced the method of building energy and seven small children. I was one of them. Because of the survivors' early work, emotional release practice continues to this day."

He gives a last wipe across his ancient face. "Seldom do any of us even get small colds. The word 'sick' isn't used anymore."

"What do you mean, no one ever gets sick?"

"Oh, sure, sometimes, but we don't call it sick. Instead, we refer to it as a loss of energy. Funny, how things work out."

"What does a scream have to do with sickness?"

"I got so caught up in the story, I forgot you asked the question. My short-term memory is not as sharp as it was, nor as it could be. I'm getting older.

"When we scream into our hands, it does two things. We blow out the immediate stress of the situation, and it saves the ears of anyone around us. To openly grieve has similar effects."

"I don't get it. What does 'blow out' mean?"

"I can't explain it rationally. The intellect doesn't get it, but the body does. I feel your nervousness. You want to give it a try to see what happens?"

"No, thanks," I say, feeling put on the spot.

"It's all right if you don't want to try, but now that you're anxious, it's the perfect time to experiment." He goes on like I'd agreed. "Put your hands over your mouth so your fingers seal all the air."

I don't know why I do it, because I don't want to try, but I put my hands on my mouth.

"When you scream," he says. "Don't do it from your throat. Scream from your gut, more like a guttural burp. If you scream from your throat, you'll hurt your voice." He holds his hands to his mouth. "Keep all of your body parts moving; it will help loosen the stuck energy. The motion is awkward at first, but your body will soon take over and do what it already knows how to do."

When he screams, I follow. At first, a muffled scream hurts my throat, but I get a feel for it. The sound deepens and originates from my solar plexus. My scream unravels nervousness, but the fluttery feeling embarrasses me. I stop and let my hands drop.

"That's great," he says. "I'm happy you got into your gut so quickly."

"I don't feel as nervous." I say. "I really don't."

"Good! Now try it again, and this time stay with

the feeling and scream longer, if you can."

My anxiety rises again. The screams must look silly. I look around for Leigha. She sits on a bench talking to an older woman, her back to me. I turn to the old man and put my hands to my mouth. The scream comes directly from my stomach. I roar as my body vibrates. I feel a hidden frustration well up from deep inside. I can't put a name on it, but I feel it, just the same. Three deep breaths and three hand screams, then I stop. When I do, I feel a tingle. I'm not sure if I held my breath for too long, or it's the release of my tension, but I feel light-headed, and I lean on the table.

"That was great," he says as he absently reaches for a bean pod and splits it open. "How do you feel now?"

"Dizzy."

"But, do you feel as tense as five minutes ago?"

"I feel a bunch of other stuff I can't put my finger on, but I don't feel tense."

"That bunch of other stuff is years of energy trying to bubble to the surface. It has nearly killed you."

"Killed me? What do you mean?"

"Have you had a good look at yourself lately?"

I shrug.

"You look like death warmed over because you've depleted your energy to a critical level. You need to slow down and take care of yourself."

"Normally I don't look so wasted," I say, "but I've been lost in the desert most of the last six weeks."

"It takes more than six weeks to get as run down as you are."

"I've been, well, traveling a lot. . . through time."

The old man's face twitches and his eyes widen. I'm positive he'll berate me for lying. He opens his mouth and says the last word I would have expected to come out of him. "Maranther!"

"My wife and I slept upstairs in a room. When we awoke, the entire structure was quiet. You're the only people around. By the look of things, we must have landed a hundred years into the future."

His nervous twitch relaxes, as if he's already come to terms with the revelation. With a calm smile, he picks up another bean pod. "There's a purpose for why things happen. I'm sure you're here to learn our energy release methods."

A somber look floods his face as he strips the beans into the bowl. He says in a much more serious tone, "First on your list is plenty of rest. The second part will be the hand scream technique, the cornerstone of our philosophy. It will take a while, but we'll show you how to rebuild your energy and keep you from falling victim to the likes of Maranther or Nathaniel Bishop."

"You know Nathaniel?"

"Let's say we've had to deal with each other. I wouldn't go so far as to say I know him." He picks out another pod. "Maranther is your main problem right now. I'll show you a way to get free of him, but it'll take a while."

I frown, then grab and strip a bean pod of my own. "We don't have much time. We must sleep at some point, and when we do, we'll make another leap."

He turns to me and winks. "There is a way to stop your traveling. Maranther isn't the only one with tricks. If you're ready to spend a month or so with us, we can take you through a training that will give you enough energy to overcome certain outside influences. Oh yes, and one other advantage; by the time you're done, you'll be healthy again."

"I don't have much choice."

"Is your woman ready?"

"She's probably more ready than I am!"

"In the morning, we'll begin preparations for both of you. It won't be an easy process, because there's much to learn. For the remainder of the day, I suggest you take a stroll in the gardens or outside in the forest. Soon the farmers will return, and you'll meet the rest of our family at dinner. After we eat, we'll see what we can do to keep you in our time.

"Tomorrow will be the first day of your apprenticeship. I have many things to do, so I'll excuse myself and see you at dinner." He struggles to get to his feet. Slightly bent, he slowly moves along the narrow path and disappears around a shrub.

Apprenticeship?

As if on cue, Leigha turns away from the old woman and looks in my direction. I get up and walk to her. She stands, greets me with a hug, and says, "Martha thinks their family can help get us out of Maranther's grip."

"Oh, really? The old man told me the same thing. Let's stick around for dinner and see what they have to offer."

"Do we have much choice?"

We excuse ourselves, stroll through the front doors, then outside to greet the end of a perfect desert day.

She points. "Look at the difference in the landscape."

"It's changed. What happened to the road?"

"I'd guess it crumbled into the earth. We must have leaped many decades."

A foot path zigzags through a double row of massive elms. The forest reclaimed lawns and parks with thick underbrush and a massive canopy.

Leigha says, "I'm amazed the trees survive at all in this desert. They must get water from somewhere."

Hand in hand, we walk along the narrow path. Filtered sunlight pierces the trees. Under the spread limbs of the elms, the air feels cool. Birds chirp and chortle in a cacophony of exuberance.

In an hour, the dinner bell rings, and we return to the monolith. Inside, we find tables set, food served, and a hundred people waiting to eat.

Their food is delicious and feels good once inside my stomach. I bask in the adult talk and the chatter of children. As the meal ends, I lean toward the old man. "I'm curious. How do you plan to keep us in your time?"

He gives me an oddly familiar grin. "We've got a few tricks, too, you know. You'll have to wait for the answer, but I promise we can do it."

I go on to a question he might be able to answer. "How does the forest sustain itself out in this desert?"

He hands his dish to a young woman, then turns to me. "We think the people who built the parks created an underground water system. Twenty summers ago, when a main line burst, we had to scramble and find the valves to turn the area off. Many voiced concern that without water the forest would die. It survived just fine. Probably the aqueduct had sprung so many leaks over the years the water created an underground lake for the trees."

His crooked finger points high in the air behind him at the wall of greenery. "The water system still works inside the building, and as you can see, everything is lush. We would never take the time to water each hanging plant from those balconies."

After dinner, the building fills with the sound of the people. It's good to hear activity, but inside the monstrous structure, sound gets lost. Jokes, cajoling, laughter, and serious talk go on all at the same time. There is no head of the family, and no authority. I settle in close to the old people. I feel content for the first time since our ordeal began. After dinner, more sound echoes off the glass walls as dishes are gathered, then washed, and evening activities begin.

Gaslights are extinguished, and a single dancing blaze in a well-used fire pit lights the hundred faces who sit in the circle and reflects off the huge sheets of glass of the distant walls. Three babies fuss, but soon no noise can be heard. Once things become silent, the old man stands and walks to the center of the circle. "Tonight, not only do we have our first visitors in many years, but they come from another time. Both have brought stories with them to add to our evening."

Murmuring arises and in the silence, I hear echoes off the sixty story tall ceiling.

I lean close and whisper to Leigha. "What story do we have to tell?"

"I don't know."

"Am I supposed to tell a story?"

She shushes me.

I can't think of a worse nightmare than telling a story in front of a crowd.

With a showman's dazzle, the old man lifts a hand and commands silence. "Tonight we'll hear about the time before the great sickness and the people who came before us. We have guests among us who can give us a firsthand view of the time that has gone before."

There's no doubt he wants me to tell a story. The thought of speaking in front of so many people makes me freeze. I've experienced this kind of terror, but it's been many years. I look around at the huge circle of people. I feel perspiration beading on my forehead, a flush of embarrassment, the rush of adrenaline, and a ring in my ears. The old man can't see how nervous I am. He doesn't see I won't be able to speak without passing out. He simply continues his long-winded introduction. I hear his speech, but I'm too busy fretting about the crowd to catch more than a word or two.

When he says, "Welcome our two new visitors, Leigha and Martin Vandorfor." Leigha grabs my hand and pulls me to my feet. Oh sure, she's calm and excited. She takes a small curtsy as an appreciative applause rings out. I'm frozen.

When the noise dies, the old man gives us a slight bow and says in an official voice, "I am Chelone, elder of this community." He steps between us and slips his gnarled hands to the small of our backs, then slowly guides us around the huge circle, presenting each adult and every child by name.

By the time we've been individually introduced, my breath has completely constricted. Leigha looks a million miles away. I don't know how, but I'm able to stay on my feet to the end. Once Chelone releases us, Leigha grabs my hand, and we retreat to our place. To my dismay, before she sits, she lets go and nudges me toward the center of the circle.

I stumble out and stand frozen. My heart pounds. Sweat rolls down my forehead. I feel all eyes on me. I hear the old man's voice, but without knowing what to do, I'm lost in my own dizzying world of anxiety. Finally, I feel a hand grab my elbow, the grip of redemption. The hand, and it's all I perceive, gently turns me, then leads me out of the circle of hell. The farther from the crowd I go, the safer I feel. I'm led away from piercing eyes, from the intensity of people, then guided into a minuscule chamber. On the floor, a small bowl sits in the center of the room. In the bowl, the soft glow of a candle flickers. I'm instructed to sit in front of the flame.

Chelone sits on the far side of the single light and gives me a gentle gaze. "Follow your anxiety to its origin," he says in a singsong voice. "Stay with your fear and go back to the day it began."

"I. . . I—"

"Don't speak," he says. "Stay with the feeling."

The instant he makes the suggestion, I get a glimpse of what my fear is all about. As soon as I focus on it, as if it's too frightening to relive, the memory vanishes. I feel myself leap out of the altered state. With masterfully spoken strange words, he reawakens that frightened part of me. Gentle, patient suggestions coax me to go deeper. Each time I come close to a memory, something catapults me into the room, bringing me back to the candle.

After what seems like a short ten minutes, I return to myself without remembering why I had to search my memory.

I look at Chelone, as the old man talks in his storyteller tone. "You've made your first journey into a world you haven't visited for many years. In this world will be found the key to your healing and a way to get free of Maranther."

"What world?"

He puts his finger to his lips. "You'll need to go into your past many times during the next month. With each visit, your journey will get easier, and it will be safer to stay."

"But why would I want to go there?"

He shakes his head. "Right now it's frightening, but when you had the original experience, it was deadly."

I try to comprehend his words, but the message feels like it's leaking out of the back of my head.

"Don't worry about what I'm saying tonight. I'm not speaking to you, the conscious Martin. I'm talking to your unconscious."

I give him a look of utter confusion.

"Right now, things look scrambled, but they'll clear. By the end of the month, you'll feel at home in your new frame of mind."

He picks a small twig, then holds it over the flame. It smells of desert sage. "Close your eyes," he says, "but don't go to sleep."

As if they have a will of their own, my eyes close. I sit inside the darkness behind my lids.

Eight

Going Back

Martin blanches when Chelone wants him to tell his story. I know my husband and have no doubt he'll go into overload with the mention of speaking in front of people. Personally, I enjoy the rush of talking to groups, and I never could understand why it affects him so negatively.

The old man whispers for me to coax Martin into the middle of the circle. After Martin stands dumbfounded for thirty seconds, I want to jump up to protect him.

Martha, the old woman who sits next to me, lays her hand on my arm. "Leave him be, child. He'll be fine."

"But you don't know what—"

"He'll be okay. Chelone is a master. He will help your husband move toward his healing."

"What healing?"

"You will see."

When Chelone grasps Martin's arm and spins him

around, to my surprise, Martin stumbles out of the circle and disappears into the darkness with the old man. I'm startled when the rest of the group focuses their attention on me.

Martha combs her tangled hair by pulling a gnarled finger through thick, gray curls. "Tell us a story about your time."

Telling stories is my forte, but I already know I'm playing to a tough crowd. It won't be easy to share a story with a group that hears tales every night. Also, except for the English language, I have little in common with these people. If I must tell my yarn, I'll have to describe every detail, every appliance, every tool of a civilization that existed many years ago. Am I up to the challenge? A hundred expectant faces look at me.

I take a deep breath and begin, still not sure where the story will lead.

"Far to the north, as many people lived in my city as once lived in this building. They didn't have such a well-planned community, though. The houses were spread out on small pieces of land. Although everyone here got sick and perished, this building seems more thought out and workable than the housing of my day."

I spend the next half hour with a story about Nevada City, then field a battery of questions. I'm not sure they understand the answers.

Once the old ones complete the evening functions, much of the group disperses into apartments on the first three floors. The remaining people form a tight circle around the diminished fire.

Each person lies down with his or her head on the

outside, feet touching, creating a wide circle around the fire.

"Come here, child," Martha says, "Lie on your back and touch feet with your neighbor."

Chelone ushers in my dazed husband and coaxes him down across the circle from me. He settles in next to Martin with another elder male on his opposite side. Eight men are on one side of the circle, with eight women, including me, on the other.

A tingling sensation vibrates through the contact of one foot on my right through my lower body to the other foot on my left. The prickling gets insistent as I become more expectant. Something is about to happen. I watch a thin finger of smoke rise out of the dying embers. It lifts through the trees toward the impossibly high ceiling.

A young woman ties my ankles to my neighbor's. She continues around the circle, binding all of us together, as Chelone leads the group in deep rhythmic breathing. I hear a long sigh as everyone exhales. The sound lasts fifteen seconds before each new breath is taken. On the thirteenth sounding, my head clears. It's the same feeling I get when my ears pop.

The unkempt lawn of the ancient indoor park feels like a soft mattress. The last thought I remember is feeling safe and warm.

In the morning, I awake to a drum of human noise that echoes off the glass walls. I raise my head. The hard earth should have left me sore and stiff, but I feel rested and as comfortable as if I'd slept on an air mattress. I get up to one elbow and look across the cold and lifeless pit at Martin, who gives me a sleepy grin.

"How are you doing?" he asks.

"Slept wonderfully. How about you?"

He habitually looks at his watch, then says, "Are we still in the same time?"

I point to my left. "I recognize that couple, and they look the same age."

He gets to his feet and stretches. "I'll be happy if we're still in the same decade."

Chelone unties himself and walks over to Martin and I. "Get yourselves some breakfast. Eat hearty, because you'll need the nourishment. We have a long day ahead of us. I'll be back when you're done." Without waiting for a reply, he saunters away toward the building entrance.

We eat oatmeal pancakes with wild honey and fresh butter. I finish off four large cakes before I push my plate away.

When Chelone returns, he puts his right hand on my shoulder. "Let's go to the second-level roof. We'll start off this morning with slow movements to open the blood vessels and get your heart energized."

He leads the way to the stairwell, then disappears up the same stairs we came down yesterday. Although I hear the click of his sandals on the steel, the sound continues to fade as Martin and I are forced to take breaks every fifth or sixth floor.

"Where in the hell did he go?" Martin says on our fourth stop while gasping for breath.

"I don't know, but he isn't like any old man I know."

"How many floors do we have left to climb?"

"He said forty."

"Holy shit, we're not even a quarter of the way, and I'm exhausted."

When we reach the fortieth floor, Chelone greets us with a casual grin. Both Martin and I are swimming in perspiration as we step onto the rusted steel platform.

"Let's go out where the air is fresh," Chelone turns, pushes through the two creaking doors and into a glass enclosed room that looks out onto a brightly flowered platform easily the size of a football field.

I take a deep breath and inhale the fragrance. "Wow, it's beautiful."

Chelone's face blushes. "My Creation. Mine and my grandson, that is.

We walk out into the warmth of the day and smell the aroma of hundreds of flowers and blossoming trees.

The flagstone path wanders through the garden as the old man leads us into an open square.

"Follow my movements," he says, "and we'll loosen our bodies."

I'm still out of breath. "Trust me, after forty flights of stairs, I'm very loose."

He ignores my statement and starts into a very slow moving dance that looks like a variation of tai chi.

Patiently, he explains simple moves and gives us time to practice. His delivery is slow and deliberate, but it takes concentration. Like a ballet dancer, he flows effortlessly from one position to another.

Within the hour, I've got three moves memorized, but I feel awkward and my legs ache.

"Now we're ready to begin the day's lessons," he says.

"We'll get together every morning for movement. After a week, I'll separate you, but for now, the information you'll need to learn can be provided to both of you. Use these movements. When you can, try to speed up and accentuate them. Do it to your maximum, but stay inside your safety margin. We don't want any twisted ankles or broken legs."

Beads of perspiration run down my neck. My shirt is soaked. We're supposed to accentuate our movement, but I feel resentful for having to move at all.

He flashes a wily coyote grin. "Resentment is good, Leigha. It'll help you do our next exercise with more gusto."

"How do you know what I'm thinking?"

He ignores my question, steps over to the brush and produces a small drum, then expertly beats out a rhythm that resonates with my body. Soon, I find myself moving quickly, able to keep up with the tempo. A minute into undulations, he speaks with the beat of the drum. "Feel. . . the level. . . of rage. . . inside your soul." He repeats his eight words, and they strike deep. My resentment builds toward him for forcing us into this ridiculous dance.

"Feel. . . the level. . . of rage. . . inside your soul," he repeats in time with his drum.

"Feel. . . the level. . . of rage. . . inside your soul."

"Feel. . . the level. . . of rage. . . inside your soul."

We dance harder and with more purpose, until I'm a bundle of rage.

The rhythm of his drum and the monotone chant gather inside me. I focus everything toward him. I want to scream at him, yell as loud as I can.

He changes his chant, though I'm not sure he's been chanting. "Feel. . . the level. . . of rage. . . and scream your anger. Feel. . . the level. . . of rage. . . and scream your anger."

I hear it for the ninth or tenth time; I'm not sure. I'm aware of a deep-seated scream gurgling from my belly, finding its way to the surface. I want to stop dancing. I want to halt the drum. I want to hold the fire inside, but I'm powerless. My dance becomes more frantic. I'm no longer staying within normal dance patterns. I make strange movements, which brings my rage closer to the surface. My arms flail high in the air. The twisted fury finds its way to my throat. I try my best to contain it, but the flame will not be restrained. My mind is not in control any longer, and I'm unable to stop the inevitable.

A growl sneaks past my larynx. Like the prelude to a volcano, a snarl bubbles up, followed with a shriek, higher pitched and more piercing than I've ever heard my voice reach. My scream surprises and scares me. I try to cut it off, but the storm overpowers me and pushes the scream out, a high-pitched keen, like the wild howl of a coyote. When I run out of air and suck in a deep lung full, I'm compelled to continue my insane wail.

During the few seconds it takes to refill my lungs I hear Martin's voice undulate next to me. I look and see his face twisted and contorted. His lips are drawn into a snarl.

Finally the drum stops, and both of us collapse onto the stone gasping for air. I'm completely exhausted. We grab onto one another for physical support, then burst out laughing.

We hold one another and sob, then I cackle, next cry again and giggle, until I have no more. When I'm calm, the last snicker bubbles out and a final tear rolls down my face, before the old man speaks.

"This is a little sample of what you have inside."

"What do you mean?"

"You've experienced a taste of your buried emotion."

"I've never felt so light," Martin says.

"Feel how freeing it is to unload a fraction of what you have stored?"

"How did this happen?" I ask.

"The dance, or maybe the drum, who knows? Even breath and screams help free the energy."

"I've danced and drummed before," Martin says, "but I've never been so light."

"Feel the lightness in your bodies and use this as a reference to what we humans can obtain, a life without cumbersome baggage."

Chelone looks angelic, like a holy being.

He smiles and tosses one hand into the air. "I'm not a holy man. I'm only human, like you."

I grimace. How does he know my thoughts?

"As soon as I leave," he says, "you'll be alone. For the rest of the day, walk in our garden. Enjoy the trees and flowers. Walk together without saying a word. Don't try to communicate with language of any kind, but feel each other's presence and whatever you do, don't go to sleep.

"Tonight, when we're all together, tell everyone about your experience." He reaches out, grasps one of each of our hands and gives us another angelic smile. "If you could see yourselves right now, you would think you were the angels, not me." He squeezes our hands, stands, turns, and disappears behind the bushes.

I turn toward Martin. "He's right, you know. You look radiant. Your face is smoothed out. All the deep lines of age from an hour ago are gone."

"And you're the same," Martin says. "Your girlish glow has returned. I haven't seen it in years."

I scoot close and face him, then say words of love. He reaches out and gently touches my lips. "We shouldn't talk." I lean to kiss him. When our lips meet, passion springs upon us. In seconds, we're groping one another. I search out Martin's skin under his shirt. Quickly, our sweetly placed kisses become passionate ones. Clothes fly, and we make love in wild abandon.

Leigha, Chelone, and I spend the morning dancing on the lower roof gardens. He shows us movements that evolve into screams I've never experienced.

When Chelone leaves, I comment on Leigha's beauty. After a few exchanges and some wild sex, we spend the rest of the day without speaking. In my altered awareness, I can read her thoughts.

When we take a walk in the roof garden, I notice my perception has changed. My entire view of the universe has shifted. The flowers are more beautiful. Bushes and birds have a glow around them I've never noticed. The entire day has a crystalline quality, a brightness unlike any I've ever experienced. We walk slowly through the plants and trees. Of the thousands of different flowers, I find myself engrossed in each petal. The sky is bluer, sun brighter, earth richer, plants greener, colors much more vivid than I've ever noticed.

The sun leans into the western sky when a girl appears with two small trays of food. Until I see the food, I haven't felt a hint of hunger. Leigha and I devour the meal. Like everything else today, the food has a holy quality about it. I feel its healing powers in my stomach.

Later in the day, without saying a word or signaling to one another in any way, we both walk down the long flights of stairs to the ground floor and into the huge open area as dinner is being set on the table. Everyone smiles, but I don't need to return their gesture; a permanent grin has plastered itself on my face.

When we finish the meal and clear the dishes, Chelone stands and clinks a teaspoon on the metal table. The hall becomes silent as he speaks. "Today our two new friends have experienced a shift in their perception." He points at us, and I feel a twinge of embarrassment.

"They've started on the long road to recovery, and I honor them for taking the first step on their journey." He turns to us. "As a way to integrate into our community, I encourage the two of you to share your experience."

My old fear crops up. For a moment I freeze, but from deep inside an inner strength arises. In spite of my fear, I get to my feet and tell a tearful story about the day. I end with a thanks to Chelone and the people around the circle for their hospitality and generous help.

When I finish, I sit and the circle falls silent.

Leigha stands and tells her story, but I'm too involved in my newly acquired ability to speak in front of the group to hear much of what she says.

When she's finished, the same silence fills the huge hall. Minutes go by before Chelone stands and gives a long dissertation, but I hear nothing. My mind is filled with a euphoric feeling of success.

When Chelone is complete, everyone around the pit falls silent again. There are no stories, only the blaze to light the face of each person.

Later, the same sixteen people lie around the fire and a small girl lashes our ankles together. I fall into a deep sleep with no dreams.

When I awake, Leigha and I are alone. I sit up and look across the cold fire pit at her. "I don't feel as buoyant."

"Me, either."

I stretch. "Yesterday I felt like an angel. It was almost more than I could handle."

She stands and stretches. "But, today it's gone."

I'm on my feet. "I thought it would last longer."

"I hoped it would last forever."

After we eat and climb those god-awful stairs again, we meet Chelone in the middle of the roof garden.

I speak first. "The lightness is gone."

He flashes a smile. "What you experienced yesterday is something I helped you attain. I did it to give you a working knowledge of what life can be like, truly free of anxiety. The less dread, the more room in your lives for heightened awareness."

My voice is sad. "Yesterday I felt no fear."

"You have a long journey ahead of you. Someday you

may be able to attain the state on your own. For now, I'll have to help you reach that level of awareness."

"How long will it take to get there ourselves?" asks Leigha.

"Who knows? Some take years, and many never get there at all. The two of you have a start, though. Because of your predicament with Maranther, you have incentive. I'll spend extra time giving you a condensed version of our training. Extra work will be necessary to get you free of Maranther's influence. It will not be easy, so before we begin, I'll want your full commitment."

I look at Leigha for confirmation, then back at him. "After yesterday, you have my complete attention."

Her head bobs. "I'm committed. Anything to get free of that meddling old woman. If we learn to find elation, all the better."

"Okay then, let's begin. I hope we can get a good start within the next month or two.

I give him a suspicious look. "Month or two? I thought you said one month."

"Some people work faster than others."

Leigha looks away from me and at Chelone. "But who will take care of our kids? We're already late. They'll have rescue teams out for us."

The old man smiles. "Stay with us as long as you need to. When you're finished, I'll place you on the day you planned to be home. You can stay years, and you'll never be missed."

Leigha takes a step aside to give me room to move. She takes a pose. "Time travel is still difficult to fathom, but if that's the case, and we won't be missed, then I'm ready for whatever you have in mind."

"Heightened awareness is a delight," Chelone says, "but it can only be attained when a person has gathered enough energy. Storing energy is the work of everyone in our complex. For some, it takes longer than others, but the two of you have a natural ability. You should be able to pick it up fast."

"I'd hoped to go back into the altered perception," I say.

He ignores my statement. "Martin, you'll need to nap for two hours every day to recharge your lost energy."

He looks at Leigha. "You're in much better shape. You may not need to nap as long, but take one every day."

"What time of day?" I ask.

"Our usual siesta time happens after lunch."

Leigha rotates her pose and stretches to the right side. "How do we keep from going to another time zone?"

"You'll have to be lashed to a circle of our people, but we've already arranged that.

"For task two, practice the movements I taught you yesterday, until you can do them in your sleep. Any specific motion isn't important, but perfecting physical rhythm builds your energy. Find something to build balance. Nothing is written in stone. If you discover alternate moves that reach the same goal, explore those as well. I'll be with you every morning for an hour. When we're together, you can ask questions."

He steps over to a flowering plant, plucks a blossom, and takes a deep breath. "The third assignment," he says on his exhale, "and the most important one, is to clear yourself of negative experiences; in a sense, rewrite your personal history. You want to leave room to replace past encounters with present, positive ones."

I look at him with a question, but I'm learning I don't have to voice it. He knows what I'm about to say.

He hands the flower to me, and speaks as I draw in the scent. "A better way to explain it, is to open room in your psyche. Get rid of clutter and make space for new information."

I look from the flower to Chelone. "How exactly do we accomplish that?"

"It's a small exercise, and it won't seem like anything is happening. The process takes years, but you can get a good start on it in the short time we will be together."

I don't trust things that are supposed to be easy, but I keep listening.

He takes in a deep breath while turning his head as far to the right as possible. When he exhales, he rotates his head slowly to the far left position, expelling all his air as he turns. He speaks when he returns to the forward position. "The job here is to bring up an old mishap or trauma that happened to you during the inhale, then expel it into the universe as you exhale."

I rotate my head, but don't draw in air. "That's all? That looks too easy."

Chelone flashes me a patient grin. "Yes, but consider how many traumas we've suffered over the decades. It may take you the rest of your life to systematically expel each one."

"Oh, I see."

"Things like this take time, but if you work hard, in the next two or three months, you can get started."

"Now we're up to three months."

"Some students take longer than others. You two will do great, though. Today, let's start with a tiny exercise. Like yesterday, stay as close to the original movements and be as graceful as possible. Later, each of you can make adaptations."

We dance for an hour; every minute I feel lighter. At the end of one final set of movements, he stops.

"Sit with your back against something comfortable and look out onto the desert. How does it feel when you've tuned your body and mind? Close your eyes and feel how expansive you are."

I sit, and my body is reeling. I look over at Leigha and her face is aglow.

He speaks. "You're beginning students of an ancient Toltec tradition. It has been passed from one generation to another, much further in the past than when the first Spanish explorers arrived. I learned from my family, but not my blood family. If you prove worthy students, you'll get free of Maranther's trap."

"I'm not interested in being a student of a tradition," I say, "but if we have to do this to get free of that damn Maranther, then I'm ready."

"You'll have to practice with unbending intent."

He gives us a number of meditation instructions, then stands. "I'll see you at lunch. Oh, I almost forgot, don't talk to one another, and at this point, sex will drain your energy. After lunch, spend the rest of the day walking in the forest in silence." He turns, then disappears behind the shrubs.

We sit through the morning until a young man with

long, blond hair approaches us. "Will you come join us for lunch?"

We descend the forty floors and eat in silence while the noisy group jokes with one another. After lunch, with pencil and paper, Leigha and I go outside into the forest and spend the rest of the afternoon walking and taking a nap.

When the dinner gong sounds, without having said a word all day, Leigha and I stroll, hand in hand, into the building to eat.

After two days of concentrated effort, I feel magic in the air, something sparkly and bright. I consider myself a content person, but I feel lighter and happier than ever. We're lashed to the same people in the star configuration around the dying embers. Once I fall asleep, my dreams become so vivid, I can almost reach out and touch them. They are happy and playful for the first time since our Maranther saga began.

Nine

Into the Future

When I awake, the sun filters through the trees, and birds twitter in the branches above me. For a time I lie with eyes half closed, thinking of Leigha and the kids. Unlike other nights, my back is sore and stiff. One arm has fallen asleep. Something is wrong.

Once my sleepy eyes fully open and my mind comes awake, I sit up with a startled gasp.

"Oh, my god," I say aloud, and my voice dies on the thick foliage. I'm not able to immediately accept, or fully comprehend, what I'm seeing. I stand and stare at a thick, weedy bush growing in the middle of the pit. I scan the area for Leigha.

"Leigha," I say aloud in a quiet, not yet hysterical panic. I call louder, hoping my voice will carry. It doesn't. Each successive try gets louder. Each time, the sound dies. I hear no echo; there is no feeling of expansiveness.

I've yet to begin a search, but I already know not a living soul exists in the structure. No one has been in here for a long, long time.

The soft grass I fell asleep on is now a tangle of roots and spiky vines. Some climb the massive trunks into the high branches of the ancient trees. I thought the huge trees were old when I went to sleep, but now the trunks, five times as thick, arise as columns of bark, volcanoes of wood, spewing out of small mountains of earth. Yesterday the ceiling was canopied, but today monstrous trunks rise into a thick mat of greenery and leave no room. Small amounts of sun filter in, bouncing off walls and through lower windows.

"Leigha," I yell louder. My voice carries to the nearest tree trunk and dies.

I cup my hands next to my mouth and scream, "Lee-ahh." I'm probably hundreds of years into the future. In despair, I drop to my knees and moan. What happened? Have I lost her again? Maybe this time it will be forever. Chelone assured us we would stay together. Has that damn Maranther interfered again?

After a long time down on my knees lamenting my predicament, my survival instinct reluctantly kicks in.

I'll need food and water.

I spend a half hour climbing over thick vines, around entangled branches, moving slowly toward the outer wall. Once outside, I look up into a cloudless sky along the impossibly tall wall of glass. Out of the thousands of huge panes, ten or twenty are intact. Thick tree branches and heavy vines wind their way in and out of the missing windows. They twist their way out around the massive building, obscuring all but one of the sharp, crisp lines of the structure. It looks like a tower of shrubbery.

The earth surrounding the building has reverted to desert. Ancient saguaro cacti grow within feet of the broken remains of the monolith. All traces of the huge forest I walked in yesterday have vanished. Not a stick from those immense trees remains. How can all of this happen in one single leap? How did I jump so far into the future? The enormous elms have grown old, died, completely decomposed, and disappeared. Have I leapt far beyond even my own imagination?

After that month of being all alone in the desert, in automatic response, I reach into my pocket and pull out my trusty fish line. If I'm forced to be alone in the desert, I'm sure as hell not going to starve.

Within minutes, I set a snare.

My next job is water.

Inside the building, plant life flourishes, so I turn my attention to finding the source.

Chelone told me the building automatically watered itself. There must be a series of drip lines under the roots and bushes.

I snake my way into the center of the foliage-choked hall and search along the ground. I look for wetness in the soil, signs of a broken or leaking line. The upheaved earth is riddled with a dense mat of gnarled and twisted roots, but no trace of a watering system exists.

I'm not thirsty, but the day feels warm. The desert air smells dry; I know from experience, I'll be thirsty soon. In this hot climate, simple thirst will turn to dehydration too quickly. I won't suffer that mistake again.

Whoever designed the watering system designed it too well. After an hour, I find nothing.

In the middle of my search, it dawns on me that water might be easier found on the balconies, where pipes run through the long, concrete planting boxes. I snake my way to the stairwell and pull at the rotted steel door. Only the stainless steel handle looks like it has weathered the passage of so much time.

I grab the lever handle and tug on the heavy door, but it doesn't budge, though I'm sure it isn't locked. I brace my right foot against the corroded steel jamb, lean back, pull, and hear a long squeal of a reluctant hinge. The door slides slowly away from the jamb, and opens no more than ten inches before it becomes hopelessly stuck. I squeeze through the opening and start up the crusted steel steps.

On the tenth floor, I push against another door, which barely allows me through. The balconies and walkways look so tangled with overgrown greenery, I can't see the original concrete structure. To move either way on the walk forces me to climb on hands and knees atop thick rolls of vines. Any attempt to find pipes in the chaotic mess is hopeless.

I brave the mountain of shrubbery for twenty yards, as far as the first apartment door, turn the peeled brass-plated knob, and push inward. The door moves with surprising ease, and I step into a musty, dust-riddled entry leading to the living room. I turn right and walk into a dark kitchen. Beyond the next wall lies a single bedroom. In the kitchen cupboards, I find a corroded can of something not recognizable. In one corner, a large glass jar holds pinto beans. I open the lid expecting them to be musty. The smell of beans wafts out into the stale air and fills my nostrils. If necessary, I'll save the pintos for tonight's dinner.

I close the lid, leave the jar on the warped plastic counter and step into the bedroom. On the bed, under a rotted and stained cover sheet, a mummified corpse lies entombed.

I skirt around the gruesome carcass and go into the bathroom to pee. When finished, without thinking, I push the handle, and the toilet flushes.

"There's water," I shout. "There's water in the toilets." It won't be the best water in the world, but with the old evaporation reclamation trick and tens of thousands of toilets as a source, I won't be dying of thirst anytime in the future.

I move through the bedroom, and rotate the faucet handle of the kitchen sink. After a number of short spurts of air and horribly rusty water, the tap runs cleaner. It's not clear water, but running.

"Water!" I sigh aloud. "At least I've got water."

"Of course you have water," a voice from behind me says. I spin, and Chelone stands in the hall.

"Shit, you scared me. Where'd you come from?"

"It hasn't been easy to find you," he says. "I've been searching through time for a week. I'd given up, when I heard you banging around."

"Your building is so old. We must be a hundred years into the future."

"More like five hundred," he says.

"How did you find me?"

"Let's just say I have my ways."

"How did I get here?"

"I don't know for sure. We think your straps came loose in your sleep. In the time-loop phenomenon, if you don't travel for a while, you save the energy like a rubber band. When you do, you spring wild and land far away from where you began."

"You know a lot about time travel," I say, "and you seem to have the ability to leap about at will. You sure you're not connected with Maranther?"

"At one time I apprenticed with Maranther, but that was many years ago."

"Can you get us back?"

He nods absently.

After an overly long day of exploring the defunct building and surrounding desert, when night falls we tie our ankles together and take our place in the exact location where the circle of sleepers lay five hundred years earlier.

During the night, my dreaming has a gap. Something happens, but I can't recollect any of the particulars. I awake at dawn and find myself in the group circle. I sit up and look across at Leigha, who's still lashed to her neighbors.

Chelone and I are awake. I lean over and whisper, "How did you do that?"

"I've had practice with traveling, but in my old age, my accuracy isn't always perfect. Our people," he waves his arm indicating the others in the circle, "helped us pinpoint the date. They got us back. With practice, you could be accurate, too."

"Really, how?"

"Keep up the work, and you'll manifest your intent."

Chelone unlashes himself and we walk outside until everyone wakes up.

My reunion with Leigha is frantic. She acts like I've been gone for a year.

After breakfast, once again, we climb to the lower roof and practice our movements. As we finish, Chelone appears out of nowhere and sits with us. "I want to show you The Fire Breath."

He opens his nostrils and takes quick, short blasts of air. After twenty or thirty breaths, each growing in intensity, he lets loose with a deep guttural growl that quickly builds to a lion roar, much more voluminous than I ever guessed could come out of the frail old man. He jiggles and shakes until his body movements become so pronounced he's bouncing off of the ground, sometimes a foot into the air. His arms flail, face grimaces, tongue wags and is extended as far as possible. He's a wild man in the trance of a voodoo dance.

Leigha moves behind me, but I'm also looking for a place to hide.

With a flair, Chelone lands both feet on the ground. Breathing heavily, he gives me a wild-eyed grin.

"I held back," he huffs. "Because I," he huffs again, "could see you were. . . concerned."

I look at him. "Held back?"

"Like I said. . . this is an extreme example. . ." He takes another breath. "Of what I call the release of built-up emotions." He draws in a deep inhalation. "For short, we call it Emotional Release. . . or even shorter, E.R."

Leigha's face scrunches. "Why would people want to bounce and scream their lungs out?"

"We all walk around. . ." He takes another breath. "With years of frustration and anger. It results from hundreds of little things that happen to us every day. Some events are so small we hardly notice, but they still happen. They get filed in the storage cabinet of our bodies. E.R. gives us a direct method of moving the stored energy out of the body. It frees the psyche. This particular form of blocked energy contributes to chronic illness such as ulcers, heart disease, cancer, and others, to say nothing of the emotional harm it causes."

I say, "You're telling me stored energy carries with it all of the diseases of humanity?"

"More like stored energy keeps our bodies so busy, we don't have the time or strength left to fight everyday diseases like colds and flu, much less the more devastating ailments.

"The reason the medical community, with all of its technical skills and machinery, couldn't find a cure for cancer was the malignancy that grew in humans was not a disease in itself, but each person's inability to deal with stress and buildup of negative energy. Cancer lives inside every one of us every minute of every day.

"Normally, our bodies will be able to fight the mutant cells before they reproduce and take over. Without extra energy, we don't have enough of what it takes to fight off the cells. They quickly multiply. With the help of local herbs, even common colds can be dealt with by the E.R. application."

"If we're your first visitors in a long time, couldn't it

be your community is so isolated that you don't come in contact with disease?"

"We thought about that, but it can't explain diseases like cancer and arthritis. There hasn't been a single case of either since the fall of Yuma."

"You're attributing all of this to screaming? Your E.R. work?"

"Directly connected."

"Well then, show us again how it should be done."

Chelone steps back and begins the blaze breath again. After twenty inhales and exhales, he transforms into a foaming-at-the-mouth crazy man. It lasts a minute, but feels like eternity.

By our third attempt, I feel dizzy and light-headed.

From his seated position on the rim of a planting bed, he speaks. "You feel lighter because your body responds to the extra oxygen. Right now, hyperventilation causes your euphoria, but the feeling is valid and one we call heightened awareness. Like the other day, look around and view your surroundings in a different way.

He stands and walks toward the building. When he reaches the door, he turns. "Practice three times every morning. When you feel yourself settle into the regular everyday view, get up and do more. Don't do E.R. every minute of the day, but for now, you need to get extra energy to confront Maranther. In a month or so, you might want to cut back to once or twice a day. I'll send someone with your lunch. After a nap, continue until dinner."

The first few tries exhaust me, but later something shifts, leaving both of us feeling invigorated. By the time the young man brings lunch, we're bouncing like children. The afternoon flies by before we know what's happened. Neither of these exercises excites me, but I love the increased energy. Once we get into the rhythm, time rolls by.

Ten

Mosquito

We dance and release until the hot sun is low in the west, then during a short one hour meditation, I hear a buzz and feel a stab at my neck. I swat and bring my hand back, then stare in wonder at a squashed mosquito the size of a hummingbird. My hand shines bright red with the blood the creature has drawn. I reach over to show Leigha, but she's deep in meditation. I decide not to bother her. I stand to wash the dead pest and what seems like a pint of blood off in the small brook meandering through the roof garden. While I swab, I feel another sting on my shoulder blade, but I can't reach it. I lie on my back and rub the spot on the ground. When I stand, another wide patch of blood spreads around the dead insect. I touch my neck and feel a swell the size of a Ping-Pong ball.

I look toward Leigha and see her swat the air. I pull her to her feet and scream over a growing buzz high above our heads. "Let's get the hell out of here!"

We sprint for the door as the hum turns into a swarm. We reach the door, run through, and I slam it behind us just as the horde closes in on us. A splatter of the gigantic mosquitoes hits the glass. It sounds like hailstones.

Within seconds, the window is covered with smashed insects. I feel another stab on my foot and look at a bright red insect filling itself from a vein. I lift my other foot and kick the blood-engorged body over with my toe. "At least they fly slowly and are easy to kill."

Leigha stares at the spattered glass. "Would you look at them. Where did they all come from? They're so big and quiet. Where do you suppose. . ." Her face turns three shades whiter. "Martin, your neck. We've got to get you out of here."

My neck continues to swell as we run the long flights of stairs to the ground floor for help. When we reach the bottom, the swelling closes my airway. I sit on the final step and try unsuccessfully to gasp for a breath. Leigha runs screaming the last hundred yards across the courtyard. "Martin can't breathe."

Chelone and two men sprint toward me as I try to draw a breath.

Chelone digs into his pouch and pulls out an overly large syringe. "The giants have returned."

Unable to draw a breath for a full minute, I see black spots.

Chelone holds the syringe in the air and studies it as he pulls a septic swab from a plastic bag, then wipes the needle. "Grab his hands and sit on his arms."

I hear what they say, but the meaning of it slips past

me. Two men pull me to the floor and put their weight on my stretched arms. They don't need to, because I'm weak as a kitten. I feel the pain of the syringe stab my neck. In a moment, I suck air past my constricted throat, gulp in a deep breath of fresh air, and choke from the surprise. I exhale and take a second breath, then a third.

Chelone searches my arms and chest. "Was he bitten anywhere else?"

Leigha points at my two other blood-stained lumps. He jabs the syringe into my foot and draws out more poison, then rolls me over and repeats the procedure on my shoulder blade.

Leigha's bites are tended to, as I take long, grateful breaths of air.

Chelone stands and looks toward the big front doors. "We need to get those doors closed. Today our hands will be full from attacks in the fields." In a frenzy, they leave to help other victims. We're left to struggle to the tables on our own.

I'm so weak, I'm almost not able to sit. One of the old women hands Leigha a salve, and we dab it on our bites.

Eight people outside of the monolith get brought in. Once Chelone and his people have assisted the eight, they set the tables for dinner. We wait for the workers to come in out of the fields. I croak, "I've never seen such big mosquitoes. Where did they come from?"

An older man answers; I think his name is Sanders. "When I was a young man, the mosquitoes came one spring day. We had no idea where they came from, or why they had grown so big. Over the years, we've lost a few of our people to the pestilence. If the full force of the swarm had attacked you, there would be nothing we could do. They would have sucked so much blood and replaced it with their poison, you would never have survived."

Leigha scratches a mosquito bite. "Where do they come from?"

"We're not sure. We thought it might be a mutation from the nuclear power plant twenty miles from here."

"Do you always carry the syringes?"

"Someone always carries at least one, and we all have plastic sheets to get under when the mosquitoes arrive. More than three stings, without drawing out the poison, and things get sketchy. Luckily, the monsters come only three times a year. As suddenly as they arrive, in a few hours, they're gone, and we don't have to worry about them for another four months."

"So, what do we do, lie around and wait for them to leave?"

The lanky man grimaces. "That's about all there is to do."

The evening after the mosquito attack, Martin and I sit in the circle and listen to mosquito stories. Some I barely believe. Others aren't meant to be believed. Each person who wants to tell a story stands, and everyone listens. Some have a gift and tell stories that come alive.

Most become hesitant and stilted. Chelone tells elaborate sonnets, winding psychic cords around imagination, spinning intrigue that does not let go until the story ends. Whenever he stands to tell a story, the circle goes silent.

Itching and scratching distracts everyone, as does the constant application of salve and much passing of the jars of ointment.

After an older woman tells the children a story, the same Martin who has always been terrified to stand in front of a group, though shaky, tells a tale of his youth. "I was probably eight or nine when my friend and I decided to hike to the top of Mt. Tamalpias. We'd spent the week at a summer camp at the base of the mountain. Jake and I left a note, then slipped off one morning.

"The day started off cold and foggy as we hiked up the trail, but later it warmed. We wound our way along the path and got glimpses of the mountain peak. All day San Francisco was at our backs. I remember the hike as clearly as if it were yesterday. The spires of the Golden Gate Bridge poked out of a blanket of fog. We saw it many times during the day.

"By early afternoon we reached the summit. With plenty of time to return before it got dark, we decided to stay for a while and rest, but both of us fell asleep and didn't wake until the sun was almost down. We wanted to make it back to camp before dark, so we sprinted along the trail in a race against time. Although both of us packed food and water, neither of us remembered a flashlight."

Giggles arise from the younger section of the circle.

A dark-haired girl in her early teens asks, "What is a flashlight?"

After Martin explains, he continues.

I've never seen him speak in front of a crowd of people, much less enjoy himself. I've also never witnessed his newfound strength. It must have something to do with our practice.

"About three quarters of the way down the hill, the sun dropped into the ocean and darkness surrounded us. We had to stop running and carefully walked along the path. When the coastal fog came in, which made seeing even more spooky, we blindly felt our way as we crept toward camp.

"We'd been warned about rattlesnakes, bobcats, and cougars. I was sure every bush hid a dangerous animal. It took two hours to get from the top of the mountain to where we had to stop running. The two-hour sprint was nothing, compared to the final hour of stumbling, one step at a time, the last mile to camp. When we saw the lights of the compound, it was way past curfew.

"With six boys in our little cabin, we knew us our little escapade would not get past Dan, our camp councilor, but we hoped he was asleep. He hadn't been around much, anyway. We assumed that he wasn't interested in us kids. Except for assemblies, where we had to be seen together, he ignored us and kept an eye on us from a distance.

"Sweaty and dirty, exhausted from running on the trail, we reached the cabin and quietly opened the door. We knew we were in trouble, but we hoped to slip into bed before anyone, especially Dan, awoke."

Martin nervously clears his throat. He blanches with an expression of terror. His slightly wrinkled forehead transforms into deep furrows. He turns, as if to look for a way out. His face scrunches, and his eyes go blank. His body tightens. His breath comes in shallow spurts, and his face is three shades whiter. When his eyes roll to the whites, he collapses.

Some of us spring to our feet. I'm close to my fallen husband when a blinding glare, like a gigantic flash from a camera, goes off in front of my eyes. Afraid to trample Martin, I stop.

The circle drops into silence when the old man barks, "Let the man do his work!"

"Sit," he commands. "Martin will be fine. When he awakes, I want the circle to be silent so I can continue with him."

No one gives him a dissenting vote. The six of us on our feet, though still stunned from the flash, carefully find our way back to our places.

After five minutes of introspective silence, Martin stirs. During the interminably long minutes, even the smallest child does not make a peep. Finally, Martin breaks the silence with a moan. When he moves, his color has returned. I grin with relief when I see his pale gray eyes again.

As he awakens, his face has a baby-like quality.

"What happened?" he murmurs into the silence.

When he sits up, the worry lines in his face re-form. He looks around warily until his gaze lands upon the old man. Their eyes lock.

Chelone breaks the silence. "You tell a good story."

"You think so? Unfortunately, there's no conclusion even the slightest bit interesting."

"Continue with your story."

Martin's body gets rigid. He sits at attention.

"I'll tell another story. The one I told has no point."

The old man speaks in a singsong voice. "Continue."

It's obvious, he wants to coax Martin, rather than command him.

"I don't know where the story came from. I don't remember doing anything like that. I can't tell this story, because—"

"Continue with your story," the old man interrupts, this time in a soothing, but firm voice.

"I don't remember the rest of the story. I. . . I. . ." Tears well up in Martin's eyes. He frantically wipes them. With a deep sob, he moans, "I can't remember."

"Continue with your story," Chelone says again in a soft voice, but with more command.

Martin puts his hands over his face and breaks into more sobs. I hear a barely audible, "I. . . ca. . . ca. . . can't."

The circle is quiet. Only Martin's crying cuts through the emptiness. He breaks the silence with two words, "I can't."

I jump when, like a sea captain, Chelone barks an order. "Continue!"

The sound of his voice booms off the distant glass walls. The feel of his authority echoes in the cavity of my brain. The intensity of his demand bounces around in my heart. I want to come to my husband's aid. I'm ready to yell at the old man to stop badgering Martin.

I begin to speak the first word of my demand, but the second my word forms, Chelone snaps his head around and glares at me. I've never seen so much intensity. The formed words rushing past my larynx are popped like a balloon. I can't speak.

I'm exasperated as Martin continues to sob. Chelone repeats himself, this time more gently. "Continue with your story."

"I . . . can't," Martin moans.

Other than the sobbing, a second minute of silence goes by. I wonder why Martin doesn't flee, but if the old man can stop me from making a noise, then he can also compel my husband to stay in the middle of the circle.

Five slow minutes pass before the sobbing ends.

"Continue with your story," Chelone says.

His monotonous sentence is getting on my nerves, but there is nothing I can do.

Melodically, he repeats the sentence again. "Continue with your story."

Martin looks at him with a tear-stained face and red eyes. With a shudder of grief, or resolve, he says, "We sneaked. . ." He once again breaks into a heartrending sob. Another minute goes by before he continues. "We slipped into the cabin, but Dan grabbed our arms and pulled us outside. Once away from the cabins, he yanked us behind a huge tree. He whispered the punishment in an eerie voice, frightening me more by his diabolical tone than any threat of discipline."

Martin halts, looks at Chelone and moans, "I . . . I can't say any more, I just can't."

"You can and you will," orders the old man.

"But, I can't. It's too. . ."

With a menacing glare, the old man gets up and walks over to Martin. He looks angry enough to hit him.

In a lightning-quick movement, I think he intends to grab Martin by the shirt collar to shake the story out of him, Chelone surprises me when he snakes in behind where my husband is sitting and snatches his backpack. Before Martin has a chance to respond, in another quick move, the old man leaps back and sits in his original position. "You will continue the story or I will destroy the possessions in your pack."

"Hey, you can't do that," Martin protests.

"Hey," the old man mocks, as he digs into the pack, "I can. Continue the story, and I'll stop."

The first thing out of the bag is Martin's six-inch buck knife. He slips the knife from its sheath and holds it in the air. Martin screams, "Hey, that's my knife. What are you doing?" He makes a futile attempt to get up, but, like me, he's stuck.

With both hands, Chelone bends the polished steel blade in half, like a piece of taffy.

He throws the knife into the center of the room. I look around, see gleeful faces and think how sick these people are to get pleasure out of this.

The next object out of Martin's pack is his shaving kit. The old man opens the little zipper and flings its contents into the middle of the circle. Each article slowly floats through the air; two plastic razors, a small bottle of mouth rinse, scissors, a tube of shaving cream, nail cutters, a plastic lighter, a tube of deodorant, and three Band-Aids. They reach the summit of their flight, pop like firecrackers, and disappear. The circle remains silent, the hall pregnant with expectation. Everyone, including me, waits for the next surprise. Martin, however, is not amused. "Hey, damn it, that's my stuff."

The next item is a leather pouch. Chelone opens it and comically peeks inside, then at Martin. With an impish smirk, he looks back inside the pouch, then at Martin again. When he looks at me, his grin turns to a devilish smile. "What do we have here?" he says.

I know what's inside the pouch. I want to protest, but I can't speak. I search for help from the rest of the people, but only see curious faces looking from me, to Chelone, and across to Martin.

He yanks the zipper and withdraws a wad of cash.

"Hey, that's mine. Put that away, or I'll—"

"You'll do what?" the old man mocks again. "You'll come over here and punch me out? You'll clean my clock? You'll put my lights out? I think not. You'll continue your story, before I give all your money away."

"I can't," Martin mewls.

The old man fingers through the wad of cash.

A glare spreads across Martin's red face. His anger is palpable. In a growl, he says, "I'll kick your ass, you son of a bitch."

I've never heard him use such language.

The old man taunts him, pulls a handful of bills away from the wad, and carelessly tosses them. The bills lift into the air like floppy butterflies and spread out. As if in a choreographed dance, each separate bill flaps over and lands in a person's lap. Chelone reaches in and tosses another handful into the air. "Will you continue the story before I have to give all your fine money away?"

"Damn you," Martin growls. "When I get free. . ."

Another handful goes into the air and repeats the same floating dance, landing in more laps.

Chelone's voice booms. "I'll give money away until you tell the story."

Martin snarls and makes another effort to break the invisible bond.

Chelone gleefully tosses one more handful into the air, and the invisible bonds snap. Martin breaks free. He stumbles across the room toward the old man, so enraged he continues his forward movement until he trips. His fist is doubled, as he regains balance and momentum. I'm afraid he's going to kill the old guy.

Chelone's expression shifts to a look of dumb surprise. He ducks and holds his arms out to protect himself.

With the intensity of a freight train, Martin's right fist slams toward the face of his tormentor.

I look around for help, but I'm the only one concerned. I see only gleeful faces. I watch in terror as Martin's fist plunges into Chelone's nose. I imagine the result. There will be blood, and I hate blood. With no way to stop the inevitable, I find myself compelled to watch. Not only can I not move, but I'm forced to keep my eyes open.

Chelone's skinny arms will not protect him.

Martin's fist comes within inches of the old man's face. There's murder in Martin's eyes. He may actually kill Chelone. I want to stop it, but I'm unable to move.

I'm able to scream the second before Martin makes contact. I expect to see a smashed nose, blood spewing over the old man's clothes. Martin's fist makes contact, but something unexpected happens. I can't believe it. I didn't blink. In one second, I imagine a broken nose. I witness murder. We're going to get kicked out of here, the one place that might help us get free of Maranther. We'll be destined to wander the desert, forever cycling through history.

In the next second, Martin disappears.

I blink, sure I'm hallucinating. Was it a sleight of hand? My gaze shifts to the old man. I'm ready to demand an explanation.

"Where is my. . ."

Chelone has also vanished.

The crowd talks in hushed tones. I turn to Martha. In a shaky, unsure voice, I ask, "What happened?"

"Since your husband was unable to bring the story to the circle, Chelone took your husband to the story."

"What story?"

"Into the trauma that affects his life. Our magician took him back to the moment the ordeal happened. You watch; they will carefully study the drama, and your man will return transformed."

"What is he going back to? I don't know about any trauma."

"Chelone is powerful. He will take your Martin back and help heal the old wound that keeps the two of you stuck in Maranther's trap."

"Like your accident in the desert. Even now, though you're an adult, and logically it was truly an accident, you continue to see the event as your fault."

"It was my fault. But wait. . . how do you know about what happened to me as a child?"

Martha smiles. "We know more than meets the eye. The work we do helps us see beyond our own lives. Relive your desert event with Chelone, and he will guide you through the experience, then help you understand."

"Understand what?"

"It was an accident and not your fault."

"Yes, an accident. Everyone tried to convince me."

Martha puts her hand on my forearm. "You believe it happened because of you."

"It had to be me. I talked Sara into sneaking off. I couldn't find our way back. I was the one. . ."

She slides her hand to my shoulder. "Yes, but it was still just an accident. Reliving the experience will prove it to your adult mind. All of your proof comes from your childhood perspective. The burden you've carried from that one weekend has been heavy. Chelone's magic can relieve your burden."

"How?"

"The first time I went with Chelone, my life forever shifted. Instead of growing denser, I've opened space in my life. It's not an easy process or quick, but well worth the time."

While I think about the events, she says, "Guess my age."

I suppose a well-preserved fifty-three, but say forty-nine.

"Last month I celebrated my seventieth birthday."

"This can't be. Your skin looks so soft and supple. Your eyes look bright and sharp. You're so shapely and trim."

She points at a woman I guess no older than sixty.

"Last month, Louise had her ninety-first birthday."

"Where do I sign up for your beauty treatments?"

"You already have, but I don't think you two have any choice in the matter. Continue the process. Go into your past with our Chelone. He will help you relieve yourself of those unwanted stresses. You'll relive those days that haunt you and gain strength."

"You mean if Chelone helps me, I'll look younger?"

"Not exactly. More like if you remove the stress, you can slow the aging process."

"Doesn't that put a lot of faith in your leader?"

"Chelone is your next step. Maranther will eventually be your teacher. Maranther was also your student."

"What do you mean? I have never had any students, especially that old woman."

She raises nervous eyebrows. "Much like our traumas, Maranther is a curse and a blessing at the same time."

"Maranther will forever be my curse. I wish I never heard that name."

"Don't be so quick to jump to conclusions."

I'm racing across the inner circle to attack Chelone. I want to kill that old man. When I reach him, my arm swings down on his nose. In a split second, I'm standing next to Chelone in front of the cabin at Camp Rotunda. While the situation plays out in front of us, I'm compelled to watch.

Dan grabs both boy's arms and pulls them outside to the dark compound. Once away from the cabin, Dan yanks the two behind a tree.

I turn to the old man. "I don't want to watch this."

Chelone gives me a wry smile. "Why?"

"I've already experienced it. Is it necessary again?"

"Didn't you forget this happened?"

"I don't want to see it a second time, if that means anything."

The old man gives me a pat on the shoulder. "Let's see how this is going to unfold. It might be interesting."

"Trust me, it's not the least bit interesting."

Chelone points toward the scene under the tree.

Dan speaks in a dark, sinister voice I haven't heard since that night. Once again, I find myself unhinged by his tone. Little Marty Vandorfor knew he had some kind of discipline to endure, but Dan's tone was frightening.

Tears well up in my eyes. After all these years, will I be forced to relive every detail?

In his demonic tone, Dan says, "Everyone knows you disobeyed the rules. I've been appointed to hand out the punishment. We'll just see if you little pups can pay the price."

Standing next to Chelone, I watch a rope snag around my boy wrists and pull Marty into the tree. When his feet leave the ground, the hoisting stops, and Dan ties the rope around the trunk. Marty reaches out with his toes to get footing. I remember how painful it was.

With his back to Dan and Jake, Marty shifts weight, so he can spin and see what kind of awful punishment Dan has in mind.

"Don't turn around," Dan growls, "or you'll get it ten times worse than little Jakey here." He stops shifting. I hear whimpers and sinister, hushed commands.

A belt buckle clinks, and I remember being relieved when I knew Jake was going to get whacks with the belt. My dad whacked me, sometimes. Even with my pants down, though it stung like crazy, I survived.

"Hold still, you little sinner," Dan whispers. "Be very quiet, or you'll get it worse."

When Jake's whimpering rises three levels, my heart skips. Although he doesn't cry out, he's barely able to hold back. Little Marty wants to turn and look, but he's sure Dan will see him. I remember listening for the first whack of the belt, but it never came. All goes quiet, only the sound of the belt buckle and a clear ratchet of a zipper.

"Okay, Jakey," Dan whispers in a nervous titter. "Your punishment fits your crime. Now, tell no one, or you'll get another harder punishment. Do you understand?"

Jake murmurs in a broken sob, "Yes, sir."

"Now, get yourself directly to bed. I want you asleep before I return."

"Yes, sir," Jake whispers and runs toward the cabin.

Dan murmurs in a hysterical tone. "I've saved you for last. You're the right age for the plucking. With you, I'll take my time."

The scene changes to the next morning. Little Marty Vandorfor hasn't slept. When the bugle calls, I watch my four untouched cabin mates get up. They're excited about the canoe journey. Canoeing is the last thing on little Marty's mind. Dan comes in and gives Jake and

Marty a hard look, then leaves the cabin. Both of them clamber out of bed and dress without saying a word.

Next, we're outside the cabin. I watch as the action slows, then stops, not like someone calls a halt to activity, but everything slowly comes to a freeze, like a low battery on a tape player. Chelone and I stand in a yard with forty or fifty boys and five adults, and they're all frozen.

Chelone points toward the frozen scene. "Okay, now that you've experienced the trauma again, what would you change if you could change it?"

I look over and see he's serious, but I ask the question anyhow. "What do you mean?"

"If you could change events in this scenario, which would you change?"

I look out at the frozen people and see Dan bent to help Tommy Danfield with his shirt. I sprint over to him, fist drawn, and slam it into his angelic, smiling baby face. My fist splits and blood pours down my fingers. His face has not one little scratch. I feel like I've hit a brick wall.

The old man shakes his head. "It may have felt good, but now we'll have to deal with your hand. I wish you had thought about your action first."

I open and close my fist. "It didn't faze him."

"Oh, yes, it did. You just can't see the change, yet. We are the ones moving slowly inside our little bubble of time. Six teeth will be missing before he hits the ground. His broken jaw will be wired for the next few months."

"Then it was worth it."

"Do you have more changes?"

"Can we erase the entire event altogether?"

"I guess you can, but there's a small problem. Your

experience will have to change to accommodate it. With each change, there's a snowball effect that will shift your life. The revisions you make can only be ones that don't affect you directly."

"I see. Not to change the subject, but did Maranther teach you this stuff?"

He gives me a wry smile. "Maranther and I have spent some time together."

"Can we speed the time frames three or four notches? I want to see Dan's face splattered. I deserve to see it. I want to see him sprawled on the ground. No, what I really want is to cut off his dick and feed it to him, but I'll be satisfied to turn him in to the authorities so he can't do this to any other boys."

"Even if you did cut off his dick, he would still find a way to violate boys. I don't think he does it for sex. He does it for power. Turn him in to the authorities, and it might change things. It took a lot to convict Dan for his crime back then, especially without corroborating evidence."

"Well, if I have the chance to reinvent my story, I have to do something. Do you have any ideas?"

"This is a very unique situation," Chelone says. "It's one exclusively for you to decide. The answer must come from you."

"Can we put everything aside for now? I need to think about it. Can you jump me back here later to finish him off?"

"Yes, but it won't be as easy. You'll have to do a lot of conscious preparation to make a leap again. I can't trick you again, because you'll know. Surprise makes it easy."

"Then it'll be much easier to take action now, before we return?"

"Much easier."

"I don't want to make a stupid move and accidentally erase a part of my personal history I want to keep."

"It may be too late as it is. When you hit Dan, you could have already caused changes."

"I want to think about this," I say. "If I'm to make changes, then I'll want to figure out where it'll have the least effect on my life. I assume, because you know this exists, you also know how to help me make effective choices."

He cracks a wily grin. "Careful thought is the first step."

"Let's go back, but if the damage is already done, if some part of my history has already changed when I hit Dan, then I definitely want to see him take the fall from the punch."

He points. As if in time-lapse photography, people move ever so slowly, then faster and faster. Mesmerized by the reconstruction of moving life in the concrete-looking objects, I watch Dan's fingers clasp the top button on Tommy's shirt. At first in slow motion, but when time speeds up, his head snaps, and he loses contact with the ground. I feel a sense of satisfaction as splatters of blood and white ivory chunks fly free of his stupid grin. He lands hard on the packed earth. I watch the bone-jarring crunch twist his body.

A bloody nose spatters his baby face. I close my eyes. For a moment, I'm afraid the single sock on the jaw may have set a ripple of change into my future. It may have shifted something critical and compelled me not to turn the corner at Macy's and run headlong into Leigha, our first meeting.

I open my eyes and find myself in front of my wife. Everything seems the same, but time will tell. I'm in the middle of a hundred silent, expectant people.

"Continue with your story, Mr. Vandorfor."

I know the story, now. It's been locked inside me all of these years. It has twisted my guts, my guilt, my self-confidence, and I never knew it existed.

Although embarrassed, I continue. "We were sweaty and dirty from running and a hundred slips and falls. When we opened the door of the cabin, I hoped to slip into bed before anyone, especially Dan, awoke."

For the first time in my life, I tell the entire story, not only to myself, but also to the people who sit in the circle around me. I stop and start many times, but Chelone's supportive gaze keeps me going. Finally, I'm able to tell the parts not easy to speak.

Eleven

Martin's Return

Suddenly, my Martin and the old man Chelone disappear. A minute later, in reverse, they fold back into existence. I sit in awe and watch in wonderment as my husband of sixteen years, a man I think I know better than he knows himself, finishes a story of childhood rape I've never heard. My mouth hangs open. I'm surprised he's able to stand in the center of this circle at all, much less tell a hundred people such a dark secret. I look at his face. Tension has released. I see his eyes, free of the secret, after so many years. I watch his body move more freely, replacing his usual stiff manner. I always thought he'd protected his backside more than necessary. I've always wondered about his bent-kneed gait and the way he twists his spine when he stands. The further the story progresses, the more his slouchy posture disappears. He stands tall and self-assured as he reveals himself in the circle.

I hear a sureness in his voice I've never experienced, a power I've never seen. When he gets to the hardest part of his story, the most painful part, with tears in his eyes, a quaver to his voice, he speaks with an intensity I've never heard come from him.

The evening ends when Martin completes his story. Without a word, without a sound, everyone simply gets up and retires, leaving the remainder of us to lie in the circle and touch ankles. Calmness permeates the group. When we all settle in, I fall into a deep slumber.

During the night, I dream of Sara Britton. Although Sara has been on my mind ever since Martin and I drove into the desert, I have not allowed myself to think of her. I know why Martin made the deal to get me here, but until now, I refused to delve into that part of my past.

The dream opens me up. I find myself inside the small cave Sara and I stumbled upon. I'm not sure if I'm an adult now, experiencing then or a child then, living it now. Either way, I'm inside the cave. Little Sara's head lies on my lap. In her dehydrated state, she speaks long, unintelligible sentences. I stroke her hair and cry. I wish her parents would find us before it's too late. I'm thirsty and scared. My guilt for bringing her here turns into a monster and consumes my every thought. I look out of the mouth of the cave on a blazing hot desert floor with nothing to feel but despair. I listen to Sara's babbling and hold her. My best friend withers away. I'm in terror of being alone.

By late afternoon, Sara goes into convulsions. When the sun goes behind the hill, leaving us with relief from the unending heat, Sara draws her last exhausted breath.

She simply exhales, chuffs, then stops moving. I want to wail. Although I feel grief, I'm unable to shed another tear. Night comes, the heat subsides, and I'm relieved to lie in the relative coolness of the cave, next to my best friend, whom I've killed.

My nightmare shifts. I'm walking in that frightening first day of school after my recovery. The children look at me, teachers watch, even the janitor stares. No one asks about what happened in the desert, but during third-period break, Billy Sanchez, the jerk of all time, leans over to me and whispers, "You killed her, didn't you?"

I look around to sideways glances. Although no one speaks the words, I'm sure everyone says the same thing, "You killed her. You killed her." I run through the hall, out of school, and home to safety.

"I killed her," I say to Mom.

"It was an accident, honey; just an accident."

I break down and cry. "Everyone says I killed her."

For months, until I learn to ignore them, I cry often.

I won't trust myself to have another friend, for fear something might happen. Much later, thank God, my parents move to another town. I'm able to start over in a school where no one knows what happened. No one can point and say, "You killed her."

In my new school, I learn to trust myself and make one or two new friends. I've created a new life. My past disappears when no one speaks about the trauma. One day it happens; I've completely forgotten about it. Except for odd quirks I picked up, I have no recollection.

The strange dream shifts to thirty years later. Martin and I sit at opposite ends of the therapist's couch, working on differences. One day in her office everything gushes forth. I relive every horrid nuance of the ordeal.

Here I am again, two years later, after I conveniently tucked everything into my memory. It's back.

The therapist's office fades, and Chelone stands next to me. We look at one another.

His body is illuminated, like he's an angel. "Do you see it now?"

"See what?"

"It wasn't your fault. All of those years of guilt were just misplaced feelings. Billy was a jerk, and you thought they all felt the same.

"They did feel that way," I scream. "After the accident, nobody talked to me."

"You expected them to accuse you, so you pushed all of them away. I'm sure they felt awkward, but few actually thought you killed her."

Tears roll down my face when I realize I had pushed them away. Susan Hillary repeatedly approached me, but I couldn't see her attempts. In my grief, I isolated myself. My teachers tried to get through to me, but I only remember jerks like Billy, who taunted me, or worse yet, the ones who ignored me. I was so sure everyone talked about me when I wasn't around.

My tears flow for all the people I turned away. They tried to find me in my fog of self-pity and guilt. I cry for little Leigha who took responsibility for something that wasn't her fault. I cry for the thirty years I hid from myself in a effort to protect my wounded little girl.

"What do I do now?" My face is buried in my hands.

"You have the tools to begin your healing," he says.

"It'll take a long time, maybe years, but the more you relive the old story from your new perspective, the more room you'll have for something else."

"Something else?"

He smiles and winks. "Wondrous new things you can not even imagine. Even the knowledge of such things is not available until you heal the past.

"One thing, though, by the end of two weeks, you'll be strong enough to overpower Maranther's influence and go to your own time. Your life has already made a critical shift. Your old life will not have as much appeal. At the least, you'll travel a new path. Even your home in California, with this small change of perspective, will be less fulfilling."

I look up. "My life at home is very fulfilling."

"I assure you, now that you have started on your path of discovery, your old life will no longer satisfy. At some point you will want to return and continue the work you've begun. You'll always be welcome here."

"The experience we went through before we met you changed my life," I snuffle. "This dream has forever shifted my outlook, if I only can remember."

"Technically, we are in a dream, but a much different kind. You'll remember every word. When you awake, write down your thoughts and experiences. Oh, yes, and write how you're feeling."

With his last word, I pass out of the dark void of the dream. I open my eyes and witness the fiery crimson of dawn. I feel nurtured by the silence of the room and the familiar faces asleep in the circle. I roll over to get up. At my feet I see a faded legal notebook and sharp pencil.

When the sun slips over the horizon, the morning shifts from soft mauves and pinks to a saffron brilliance. Although my three bites itch, my body has rested more than any time in the last month. I'm happy. I watch the birds inside the glass walls of the building. They fly from limb to limb, warbling and chirping. I sit up and Leigha sits at the other end of the disbanded sleeping circle. She writes on a yellow notepad.

I stand and step over to her. "Good morning."

Her head snaps up. She quickly interprets who I am, then returns to frantic scribbling. Her left hand fingers the amulet. "I can't talk, now," she says. "I can't break my train of thought."

I saunter sleepily to the kitchen to grab a bite. With an apple and a handful of almonds, I sit at an empty table. I eat and go over last evening's experience. Something has been lifted from me.

Because Leigha's journaling looks like it will consume her entire morning, I hike upstairs and find an empty room to do some moves. Thirty minutes later, having screamed my voice till it hurts, I sit and breathe. After an hour, Chelone appears and sits beside me. I turn and acknowledge him.

He produces my backpack. "Everything is here."

I draw the blade out of its leather sheath. "How did you straighten the knife?"

"A better question would be, 'How did I bend it?'"

"Huh?"

"Hokus pokus. Magic. It was an illusion."

"How did you do it?"

His grin is more like a grimace. "Any ideas on how you want to change things with Dan?"

"If all I might do has a possibility of changing the world enough that my life may be different, I'll have to do something so subtle it affects Dan and no one else."

"If it could only be done," Chelone says.

"I want to come as close as possible."

He nods. "Close will still change things for you."

"How about if we go into the government computer files and change his police record? He's guilty of raping young boys. If we add convictions to his record, whenever he applies for a job working with kids, he won't get the job. That should change things a little."

"Good idea. How can we get into the computers?"

"I assume you can place me at a computer terminal. Being an old hacker, I'll do the rest."

"I'll get you into a computer terminal, but only if it is an experience you have in your memory. I can transport us to a point in memory, not to a place."

"Plenty of times, I went to the police department to bail out my younger brother, who had a propensity for trouble. Will that help?"

"That'll do, but here's another difficulty."

"What?"

"Last night I got you pretty pumped when I threw your money around. Because I'll no longer be able to surprise you, I need to do it in another way before I transport you anywhere. You have the potential, but to store that kind of energy takes time and effort."

"Whatever is needed," I say. "I'll do it."

"You need to go into meditation for at least two days, maybe more. I'll bring you food and water, but even while you eat and drink, you can't come out. When the time is right, I'll be there, and we'll go to the police station."

"What kind of meditation?"

"The kind you've been practicing, but you'll have to stay in a meditative state for the entire time. Your first tendency will be to resurface to go to the bathroom or when a meal comes. You'll be forced to arise from the depths to do those things, but you can't come all the way out or speak to anyone."

"Where do you want me to do this?"

"Because you picked this room, I suggest here, but if another room feels better, then by all means, go to that room."

"Here feels right."

"You ready?"

"Yes, but will you explain to Leigha—."

"I wouldn't worry about her," he interrupts. "She has more than enough work to do."

"What about accidentally jumping into Maranther's trap?"

"You needn't worry about Maranther. The sorcerer will not affect you during this exercise; I'll personally see to it."

"Okay, what do you want me to do?"

"First, break your sleep pattern, and I mean really shatter it. Sleep one hour, then wake and meditate for an hour, sleep three hours, meditate one, sleep two hours and so on. Don't get stuck on any pattern. You'll get spacey, but it won't give you any long-term problems. Your dreams will become much more vivid.

"Write as many dreams down as possible. It serves to remind your awake-self about your dream experience. Reread the things you write and meditate on the dreams themselves, especially the emotional content.

"After two or three days, this world and your dream world will merge. Although the journey is disconcerting at first, you will get used to it.

"It might be dangerous to break the continuity while you're absorbed. Stay with it. Surface only to go to the bathroom or eat. Remember, as soon as you end this practice, your life will return to normal, but while you're in it, things may get bizarre."

"If I get your meaning, I'm to stop all the assignments you gave me earlier and concentrate on this one?"

"The things I gave you are active meditations."

"Active meditations?"

"Move and dance, but with purpose. The meditation lies in the intent. Concentrate on moving and expressing your energy; it will help you get where you're going with less time spent in boring sedentary contemplation. To help your mind from stagnating, go back and forth in the two approaches."

"What do I concentrate on?"

"Relax at first and focus on your dreams. When you find your mind clear, bring your attention to the police station and keep your focus on it. After a while, you'll dream about the station. When it happens, I'll show up, and we'll be off."

He stands and walks out. At the door, he turns. "Keep your attention on the police station; I'll take care of the rest."

I nod, and he closes the door behind him. I sit on the floor and cross my legs like the East Indian Yogi and immediately realize I won't be comfortable for more than a minute or two. After various similar positions, I sit on the couch with my legs out in front of me like I normally sit. It's the one position I'll be able to sustain.

After the first day, I find myself trying to concentrate only on the police station, but keeping my mind on a single subject turns out to be harder than I imagined. My thoughts wander to other topics. I'm in a constant struggle to think about the police station. The further along in the mindset I go, the more my thoughts jump to other subjects. After my body gets sore, I switch to moving, and twenty minutes later my thoughts loosen, allowing me to concentrate again. I spend the rest of the second day in a constant shift from quiet meditation to sleep, to active movement. Had anyone asked me six weeks ago if I'd be involved in this kind of activity, I'd have scoffed and bet against it, but here I am, doing the things I so often belittled.

When I sleep, I have odd dreams with little meaning. By the fifth day, the scene gets more bizarre. Finally, I'm so confused, I'm not sure if my dreams are real or my real life is a dream. Dancing and writing is the only way I distinguish between the two.

In a strange, sudden shift, the scene reverses. Instead of writing my dreams down while awake, I find myself documenting my waking life in my dream, using a finger instead of a pencil. At the moment I catch myself in the dream, Chelone stands next to me.

"Are you ready?" he asks.

I nod.

He grabs my hand, and we lift off the ground in free flight. Floating high above the desert feels so safe and familiar I ask, "Have I been here before?"

"Yes," he answers without speaking a word, "We often fly in our dreams. The difference is, most people will not remember."

I recognize him. "You've been in my dreams before."

"More times than you know."

"Why didn't you tell me?"

"I've waited for you to mature."

In a short flight of five minutes, we sail over desert and rocky crags, over forest and city, until we reach a town I don't recognize from the air. We drop out of the sky to street level. Chelone points across a park, and I recognize the Burlingame City Hall.

"This is the town where I grew up."

"And the police station you have been concentrating on during your meditations."

We float down to the station. Without opening the doors, we push through the thick plate glass like yogurt squeezes through a strainer.

Three desk clerks sit on our right. An officer, paper cup poised to his lips, sits frozen on the edge of a desk to the left. We float past. No one looks up or moves. Like the scene when I punched Dan, the people have slowed enough to look frozen.

Chelone leads me along a hall to the back offices.

I point to my right. "The computer is there in the corner."

He sits next to me in front of the monitor, and I begin the tedious process of hacking my way into the federal database.

It feels like an hour, but I finally find my way into Dan's file.

"Jesus," I say, "he has five prior arrests for molesting boys, two convictions for petty theft, and a charge of assault and battery that never went to trial."

"It's not surprising. Employers didn't check too many backgrounds in those days."

"Yeah, but he worked with kids. You'd think someone would have checked him out."

"After you grew up, more in-depth checks were made, but not when you were a kid."

I rub my computer-tired eyes. "Adding more arrests and convictions to his record won't do a thing."

Chelone is silent.

"One way to get him off the streets is to have him arrested."

"Humm," Chelone murmurs.

I add a warrant into his file, but it takes time to think of something believable. Eventually, I raise my hands in surrender. "I'm not going to be able to make one change in his life."

"Not without affecting yours."

There's a long pause. I take a deep breath, toss my hands in the air, shrug, then delete my new entries and close the terminal.

I turn to Chelone. "I can't even. . ."

He raises his hand and places it on my shoulder. "Don't worry, Martin, some things are better left unchanged."

My eyes open, and I'm in the apartment.

I grab a pen and the writing pad, then recount the dream.

When I finish, Chelone enters the room. He sits across from me on the sofa. "You made a fine choice."

"Huh?"

"Not to make any alteration in your past is always a better choice. You can never tell what will happen with even the slightest change that far back. It could have disastrous effects."

"Although I never saw him again, I feel he and I are forever connected."

"Yes," Chelone says, "and healing doesn't come from revenge. You have begun recovery by coming to terms with the event and eventually honoring it."

"I'm not sure if I could ever honor what happened."

"Even so, that is the job. Continue your meditations." He rises and walks to the door. "Continue to break up your sleep for another day or two. You and your wife stand close to your leap."

"What leap?"

"I can't explain," he says, "but you'll know when it happens."

Twelve

Leigha's Revelation

I haven't seen Martin for days, but I'm much too involved in my own tasks to miss him much. I sit cross-legged in the ground floor apartment. Chelone assures me that while I'm in meditation, I don't have to worry about Maranther or time travel, so after an exhausting eighteen hours of meditation and dance, I fall into a deep slumber. I've just closed my eyes, when Chelone comes out of the surrounding darkness. It doesn't seem strange any longer that he glows like an angel.

"Where is Martin?" I ask.

He waves a hand with palm down, like my question is not important.

I fire another question at him. "When can I stop this damn meditating?"

His old man face strains to bring all of those wrinkles up into a smile, but he says nothing.

"When can we go home?"

Without moving his lips, he answers, "You're almost ready to leap. It's time to make your choice."

"What choice?"

"You'll know when it happens."

When he fades into the darkness, I awake.

The rest of the day, I ponder his statement. What will I know and when will it happen?

That evening, in an odd dream, I draw away from my prone body, then float across the vastness of the hall and through one of the huge windows. I'm weightless twenty stories above the ground in a gently undulating current of desert breeze.

Once I've adjusted to the new sensation, I push away from the structure out into open space. When I apply my will to the chore, I'm able to move with little effort.

Staying close to the building, I experiment with my buoyant body until I spot a ghost-like creature floating on the western face of the building. I move in the direction of the apparition. When I get close enough, I realize it's Martin. We come together in a long hug, which brings up forgotten memories of us connecting like this many times. I want to speak about the feeling, but can't mouth the words.

"It's okay," he says, without moving his lips. "We don't have to talk. I understand your thoughts."

In the middle of our reunion, a strong force, like a harsh desert wind, sweeps us away from the building and across the desert. Hand in hand, we're being pulled toward something, though it feels more like toward someone, at the speed of a jet. Martin points behind us as I watch the gigantic twin monolith slip over the horizon. A three-quarter moon rises above the eastern mountains and shines ghostly over the barren terrain. The mesa gives way to a deep gorge as a wide band of crystalline sand stretches the length of the canyon. Our car is buried under that sand somewhere.

"Maranther," Martin thinks to me, and I feel him shudder. "We're going back to the adobes."

With the mention of the name, I tighten. As I tremble, my grip slackens.

"Don't lose your resolve," he says. "We can do this."

I regain my intent and grip Martin as we approach the familiar boulder with its stone foundations.

Maranther calmly sits on the boulder in front of her firepit, just as I'd seen her on our first meeting more then two months ago. As much as I try to reverse direction, we're pulled to the rock, the flame, and the frightening old woman.

Without landing on the rock, or even approaching it, Martin and I find ourselves sitting across from her. I look into the black eyes of our nemesis.

"Afraid of a harmless old woman?" Maranther asks. "I would never hurt you."

I say nothing.

Martin speaks. "What do you want from us?"

"Checking in to see your progress."

"Progress?" I ask the question a little too loud.

Her face pulls up into a grin. "Why, your meditation and rage work, of course."

"How do you know about that?"

"I know many things about your life, my dear. More

than you, or your scrawny little husband might guess."

"All Martin and I want is to get out of this nightmare and return to our normal life. What do we have to do? Why are we caught in this? What purpose does it serve to keep us here?"

She titters. "You have so many questions. Oh, but you haven't guessed?"

"Guessed what?"

"Don't you recognize the places you've been?"

"I've never been to this desert. Since my childhood, I've never been to any desert."

"Think carefully before you speak, my dear."

"Other than being dragged out here by my husband, there would never be a reason for me to be in the desert. I have no need for this godforsaken place."

Maranther's face changes shape. It contorts slightly, and her eyes change color. I'm so drawn into her eyes, I don't recognize her new face. When she completes the alteration, the dreaded Maranther has transformed into Chelone.

"We've waited a long time for your return," he says. It is his voice, but with an odd quality.

"A long time?" I ask. "What do you mean?"

"You lived among us, and now you have returned."

"How did you become Chelone?"

"Dreams are limitless, but I am Maranther."

"But I see and hear Chelone."

"One and the same."

"You can't be."

His face pulls into the recognizable old-man smile. "I am Maranther, Chelone, and many others."

His face shifts again. Now, his entire body transforms into the rotund owner of Whiley's campground. Sam, who doubled as the short-order cook, still has the apron tied around his monstrous waist. A cigarette hangs from his lips.

Martin moans. "You're Sam?"

He cocks his head to the side so the smoke won't get in his eyes. "It's been a long time since you've been with us. We knew you would return."

"Return?" I ask. "I've never been close to here before last March. I've never set eyes on your damnable desert. Who are you?"

"I shift into what and whomever I please."

The face of the cook dissolves into a gurgling mass. When it reassembles, the little Mexican sits across the fire.

Martin says, "Damn, I knew that little Mexican had something to do with Maranther."

"Dreams?" the old guy asks, barely able to speak in English. "You bean to desert in dreams."

As if merely from the suggestion, old memories flood my thoughts. My teeth set on edge. My jaw clenches. A knot tightens in the pit of my stomach. I reach over and grab Martin's hand.

The Mexican dissolves and forms into Martha, the old woman who befriended me in Yuma.

"If I have visited the desert many times in my dreams, how did you know?"

Martha says, "We've visited one another more times than you remember."

"But, how—"

263

The apparition makes a fast shift to Maranther and cuts me off. "Do not try to understand such things. They are not in the realm of understanding. Simply accept that you and I are similar, made from the same cloth."

"I've spent my whole life in California," I say weakly. "I may have visited these places in my dreams, but I never lived here."

"You lived here three centuries ago as my teacher."

"Your teacher? I was never—"

She puts her hand up. "Much time has gone by, and your current life has turned out different. You have family and a home in California, but you have returned as you said you would. Long ago you asked me to wake your memory when you returned. I do as you instructed."

"If you were supposed to wake my memory, then why the charades?"

"I had to be sure it was you. In the past, I've tried to wake the wrong person. The results aren't mentionable. You are my teacher and a great Brujo. I no longer have doubt."

"Who am I?"

She grabs a stick and stirs the fire, then tosses it in. "Your old name does not matter for now. Awakening you is what matters, though I do not know what you had in mind once you awoke. I was your student, and you did not tell me every detail."

"What's my old name? I can almost remember it."

"Your name will come to you in good time. Between now and then, we have a lot of work to do and many places to go. For the moment, you must think about what you want. Would you remain here in your old home or return to your other life in northern California?"

I look toward Martin, then back to Maranther. "That's easy. I'll definitely return to California. I've had it with your crappy desert."

"You didn't say such things about the desert three centuries ago. You loved your desert and did not want to leave."

"So why did I leave?"

"Another story, for another time."

Martin asks, "You say Leigha lived another life three centuries ago? What happened to her between then and now?"

"I do not know, but I am now certain Leigha, as you call her, has another name that strikes fear in the hearts of her adversaries. She presents a presence in these parts, much stronger than me."

Maranther shifts and remolds into a native man.

Martin puts his hand to his mouth. "You're Running Feathers, too?"

"All and the same."

"The drunk at the bar?"

Running Feathers molds into Talbert, drunken slur and all.

"We are all one." He shifts to the blond-haired, goateed man I met in the monolith building what seemed like a lifetime ago.

Martin gasps. "Nathaniel, too!"

"I had to take your watch because you got too close to the answer. If you had discovered it, you would not have found Chelone and his people. Without them, you would not have been able to dream your way back to this place. The circle is now complete."

The image shifts again to the old woman, Maranther. "I am all of the people you have met."

"Why would you shift?" Martin asks. "Why not come to us and explain the situation?"

"Would you have believed me? You hardly believe me now."

After a moment of introspection, Martin asks, "What happens next?"

Maranther turns to me. "Stay here and continue the work you left behind three centuries ago or return to California and die a useless old woman."

"I'm not useless. I have an exciting job, a wonderful husband and family. I have—"

"Not that kind of useless," Maranther says with a grimace. "A uselessness that comes from not fulfilling your fate. You have a destiny here. I've waited for your return. Now you have regained a portion of your old power; you have a choice. If you do not continue your practice, the power will not stay with you long. The uselessness I speak about will be from not continuing your work. It will be a waste to leave it undone."

"What kind of work?"

"I cannot tell. I was your student and at the time very young."

"So, you say I'm three centuries old?"

"More than three centuries."

"How is it possible?"

Maranther drags a stick through the coals of the fire, then looks up. "As you suggested, I have continued the work, but three centuries is not enough time."

I look at her. "Where does our work continue? I mean, what place does it continue?"

Maranther's smile is one of excitement.

I give her a pensive look. "I'm not saying I'll decide right now. I want to look at my options."

Martin makes a shift in position. He throws his arms up. "Your options? What about your family?"

I ignore him and glance at the old woman. "I'm just curious, that's all."

"Your options are in your old memory," Maranther says. "Like your name, you will remember more when you begin the journey; until then, these things will be hidden from you."

"Now that I know who I am, can't I simply return in five or six years when my children are grown? I need to get my kids through the next critical few years until they become adults. I don't want to miss this part of their lives. I'd like to return later and see what you have in mind, but my kids come first. Can't I simply return then?"

Without anyone touching it, the fire flares.

"Yes," she says, "if you still remember."

"What do you mean? I've already remembered. Do you think I'll forget? Do you think I'll disregard the last months? It's etched in my memory." I take a sweep of my arm around the boulder and adobe scene. "How can I not retain all of this?"

"You must decide," Maranther says.

"If I am forced to select, I must choose California, but I'll never forget who I am. I will return when my kids have fully grown."

Maranther's Deception

The old woman gives me a winsome smile, opens her mouth, folds into herself, and vanishes.

Thirteen

Back to Sleep

The next morning I awake and look across the tent at Leigha. Although I don't know why, I have a deep sense of relief when I see her. The first noticeable difference is the wind has stopped. My next thought concerns my new Volvo and whether I'll find it once we get a tow truck into the valley. How will the truck get across those dunes?

I look through the cracks in the adobe and see the brightness of a sunny day. I slip out of the sleeping bag, trying hard not to wake Leigha. I remember she tossed and turned last night. I'm sure she could use the extra sleep. It excites me to get up before her, for once.

I climb into my clothes and step out into a spectacular desert morning. The boulder is strewn with decomposed pieces of adobe. It must have taken years to melt the walls, considering the small amount of rain that falls in the desert. I wander around the boulder and find artifacts left by the people who lived here maybe a century ago.

There are no tin cans, no clothing, and no evidence of any kind of modern civilized society. Out on the end of the boulder, ready to crumble into dust, stands a drying rack made of the twisted branches of a scrub tree. The setting is an archeologist's dream. I carefully inspect the six small, crumbled foundations. The artifacts appear complete and untouched. It's as if whoever lived here left in a hurry, and no one has been back since. I leave in place the stone tools, arrowheads attached to slender rotted shafts, broken vessels made from roughly fired clay. Archeologists will want this stuff left undisturbed.

I come across a small, polished green stone amulet of a wide-hipped, heavily breasted woman. I can't help myself. I pick it up. Under close scrutiny, the pendant is attached to a supple leather thong, as if it was left here last week.

I can't wait to get my archeologist neighbor out here. This place is so untouched it's unreal. I rub my finger across the smooth belly of the amulet and slip it in my pocket. I have to take something with me to prove the place exists.

"Leigha," I say an hour later when she stirs, "look what I found." I hold it out and let the stone hang from the strap.

She cringes.

"What's wrong?"

"I don't know," she says, "that amulet has a frightening memory for me. I dreamed about it last night, but I can't remember what happened."

"I had a strange bunch of nightmares last night too,

but I'll be damned if I remember a thing about what they were about."

She reaches out and fingers the pendant. "I knew it would be smooth."

"Soapstone," I say. "I used to carve it when I was a kid."

I drop the leather thong into her hand. Leigha studies the pendant. She speaks after a long silence. "It's nice."

"Why don't you wear it until we give it to Bill? He'll know more about its history. I can't wait to see his face when I tell him about this place."

She opens the leather circle to slip it over her head, then stops. "This thing frightens me, Martin. I'll put it in my backpack until we get home."

"Okay, honey, but the stone is soft, so fold it into a sock to keep it from scratching."

She carefully wraps it into yesterday's hiking shirt, and we stuff our backpacks for the long hike out.

I have a last look around the boulder, then we climb down to the gravel path. After a long march up the dusty road, signs of civilization begin to show: tossed cigarette butts, candy wrappers, a Styrofoam cooler lid. The trash is disappointing yet reassuring that our journey is close to an end.

One more night in the desert, and by late afternoon the next day, like a mirage, the big Whiley's sign appears on the horizon. We pick up the pace for the remaining two miles.

"You're a sight for sore eyes," I say to the cook, as we step inside the restaurant.

Leigha pulls me to a halt without closing the door.

"What?" He eyes are wide.

"We've been in here before," she whispers.

I push the creaky door closed. The little bell clangs. "Sure, we stopped in here on the way to the canyon three days ago."

She puts her hand to her mouth. "Don't you remember, I stayed in the car."

A chill spreads over my body. I grab her hand and walk my reluctant wife to the bar. After we sit, I whisper, "You're right; you did stay in the car."

The cook steps from the back with a faded, grease-stained menu and walks to our end of the bar. He drops the menu in front of me and pours two wondrous glasses of water. "Where you folks been?"

"We were trying to get to Mirage Hot Springs at the bottom of White Fang Canyon, but a sandstorm buried our car. Can I call a tow truck?"

He breaks into a delighted grin. "Sure, but he's got to come forty miles. You better call now, to get him here by tomorrow morning. If you need a room, I got three cottages out back. They're not much, but I keep them clean, and there's showers."

Leigha downs the water. "We'll take the room. Do you have a phone?"

He refills Leigha's glass. "Yeah, sure, it's behind the counter. Hey, Talbert, get these folks the phone."

At the end of the bar, a man in his late twenties leans over and fishes out a black cordless. He stumbles over with a drunken swagger and sets the phone on the table in front of me.

"Thanks."

The drunk makes his way back to his seat. Without rotating, probably because turning might throw him off balance, he waves a hand as he finds his stool and climbs back into position.

"Number's, 662-7898." the cook refills my water glass. "So many people get stuck in the desert in their four-wheelers, I know the number by heart. "What kinda truck you got?" he asks.

"Volvo."

He sets the full glass down, leans one elbow on the bar. "You took a new Volvo down that road? It's pretty rough country."

"I know," I say after I drain my glass. "We walked thirty miles uphill in that desert."

"How long did it take?" slurs the kid at the end of the bar.

I look at the youth through the full-length mirror.

Leigha answers, "Three days."

The cook lifts his elbow off the counter, turns his back to us, opens the ancient chrome register, inserts a loose bill, and clangs it closed. When he turns back, he looks at me. "You were out there three days?"

I nod.

He shakes his head. "Lucky it wasn't hotter."

I put my empty glass on the countertop. "It was hot enough."

He refills it. "You want anything to eat?"

"Yes," Leigha says. "I'll have a burger with fries."

He looks at me. "And you?"

"Make mine well."

He sets another full glass in front of me. "Before I

cook your burgers, you want anything to drink?"

"Coupla Coronas."

"You got it," the cook says. "You better call the tow truck. He's usually not around after five, and it's twenty of."

The cook spins on his heels and walks into the back.

I'm dialing the number when Leigha whispers, "This place gives me the creeps."

"It's all we've got, for now," I say.

"I've never been inside here, and I know this place by heart. How do you explain that?"

"You must have come—."

A voice greets me with a gruff, "John's Tow."

"Hello, my car is stuck in White Fang Canyon. Can you tow me?"

The voice asks, "Where you at now?"

"Whiley's."

"Where's your car?"

"In the bottom of the canyon, buried in the sand."

After a pause, he asks, "You got insurance?"

I dig out my wallet and read the card number.

"I'll be there first thing in the morning," he says, then abruptly hangs up.

I push the off button and set the phone on the table.

The cook walks over with two plates of fat burgers and a couple of beers. Although something about the place is vaguely familiar, I'm thinking my life can't be any better than this moment. I bite into the burger with a gusto that surprises even me. The fries are delicious. I eat as though I haven't eaten in two weeks and when I'm done, I order another.

Back to Sleep

The hike out is gruesome. Although Martin tries to make it an enjoyable trip, I barely glance at the landmarks, even when he points them out. The amulet continues to occupy my thoughts.

Other than wanting to caress the smooth fetish, my only desire is to get out of this damn wasteland. Flowers and silence are the few redeeming features, but these measly characteristics don't make up for the complete absence of human amenities. I never liked the desert, and I don't think I ever will. The thirty-mile uphill hike hasn't helped my perspective.

We come to the last rise and my last straw, when I spot the huge "Whiley's campground sign". The end is in sight. We quicken our pace, and just before sunset, I open the rotted wood and glass door of the restaurant. Although I have never been inside, I recognize the tables and chairs, the bar with its full-length mirror, and the overwhelming smell of old grease.

I stop with the door still open. I whisper to Martin. "We've been in here before."

In his normal, everything's-going-to-be-okay way, he sidesteps the issue, pushes the door closed, and guides me to the bar.

We eat and pay for a place to stay. I already know the cook will tell us the cabins are behind the faded blue door, but I say nothing.

The room is as I remember, although I've never been

here before. The shower is ugly and small, but clean; the hot water is glorious. After I dry, while I dig in my pack for underwear, I run across the amulet. I want to wear it, but Martin distracts me when he turns on the TV. We get three Spanish-speaking channels and one from Yuma, Arizona. Yuma is another landmark in my unresolved memory.

After three long days of cactus and desert gravel, I feel better once I've taken a shower. Sitting together on the bed, we watch the six o'clock news. I absently finger the pendant and almost pull the leather thong over my head three times.

I'm frightened and intrigued with the amulet. By the end of the evening, I fall asleep watching a stupid late-night talk show, with the fetish tucked warmly in my fist.

The next afternoon, the tow truck lumbers up the hill. A few minutes later, Martin, in our sand-riddled Volvo, drives into the parking lot.

"Oh, Martin, the storm wiped out the paint."

"Not to mention the glass. I'll get eyestrain driving back to the States, but I'm sure no one has new glass on this side of the border. We'll have to get the windshield replaced in Yuma.

"We'd better stay one more night," he says. "With the glass fogged up so bad by the sand, there'll be too much glare to drive in the dark."

By morning, I'm tired of greasy food and lumpy beds. I'm ready to get miles between us and this crappy little campground. I'm ready for a proper hotel with decent food. I want fluffy, thick towels, a color television with reasonable reception, and maybe a movie.

While packing, I finger the amulet a last time, then carefully slip it into a soft stocking and stuff it into the bottom of my pack.

The last of Whiley's image drops ten miles behind us before I think of the amulet again. Because we are forced to make a roundabout journey, we don't cross over the border into civilized country until late afternoon. When we drive into Yuma and find a glass shop, Martin pulls up to the steel roll-up door and a squat little guy walks out to greet us.

"Whew, you got yourselves caught in a sandstorm." He speaks in a slow, southwestern drawl. "That sand'll take the paint off right down to the metal."

He leans down, puts his arm on the window ledge and looks past Martin through the windshield. "Would you look at them patterns in the glass?"

"Can you replace the windshield?" Martin asks.

He glances at me and tips his sweat-stained cowboy hat. "Sure, I'll replace all the glass, if you want."

"Just the windshield, please. We'll have the rest done when we get home."

"I'll order the glass now, but I can't fix nothin' until tomorrow. My kid's birthday is tonight, and I won't miss it for anything."

"Is there another shop in town?"

"Don't think so. Kind of a small town, nowadays."

I ask, "Is there a nice motel close by?"

"There's a motel on fifth, next to the bowling alley."

"I'm looking for the best motel in town."

He smiles and glances at Martin, "Well. . . I guess it's the best motel in these parts. El Centro might have a better one. It's about forty miles west."

I look at Martin as he shakes his head. "I'm beat."

"Oh great," I whisper.

"What time do you want the car?" Martin asks.

The little guy pulls a pad from his back pocket and scratches some notes with a blunt pencil. "What year is the car?"

Martin says. "We got it new last November."

The guy jots the note. "Sure is a shame.

"Get it to me by nine. Barring any screw-ups, I'll have you out by eleven."

"We'll be here. Which way to the motel?"

With the pencil, he points north. "Two blocks to the stop light, then right. It's three blocks on your left. You can't miss it. Just this side of the bowling alley."

We follow his directions and pull into the parking lot of a two-story cinder block structure painted chartreuse with bright fuchsia trim. Plastic pink flamingos flock around the Kelly green kidney-shaped pool.

I grumble, "I'd hoped for something more in the realm of Howard Johnson."

Martin gives me a sheepish grin. "Don't you worry, Honey, I'll get you home."

While Martin showers, I pull out the amulet and feel its velvety smoothness. Absently, I almost slip it over my head, but Martin comes into the room.

"Can you get me a T-shirt?"

I drop the amulet into the sock and forget about it.

Back to Sleep

By two the next day, we pass from Arizona over the California border into the flatlands of Blythe.

"We're getting closer," Martin says.

"I want to see forest and mountains and water."

"If we get some miles behind us," he says, "we'll be out of the desert before nightfall."

A few times during the ride to the upper desert, my thoughts fall on the little green rock woman. Because she's in the trunk, I can't pull her out, but I want to.

We stay the night in Lone Pine, a little town on the east side of the Sierras. The room has a musty odor, but the view of the Sierras heartens me. Lots of trees and cool non-desert air give me hope that we actually might make it home.

No restaurants are open in the morning, so we pack and drive an hour north to Bishop for breakfast.

After a noisy meal surrounded by a bunch of overly loud cowboys, we get gas and pull out of town. Although I put the amulet in my backpack, it's on my mind. I have a silly urge to touch the velvety stone.

By late afternoon, we drive along the ridge above our mountain town. Martin starts down the last long grade. "I can't wait to see the kids."

"I don't ever want to go to the desert again, Martin. I don't want to see another cactus or scrub brush. I never want to smell sage. Next time we go on a vacation, let's go to the coast. I want to see the ocean. I want coolness, maybe even clouds and a little rain. I want to stay in a nice hotel. I want to go to a movie. Anything but the desert."

"The ocean it is." He pauses for a moment, then says,

"But you have to admit, we have stories. I can't wait to tell Bill about the adobes."

"You and Bill can go back to that place alone."

"There's Nevada City." He points at the white buildings protruding out of a blanket of forest. "We're home."

I smile. "I like the trees so much better, don't you?"

"I like living in the trees, but I still like visiting the desert."

"In the future you'll have to visit without me."

Fourteen

Home at Last

Martin gets the Volvo out of the garage for what seems like the hundredth time. Not only did the glass and paint need replacing from the windstorm, but everything that could get sand in it had sand in it. For the money we spent in an attempt to get the car into shape, we could have bought a new one. Lucky our insurance covered the repairs.

Martin's impatience is apparent as he is forced to wait a month for Bill to return from Peru. On the second night after his return, Martin insists that Bill come over for dinner. After dinner, Martin asks me to get the fetish.

Funny, once we got back home, with kids to tend to, school, and work, I completely forgot about the little stone woman.

It takes a while, but in the bottom of my backpack, tucked in a forgotten sock, I pull the amulet out and carry it into the kitchen.

Bill studies the stone. "This is incredible."

"It's only a carved stone," I say, "and a not very well-carved one, I might add. I'd guess Thailand or Burma."

"I don't think so," he says. "This looks like the genuine article. Without any testing, I'd say it might be Mayan from the sixth or seventh century."

"No kidding?" I feign interest. Ancient history isn't one of my strong points. I could care less.

I barely pay attention as Bill rattles on. "The piece was probably carved by an ancient medicine woman. It's a symbol of fertility. Carvings like this have been found all over the Mayan temples in Mexico, but I've never seen one in a single talisman. You say you found it in Mexico?"

I already know Martin has saved his best story for last. While Martin tells his tale, I'm mesmerized by the dangling pendant in Bill's hand. Martin and Bill's voices fade as they start a long dialogue about the boulder, the windstorm, and those three days in the desert.

My thoughts are on the little totem. I want to hold it again. I reach out and pluck it from Bill's hand. He glances over, but keeps jabbering about a trip to the site. I hear none of the details.

I study the soapstone totem and see the face. I look closer. In a long stretch of the imagination, it looks like me. I'm so immersed in the stone, before I realize what I'm doing, I slip the leather thong over my head.

I have a flash of total recall. I remember Maranther, the little Mexican, Martha, and the old man Chelone. I relive Martin's disappearance, how frightened I felt, and my relief when we reunited. Old desert memories return.

The cave scene with little Leigha and Sara washes over me.

In a blink of an eye, I'm sitting on the boulder again. The adobes are behind me, and that damnable desert stretches out endlessly in front of me. Maranther sits across the fire. She tears a strip of meat from the dark flesh of a rabbit and offers it.

"No thanks, I just ate."

"Take a bite, my dear. The wildness of this creature will give you strength."

As if I have no other choice, I take the meat. My hand mechanically maneuvers it to my mouth, and I bite off a large piece. On the first chew, my taste buds explode. "This is delicious."

"It's a special rabbit, my dear; one you chose."

Like I haven't eaten for a week, I swallow the bite and stuff a second piece into my mouth.

"Lee-ahh!" I hear a voice in the distance. I look around at the same desert, the same cacti, and the same crimson evening sky. I can't see anyone except Maranther, and I don't recognize the person calling.

"Pay no attention to the sounds," she says. "They are of no importance. I am happy you have returned to us to continue your work."

"Continue my work? I don't think so."

In a flash, I understand everything. I reach for the amulet and almost pull it over my head. In the same split second, Maranther has another piece of the meat in front of me.

I snatch the food from her hands and devour it like a mongrel dog. She hands me another, then another, and continues handing me pieces. I feed in a frenzy, consuming a never-ending supply of meaty morsels until the entire rabbit has been stripped. Only the bony carcass hangs on the spit as Maranther continues to turn the crank. I lean forward, and like a starved wild person, I dig in the nooks and crannies of the bones.

"Do you feel the power?" she asks.

"Yes, yes, I do."

"Do you feel it in the air?"

"Yes."

"Do you feel it in your feet?"

"Yes, I do." I spring to my feet and leap off the ground like a rocket, then fly into the dry desert air to a height of five or six hundred yards above the adobes.

"Do you feel the power in your heart?" she asks from her perch far below me on the rock. "Doesn't it want to explode with this energy?"

I scream into the open desert air. "Yes, yes, it does."

I float to earth and rest in my place across the fire from her.

"Do you want to use your power?"

"Yes."

"Then let us go to your real home and continue what you left behind so long ago. We have much to do and little time left to do it."

"But, I belong in California."

Before she stops me, in one fast, smooth movement, I grab the pendant and lift it over my head.

Fifteen

Return

We sit at the kitchen table and talk about the pendant. Bill explains where it may have come from. In a startling instant, while I look directly at Leigha, she slips the leather thong over her head and poof, she folds out of existence.

Bill screams and leaps out of his chair. His face goes pale. "Where'd she go?" He backs up a few steps until he slams against the wall. His shaking finger points at the empty chair.

Although I'm an eyewitness and already know she isn't hiding anywhere, in a frantic scramble to understand, I search under the table. I look in the kitchen. I run from room to room, but no Leigha. I burst out the front door, and no Leigha. Without knowing what else to do, I race around the house for a second frenzied search.

When I calm down and go back to Bill in the kitchen, he's repositioned himself at the table.

"She may have slipped away," I say.

He looks at me with a pallid expression of acceptance. He rubs his eyes with both palms. Through his hands he says, "We both know what happened, Martin."

"It's some kind of trick," I scream.

"We both sat at the table and looked right at her," he says. "The second she put the amulet on, she disappeared. It's as simple as that."

I moan, "It can't be," and run to the front door, open it, and give a long bellow, "Lee-ahh." The plaintive howl of her name reminds me of the desert, but I can't quite place it. A chill runs up my spine.

Old busybody Mrs. Grady across the street opens her front door and glares at me.

In another act of utter desperation, I run back into the kitchen, pick up the phone, and dial the first two numbers of 911. I push the last of the buttons, when, just as suddenly as she vanished, Leigha reappears in her chair, removing the pendant.

I slam the phone on its hook and race to her. I grab her and touch her face, her hair, then hold one of her precious little hands. I find my chair and park myself next to her. "What happened?"

"What are you talking about?"

"You disappeared," Bill says. He still looks ghostly white. I'm sure I look the same.

"What do you mean, disappeared?"

I reach out and, glad to see her again, I put my hand on hers. "You dissolved into thin air. One moment you were here, and the next second, you were gone."

She gives me a cautious smile. "What are you saying?"

She pulls her hand free. "I've been here all along."

Bill leans forward and looks directly into her eyes. "You disappeared, Leigha. I'm here as a witness, and you evaporated right in front of us."

Leigha's color drains. She looks from me, to Bill, then back to me once more. "Gone from where to where?"

"I don't know, Honey, but you definitely were nowhere around here. Trust me; I looked."

Leigha releases a meaty burp, then says, "I don't feel well. I need to lie down."

I help her upstairs and into bed. Once she's tucked in, I kiss her on the forehead. "I'll go downstairs and get rid of Bill, then I'll be right back."

"Hurry," she says. "I don't feel well."

I rush down the stairs, make my apologies, and usher him out. "We better keep this under our hats until we get it sorted out."

"Okay, buddy, whatever you say, but I already have an idea."

"What's that?"

"When she put the talisman pendant on, she vanished. She was removing it as she returned."

"You think it's the pendant?"

Bill flips his hat on his head. "If I were you, I'd keep the amulet in a safe place. I've heard some strange stories connected to some old Mayan artifacts."

I close the door and bolt back up the stairs to Leigha. The covers are as I left them. The pillow has been slept on, but for the second time during this odd night, no Leigha.

I lie in bed with an aching stomach. It feels like I ate an elephant. The little female fetish lies mysteriously in my hand. I distinctly remember leaving it on the kitchen table. I didn't pick it up, but here it is. The room is dim. I finger the smoothness of the stone and fondle its lines. I have an uncontrollable urge to slip the thong over my head. I feel fear in my desire, but excitement, too. I open the loop and slip it over.

In a burst of light, a flash of movement, and a rush of memory, I'm in front of Maranther, squatting on the boulder facing her small fire.

"You have returned," she says, "and so quick."

"Why am I here?"

"You must want to be here. Come with me and let us see where you truly belong."

"I belong in California with my family."

"Yes, choose California, but you have more choices. Come with me, and I will show you another existence."

When I nod, my two worlds collide. A world of my family, children, husband, the house, my job, my friends, the only world I've ever known. My safe, secure, happy life clashes with a world of leaps from one mountaintop to another while traversing space and time. I remember bolts of lightning, desert gales, magic spells, howling coyotes, three hundred years of full desert moons and I take a deep breath into my true wild nature.

Maranther and I do not fly, but simply connect to an

unseen snow capped peak on the far side of the continent then pull ourselves through the connection. We snap to our destination like a taut rubber band.

"We live here," Maranther says, as we settle atop a glacier-covered summit.

"I live in a frozen wasteland?"

"Yes, it is freezing, but do you feel the cold?"

"No."

"Mortals feel the cold. We, on the other hand, are like gods."

My Christian background springs to the forefront. I paraphrase the quote, "Do not bow down to graven images."

"Yes," she says. "Good point, but we're not gods; we simply know how to use the powers of the gods."

"But we have only one true god," I argue.

Maranther gives me a perplexed glare. "Tap into the ancient part of yourself and tell me again of your one true god."

She forces me to delve into a self that has been buried a long, long time. She pushes me into a forgotten part of myself, and I remember spoken words with many gods, not just the one Christian god I'd been raised with. I have another gigantic clash of my two worlds. I'm forced to set aside yet another contradiction for the moment to ask, "Why are we here?"

"It's your true home," she says. "You lived here long ago, and now you have returned. It is time for us to resume our work."

"What work?"

"When you left, you were evicting the invaders from

our homeland, a losing battle, because so many whites kept coming. Now, there is another threat, one of utmost importance. The earth is dying from humans abusing one another. We will work together to help heal these travesties.

"Like helping the poor and disenfranchised?"

"Not anything so simple. Humanity is our goal, and healing the wounds of nations, our work. Because we are like gods, we will do work on a much deeper, more fundamental level. Come with me, and I'll show you."

Maranther walks me along the edge of a glacier on a frozen path in ancient tundra. It leads over the top of a sheer-edged outcrop. She winds me down chiseled stairs into a small gorge. I walk with her to a narrow split in the living rock. Maranther ducks and slips behind what appears to be a solid blank wall of stone. I follow. We step around a ledge and into a divot in the wall. Afraid it will close again, I look back as we step past the entrance.

"An illusion," I say in surprise. "The rock wall is the same color, the same striped watermarks. I didn't see the separation until we were past it."

"You built this ingenious entrance," she says.

My worlds clash again.

She hunches down and leads me through a natural cleavage in the stone and along a low sloping cave. The darkness frightens me, but I am compelled to follow. We come to a place where we have to get on all fours and crawl through a crack little bigger than the width of my hips. I wonder how the old woman manages.

We crawl along a tunnel on hands and knees, until it opens high enough to allow us to stand. The light looks much brighter the farther we walk. Finally, we step out of the tunnel into a cavern large enough to be a football field. It's lit by an emerald glow.

"This is your workshop," she says. "Your true home." She scoops a finger full of green luminescent mud, then pulls a short mark across my right cheek. "The sign on your cheek will be a reminder about your place."

As she smudges a second parallel mark, my memories return. "I remember why I died. I was being hunted by the Jesuit priests. They followed me here and killed me. You were my student and I taught you well. My name is Alopay."

She bows. "Alopay, we have much work to do. Many things have occurred that need our attention."

She looks deeply into my eyes. "You are running out of energy. Go to your home in California. Be with your family. Live your life, and return when no one else will miss you."

"Now that I'm here, with so much to do, I don't want to go."

"We have much to accomplish, but you must rebuild your energy. Return when you are strong again. When the time is right, we'll spend a year in your workshop."

"But my family, what will become of them?"

"Spend as much time as needed here and return to your family on the same day you left. No one will even know you are gone."

"How will I know when my energy rebuilds?"

"I will call for you. For now, remove your talisman and return to your husband. He worries about you."

Sixteen

Leigha's Home

I'm so shaken by her double disappearance, I can't close my eyes, much less sleep, but after hours of staring into the darkness, I eventually doze off.

Far into the early morning hours, I awake and hear Leigha's quiet breath. Something feels too familiar about my momentary fear in the darkness, lying next to her, afraid she won't be here.

I reach my arm over and lay it gently across her hip. A vague memory is tickled, but no matter how hard I try, I can't bring up the recollection.

In the morning when I get up, after Leigha has been awake for hours, I ask her again, "Where did you go last night?"

She gives me an annoyed look. "I told you I didn't go anywhere."

"No, I mean the second time."

"What do you mean, the second time? I've been here

all along. I don't know what's gotten into you, Martin. I haven't gone anywhere."

"Bill thinks it might have something to do with the amulet. Do you have it?"

"What amulet?"

"The one I found at the adobes."

"Oh, that. Yes, I have it in safekeeping."

"Can I see it?"

"I don't think so. I have it carefully tucked away."

"What do you mean, you don't think so? I found it. You we're holding it for me."

"You're right, but it's too important. I have to keep it safe from outside influences."

"Leigha, you're scaring me. I want to see the amulet right now. Where did you put it?"

"You can't see it."

"It's mine!" I yell.

"You can't see it, and that's that. I'll keep it safe."

"You're acting weird. What's happening?"

"How many times do have to tell you, Nothing is going on, and I went nowhere."

"If you went nowhere, and nothing is happening. . ." I reach over, wipe my finger across her cheek, and pull away a luminescent green goo. "Then where did you get this?"

The kids are in school. My work feels more stressful

than I'm prepared for. Last week, I got permission to split my job and go part time. I want more space to write, but I have other reasons I can't remember.

I sit in the kitchen. The kids won't be home for hours. Martin is at work. The postman drops the mail through the slot. Instead of getting the mail, I have an urge to look at the fetish again.

I reach up and rescue it from a secret shelf inside a cupboard. Once I have it, a strange tingle surrounds me. I'm electrified, like my entire body is bewitched and in search of its counterpart.

I hold it in my hand and feel its pull. I open the loop of leather and almost put it on, when a noise comes from the front door. My first thought is to put the necklace on and the heck with outside influences. I lift the leather thong over my head, and it catches on my barrette. My hands shake. My whole body vibrates. It takes a second to untangle the cord. In the same second, I hear Martin's voice. "Honey, are you here?"

I struggle to release the thong from the hair clip. In desperation, I yank it out of my hair, free the leather, and pull it over my head. In the same second, Martin grabs my wrist. I shift perception from my bright peach kitchen, with every pot and pan, every dish and piece of silverware in place, away from the white tiled floor and stainless-steel sink, into a dark, dank cave, deep in the middle of some mountain.

When I've reoriented myself, Martin's hand grips my wrist. "Maranther," he says.

"Ah, yes, the desert traveler. So, you too will be a part of our little adventure today?"

"I will not."

"You are here now, and neither of us has a choice in this matter, so let us get started."

Martin demands, "Started with what?"

Leigha and I awake crumpled on the kitchen floor.

I look at her as I lift to one elbow. "What happened?"

"I don't know." She holds up the little soapstone fetish. "But my pendant has something to do with it."

"Let me see it again."

She yanks it from my reach and shouts, "No! This medicine is for me alone. No one else must touch it."

I pull back my arm. "What's gotten into you, Leigha? You're acting so strange."

She gives me a worried look. "I don't know. Ever since we got stranded in the desert, I haven't been the same. I can't put my finger on it, but my amulet has something to do with us being on the floor."

"How did we get here?"

"I don't know for sure."

I get to my feet and offer her my hand. Once she's vertical, I attempt to put the strange feeling behind me. Leigha goes to the refrigerator and opens the door. "Oh yuck!" she says. "What happened to the food?"

I expect to see that the kids have raided the fridge. I'm ready to suggest we go out to lunch, when I look over her shoulder. Everything is either thick with mold or has rotted into a gelatinous glob.

"What the. . ."

"What's going on, Martin?"

"I don't know, but it's weird. I have a funny sensation in the pit of my stomach, and I don't like it."

"Me, too. It's like something familiar has happened, but I can't remember any details."

"Maybe deja vu, like we've been here before."

She closes the door and turns to me. "Since we can't eat here, let's go out for lunch. I'll clean the fridge when we get back."

"Okay," I say in a distracted voice.

Leigha pulls a light shirt over her blouse, tousles her hair in the hall mirror, and we step out the door to an absolutely silent neighborhood. In mid-afternoons, with the kids still in school, things get quiet, but this kind of silence I've never heard. I don't even hear the distant drone of activity in town, a half mile away.

We walk to the car, and our freshly painted Volvo is covered in a thick layer of dust.

I rub my finger on the hood. "Has a volcano erupted? I've never seen so much dust settle in so little time."

We get in the dirty car and I turn the key to start the engine, but nothing happens, not even the starter click of a low battery.

"Damn this car," Leigha says. "I'm sick and tired of it constantly breaking down."

"Let's walk to town," I say. "I could use the exercise."

She snips, "I don't feel like a walk."

"If we want to eat, I don't think we have a choice."

We start out and turn the corner. The first thing we come across is Nelson's huge pine tree lying across the road. It not only crushed the Smiths' house, but it also put a deep dent in the house behind it.

Martin's face is pale. "What happened, Leigha?"

"I don't know, but the tree looks like it's been here a long time. How come no one's cut it up and fixed the house?"

We climb under the horizontal tree and walk farther along the street. By the next block, we still haven't heard one car in our busy little town, and things get more strange. The Lextands front lawn, normally the epitome of a tended garden, looks like a jungle. Vines and weeds fill the yard so high, the ranch-style house is almost obliterated.

Leigha and I walk by stunned.

The dust on the car, well, okay. The tree nearly shearing the house in half; it happens. It could've happened two minutes before we walked up, but the Lextands yard going to seed in a half hour? I drove by here on my way home and saw the trimmed roses along the entry. Their gardener had just mowed the lawn.

Leigha says nothing as we step past the property.

The remainder of the walk shows us more evidence of strange occurrences. Not until we walk across the overpass into town does the full implication hit me.

"There's no one here," Leigha says.

"You noticed."

"Where did they all go?"

"I haven't got a clue."

"The town looks so old and dirty. What happened?"

Leigha's Home

We pass the county courthouse, normally bustling with people. No one is around.

A hundred yards down the short hill we come to Broad Street, the main part of town.

"No one's here," Leigha says. "No people, not one moving car, no dogs, squirrels, not even the squawk of a blue jay."

Her face grows more pale. "Martin, our town looks deserted."

"For now," I say, "I'm hungry. Let's go to Ike's Cafe and eat lunch before we do another thing. There's always someone there."

"Is that all you can think about is food?"

"You know me," I say. "Until I eat, I can't think."

"You're right; I'm starved, too."

We walk along Broad Street through a ghost town of ancient brick buildings, curio shops, ice cream parlors, clothing and jewelry stores, but no people. The windows look filthy, the street littered with last autumn's leaves, and a thick layer of dust covers everything.

At Ike's, I open the door and follow Leigha into a dark room. The tables are set, with chairs neatly positioned. Again, thick dust blankets the room.

"I smell fresh cooked meat," I say.

She breathes in. "It's the first odor of anything except mold we've come across."

"It smells good."

"This place is eerie, Martin. Let's get out."

"First, let me see where that aroma is coming from."

"Let's get out, Martin. Things are too weird."

"I'm starved, Leigha. My blood sugar is nonexistent.

I have to eat before I can even begin to figure anything out."

A Spanish-accented, deep female voice speaks from the shadows in the rear of the restaurant. "I've prepared food for you two."

With the sound of the voice, both Leigha and I race for the front door. We sprint down the sidewalk, when it comes to me that someone actually spoke. No one is around, but I heard a voice. I reach for Leigha's arm and slow her.

"Someone is in there."

"I'm not going back. That voice frightens me."

"Listen, Leigha, the town is empty. It's obvious some catastrophe has occurred. That woman might be able to explain what happened."

"I'll wait here," Leigha says.

"Chicken. Must I go in there alone?"

She puts a hand on her hip. "I'm not going in."

"I'll feel a lot better after I eat."

"I'll wait out here."

I walk toward the café and open the door. A strong smell of cooked meat assaults my senses and draws me to the back where I heard the voice. Two freshly cooked bacon burgers and a pile of hot fries sit on a clean table, but no one is here.

I take a tentative bite of a French fry. It's delicious. I grab three or four more and pop one in my mouth as I move toward the front door. "Leigha," I say as I step out the door with a potato in my mouth. "Come on in. There's no one here except two burgers and hot. . ." I look for my wife. I see a trail of her dust prints on the concrete, but the prints simply stop where she stood and go no farther.

I run to the corner and look both ways along Broad Street, but no Leigha. I race frantically toward the next block, when a single person steps out from an alley. I stop fast. I stumble and fall. I pull myself back. I haven't time to get on my feet. The apparition comes for me. On all fours, I scramble backward. She moves very fast. Too quickly, she is upon me. I throw my arms out for protection. The old woman looms over me. I'm forced to open my eyes. I remember it all, the adobes and what they mean. I recall losing Leigha in the desert, meeting Nathaniel and the people at the monolith. I remember Chelone, but mostly I remember the old woman.

"Maranther," I say, more as an acknowledgment than a greeting of any kind.

She smiles. "It is me."

"What happened to my town?"

"Because you and your wife have leapt ahead one year into mystical time, your little city has been thrust into temporary limbo. Do not worry; when you return to ordinary time, your village will revert back to normal.

"Why are you here?"

"Your wife is my teacher, the great sorceress Alopay. After three hundred years, she prepares to continue the work she left behind. I am here to retrieve her. To attempt to follow us would be futile. We will need a year to complete our work, but I promise to have her back to you by midnight."

Maranther disappears. The streets look clean. The windows are fresh. Three people walk by and stare at me splayed on the sidewalk. A string of cars drive past. A black dog trots over and noses my hand. I'm dizzy with the knowledge that I'm home and my wife is out there in the clutches of that meddling sorceress.

I put my hands tight over my mouth and start a long, silent, mournful scream.

Channeling Biker Bob Heart of a Warrior
Excerpt

I have a bunch of questions, but I don't want to spoil the moment. I sit on the back of his machine as we roll off the miles. Eventually, I see something at the bottom of what might be a fifty-mile wide valley. In the center of the massive bowl a single light flickers, the only sign of life in the expanse, and we're heading directly for it.

We take a wind-whipping, twenty minutes to approach the flicker. The wind caresses me. The sound of his twin cylinders roaring into the night air lulls me. A strong smell of desert sage sharpens my senses. I'm alive!

As we approach, I've already guessed that the light is another huge fire, and probably one for me to stoke.

When Bob lets off the gas and allows his engine to slow, I see a line of Harleys. Twenty people wildly move around the blaze. Are they dancing? I have never heard of bikers dancing as a group. The closer we get, the more I'm sure who they are. Big clunky guys, little skinny ones; everyone dances around the fire.

Not until Bob shifts into third gear do I realize the fire erupts in the middle of the asphalt. As we pull up, familiar faces look our way. Bob shifts to neutral, kills his engine, and coasts the last hundred yards to a stop.

This time there is a difference in the party. The same people are here: Beer, Bucky, Tazz, Max, Shorty, and others, but they act different. As we dismount, their dancing stops. We walk over to a solemn circle of men.

I want to ask where the women are, but things start to happen, and I don't have time.

"A superb men and women relationship book in disguise. . . life in its most realistic, rawest form with no holds barred. . . a tough, no nonsense combination of *Men are from Mars and Women are from Venus* and *Iron John*."   Heartland Review

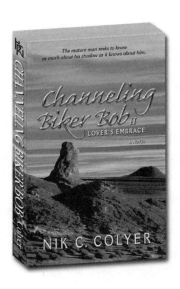

Channeling Biker Bob Lover's Embrace

Nik C. Colyer's
second novel
in the four part series.
Available through your local bookstore for $15.00
or
www.ChannelingBikerBob.com
($15.00 including tax and shipping)

Channeling Biker Bob Lover's Embrace
Excerpt

In a quick flash, one side of my hand-cuffs wrap around my thick wrist. With an effort, Tazz latches them. "Now Mr. I'm-a- Las-Vegas-police-officer, step over to the light pole, please."

"No, you wouldn't." He'll cuff me to the pole and pistol-whip me with my own gun. Now that the tables have turned, I'll be lucky to get out of this alive.

I wrap my arms around a rusted thirty-foot-tall steel pole and feel the second half of my cuffs bind around my other wrist. I prepare myself to be beaten when Tazz grabs my service revolver from Tubbo.

How many times will it take for me to learn I can't go off half-cocked and expect everything to turn out. I think of the reaming that I'll get from McKerney once I get out of the hospital. Hell, if I get out at all.

I wait for the first blow. Instead, Tazz steps in front of me. He opens the gun and drops six shells at my feet.

"I hate guns," he says and slams the pistol hard to the pavement.

The barrel digs a deep hole in the asphalt. He takes his heavy biker boot and smashes it. The open cylinder breaks away, rolls across the pavement and stops ten feet away. He continues to stomp his boot repeatedly into the body of my trashed pistol.

When he's done, he helps his little buddy to his truck and opens the door. Once Bucky is in the truck, Tazz turns to me. "We'll take Buck to the hospital now, because you ain't got a clue how to deal with your anger. Get a grip on your life, Twig and stop buggin' us."

"Nik Colyer's work is so emotionally honest it shoots directly into one's own heart. His raw, naked truths touch that hidden place we all share. Never a dull moment, his poems are evidence of a life fully lived."

Will Staple - Author of *I Hate The Men You Sleep With*

A SURPRISE MOON

Page 16
For the first time, in a predawn hour,
a full moon peeks through our dense forest
with only enough glow to spotlight my desk
in a ghostly brilliance.
I pick up a pen, seldom used these days,
a simple tool for the primitive moment.
Moonlight has centered on my paper,
from the one small piece of sky.
It hangs there for a fleeting moment,
allowing me to scribble these words,
to feel like a poet again,
after a long, dry spell.
The glow is so vague, I can't read the words,
only a formless knowledge
that the pen is still writing
chicken-scratch across a blank page.
Quickly, I write before the ghost light
disappears behind another branch.
Once the elusive sliver of radiance moves on,
I'm back in the blackness of my silent forest,
back to listening to deer crunch
through frostbitten autumn leaves.
Good-bye hoarfrost light, however uncertain,
and to you, poem,
who visits the poet so seldom these days.
11-99

Discussion Group Guide

1. How did getting lost in the desert wind symbolize Martin and Leigha's relationship?
2. The five mile hike across the sand dunes held what kind of importance to the couple?
3. Martin's first test was what?
4. Running Feathers gave Martin what gift?
5. What did the vanishing cougar give Martin?
6. What might the three rocks symbolize?
7. The trip back across the sand almost killed Martin, but what did he learn from the experience?
8. How did Sara's death affect Leigha?
9. Why did Leigha feel safe around Maranther?
10. What lesson did the real cougar give Martin?
11. When Martin showed up at the restaurant, why was everyone so surprised?
12. Nathaniel came to Martin for what reason?
13. What mistakes did Martin make once he reconnected with Leigha?
14. How did the little Mexican help Martin and Leigha?
15. At the monolith what were they trying to find?
16. What did Chelone want Martin to discover when he forced him to tell his story?
17. How did the breathing help the couple?
18. How did Martin and Leigha get back to the adobe?
19. What was Maranther's Deception?
20. Once back in their home town, what surprises lay in store for Martin and Leigha?
21. What role will Leigha play in the next novel of this series?